DRAGONS RISING

DRAGONS RISING

WARMAGE REDUX™ BOOK TWO

MARTHA CARR
MICHAEL ANDERLE

DISRUPTIVE IMAGINATION®

Copyright © LMBPN Publishing
Cover Art by Jake @ J Caleb Design
http://jcalebdesign.com / jcalebdesign@gmail.com
Cover copyright © LMBPN Publishing
A Michael Anderle Production

LMBPN Publishing
PMB 196, 2540 South Maryland Pkwy
Las Vegas, NV 89109

First US edition, October 2021
ebook ISBN: 978-1-68500-521-4
Print ISBN: 978-1-68500-522-1

THE DRAGONS RISING TEAM

Thanks to our Beta Readers

James Caplan, Larry Omans, John Ashmore

Thanks to our JIT Readers

Jackey Hankard-Brodie
Deb Mader
Dave Hicks
Diane L. Smith
Dorothy Lloyd
Paul Westman

Editor

SkyHunter Editing Team

CHAPTER ONE

"All right! Pack it in." Raven Alby grinned as her division of STAR legionaries finished their training for the day. "Everyone down to—hey!"

She ducked as Perch and his pale-blue dragon swooped toward her. Isla screeched with pride as his rider leapt from his back and landed on the grass beside the division's war mage.

Her fiery red hair clung to her face as she stood from her crouch and shook her head at the close call of being swept completely off her feet by a moving dragon. When she turned an exasperated glance onto the soldier who stood in front of her, Perch grinned.

"You know what? I've started to think I understand why everyone called me too much when I was still in school. You're good at it."

The legionary who hadn't spoken a single word since he'd joined Lomberdoon's Airborne Legion—and probably for a long time before that—pumped his fist in jubilation before he stepped back to join the line of other soldiers who gathered at the end of the day's tactical drills.

The giant soldier Farb clapped Perch on the back and snorted a laugh. "I think the mage just called you her mini-me, buddy."

Raven shook her head but couldn't hold back a smile. "No one wants that, Farb. Even him."

The three dozen STAR legionaries—who'd now been under her de facto command for the last few weeks—stepped into an impressively neat formation in the open training field on the Legion base at Havendom. Their dragons fell in beside them, tossed their heads, and stretched their wings. Leander landed behind his mage and raised his head so everyone could see him as well.

"Good work today," she told them. "Now go eat."

Laughing, the soldiers broke formation and headed across the field toward the open-air mess hall at the base of the Legion tower. When all their backs were turned, she heaved a sigh and brushed more loose hair out of her face. "Great. Now I have to worry about being clipped by my division at the end of the day."

Her familiar's rumble of amusement made her frown. "You don't believe any of them are reckless enough to do that."

"Of course not. And you didn't even bother to give me a heads-up."

"I don't have to. They know what they're doing now, thanks to you. And thanks to me..." The red dragon nudged the back of his mage's shoulder with his snout. "You're quick on your feet."

"Oh, that's right. All my best instincts are because of

you." Raven shoved his head away and he snorted a puff of hot dragon breath into her face.

"It's the closest any human or mage will get to a dragon's instincts. You should be proud of it."

"I am." She laughed, turned to face him, and stroked the sides of his scaley face. Her smile faded quickly, however, and she glanced at the tall tower of black stone that protruded from the center of the Legion base. "We should be proud of what we did in those mines too. We found the Weeping Disease fungus and burned it out of existence with Dr. Welby. And all we got from Primus Kauler after that was a nod and orders to get back to training."

Leander's purring rumble grew louder as he closed his eyes, thoroughly enjoying his mage's attention to his face. "Then why are you so frustrated? If you wanted to win awards, perhaps joining the military was not the best option."

"You know I'm not talking about awards." She scowled and stopped scratching his face until he opened one yellow eye to look at her. "I'm frustrated because we should also be out there right now looking for any other dragons who might have caught the Weeping Disease before we burned it out of those caves. We should be trying to help them but instead, we're on base running even more drills with the division and training."

"I would not be so overly eager to find these other sick dragons." He growled, the sound one of both displeasure and distress. "Not after what we had to do to the others to put them out of their misery."

"Well…" Raven shifted her gaze across the open training field in the direction of Dr. Welby's tent, which was mostly hidden by the curved outer wall of the massive tower. "I guess that's probably the last thing we're waiting for before we can do anything else. I don't like the worst-case scenario any more than you do, Leander, but finding sick dragons and…ending their suffering is the best option we have right now. For them and for any other dragons around them who might be exposed to—"

"Mage Alby!" Dr. Chui Welby marched around the curve of the tower's exterior wall of black stone and stopped to wave one hand over his head. She caught his gaze and returned the gesture with much less enthusiasm than the vet displayed this evening.

"Speaking of the dragon doctor…" the red dragon muttered.

"Whatever you were about to say about Welby," Raven said through the side of her mouth and lowered her voice, "let me remind you first that we were talking about the dragons and our mission to help as many of them as we can. We couldn't have done any of this without him but beyond that, Leander, I don't want to hear another word."

A soft, jerky hiss escaped the dragon's slightly parted lips. "You're getting nervous around him."

"No, I'm not."

"And you're blushing."

She cast him a condescending glance. "At least I don't run away from him whenever he tries to talk to me. Oh, look. There's Gruene."

"What?" Leander whipped his head up to search the sky and he launched before she could tell him she'd been joking and was merely trying to make a point. His wing-beats buffeted her red hair around her face and a moment later, he was high above the training field and darted in and out between other dragons who swooped, dove, and soared around him.

A screech of greeting cut through the already busy noise of hundreds of Legion dragons and Gruene, Dr. Welby's large black female dragon, tucked her wings closer to her sides and raced after Leander.

The mage couldn't help but laugh at that.

He can tease me about Dr. Welby all he wants but I was right too. I don't run away simply because being the center of someone else's attention makes me uncomfortable.

Her smile faded instantly at that thought.

No. I avoid the issue altogether and pretend like everything's okay.

"Mage Alby!" Welby shouted again across the field and made her jump a little before she redirected her focus to where he stood a few yards away from the tower wall and waved her forward urgently. "A moment of your time if I may?"

Raven nodded and hurried toward him.

In the sky, Leander darted over her again but it seemed that at some point. Gruene had given up her pursuit of the big red male whose actions still made it clear that he wanted nothing to do with her.

Acutely aware that all the other legionaries of both her STAR division and the other seven cohorts of the Airborne Legion had left for dinner in the outdoor mess hall, she cleared her throat and increased her pace toward Welby to see what he wanted from her.

I hope he has good news this time. I know he's working hard on a cure for Weeping Disease but we've already lost way too much time waiting for one. We burned the black fungus but there's no way there aren't more sick dragons out there who need our help.

When she reached the front of his large canvas tent that served as both his home and his private office on the base, the tall, broad-shouldered man already stood at the front with the entrance flap pulled aside. His smile widened and he nodded toward the interior of the tent. "Come on in."

Her face flushed hotly and she had no doubt that her blush was horribly apparent.

He's never asked me to come inside with him before. This is where he lives. It's a little...private.

"You can show me out here," she muttered. "I'll wait."

"In that case, I'm afraid you'll wait for quite some time." Welby shrugged. "I can't very well disassemble my entire laboratory to show you what I've found."

"Right." She cleared her throat. "Your laboratory."

"Trust me, Mage Alby, this is something you want to see for yourself."

"You know I'm not an Apothecary Mage, right?"

He chuckled. "But you are the only other person who's seen the black fungus. And I would very much appreciate an extra pair of eyes to hopefully confirm my findings."

Raven's eyes widened. "You found a cure?"

"I believe I may have, yes. So if you don't mind..." He gestured inside the tent with his free hand and nodded briskly.

"Okay." With a nod, she slipped quickly past the tall, dark-haired, handsome civilian vet contracted by the Lomberdoon military and stepped inside. The only thing she was immediately aware of at first was how much darker it was after spending all day under the bright summer sun. And, of course, that they were entirely alone together.

When she saw the aforementioned lab, her jaw dropped.

Three sturdy wooden tables claimed the center of the massive tent. Their surfaces were covered with small dishes and trays, flasks and beakers of every shape and size, vials filled with different-color liquids, books, and magnifying glasses. Alongside these were stacks of parchment papers weighted down by massive amber-colored crystals, two ink jars beside a vase holding nothing but quills, and more odds and ends than she could identify. The center table had been mostly cleared except for five small glass trays arranged around a much larger glass jar with a lid. In this, Welby had placed his black fungus samples from their first and only trip into the mines before they'd destroyed it all.

"Wow," Raven muttered. "This is…quite a setup."

"Thank you." The vet brushed past her, his dark eyes wide as he zeroed in on the glass sample trays on the center table, clearly more eager to show her what he'd found than he was flattered by her compliment. "Come take a look at this."

He pulled a sixth round glass tray from a supply chest beneath the table, this one empty. She approached him slowly and tried to take in all the work he'd done while he continued whatever he was currently doing. The man made sure to don a thick pair of leather gloves before he reached into the jar of the fungus sample to remove another piece of it with a pair of incredibly long tweezers.

"What are all these?" She pointed at the other five trays, each of them filled with a different-color liquid around specks of the fungus floating on the surface.

"I'm sure most would call these my failures." Welby snorted and shook his head. "But I firmly believe there's no such thing as failure, to be honest. Not the way most of the world tends to look at it at any rate. Merely lessons."

She nodded. "Trust me, if I called every one of my mistakes complete failures instead of lessons, my life would be completely different. So I know exactly what you mean."

He placed the new sample in the empty tray and paused to fix her with an intense gaze as the corner of his mouth lifted in a smirk. "I had a feeling you would. It seems we understand each other quite well in that regard. Among other things."

Caught in his stare, she swallowed and her face flushed incredibly warm again. "Like what?"

The mage could have smacked herself for asking the question out loud.

Why would I say that? Now he's gonna think I'm either completely clueless about all the looks he's been giving me since we came back from those mines, or I'm the idiot here who reads way more into looks and smiles. What am I doing?

"Well, to start…" Welby's smile remained as he looked at the fresh fungus sample again and nodded. "We see eye to eye on the importance of being sure we have a cure for Weeping Disease before we take any of this information to Primus Kauler."

Raven cleared her throat and forced her attention to the

vet's alchemy setup in front of them. "Yeah. We certainly agree on that."

"Good. Here's what I managed to find." With another quick smile, he selected three different potion bottles from the scattered supplies on the other tables and uncorked each of them slowly. One contained a thick, dark-green liquid, another held bright, glittering blue, and the third was completely clear but with thin red strands that looked more like hairs from some mythical creature's hide than anything else.

Where have I seen that before?

She tried to place the name of the substance in that third vial, but his ensuing explanation of his findings ripped her out of her diversion.

"These are the usual base ingredients for creature medicines," he said and lifted each vial slightly in turn. "I tried to see what each of these old ingredients might do to the fungus on their own. There wasn't any real viable reaction with any of these separately, but then I realized it might have needed a more specific combination and Bloodheart Blossom does tend to boost the properties of an intended outcome. At least when you have the right mixture."

Although she nodded sagely, she kept her mouth shut.

Nope. I'm not an alchemist or a vet, and here he is talking to me like I'm some kind of Augurer Mage who's run magical experiments for my entire life.

"It was an accident, frankly," Welby continued. "I didn't get enough sleep last night, and I'd intended to grab the jar of Etherium Root." He gestured toward another small jar that looked very similar to the Bloodheart Blossom, but the thin, solid filaments within that potion were a deep gold instead of red. "And this is what I found."

She watched intently as the vet worked and measured specific amounts of each potion into the final sample dish with carefully administered drops from a pipette. Once he'd added every ingredient, nothing happened.

CHAPTER TWO

"Um…" Raven tilted her head and stared at the unaffected concoction on the sample dish. "Dr. Welby? I don't—"

"*Expurgo.*" A burst of yellow light flared from the vet's fingertip and arced gently into the dish.

The liquid of mixed potions in which the black fungus floated rippled, then bubbled like he'd put it over an open fire before a burst of green smoke and black sparks erupted from the dish. The ensuing reaction made both mages lean away from the table. She coughed and waved aside the acrid smoke in her face.

When she looked at the bowl, however, the concoction had turned a bright golden-yellow, and the soft hiss and sizzle came from the small sample of black fungus being slowly eaten away until it completely disappeared.

"A cleansing spell," she muttered.

"You know it?" Welby darted her another sidelong glance and his crooked smile grew a little.

"Yeah. I tried to use it on the first infected dragon

Leander and I found. It almost worked, but then it made him worse."

"No, it didn't. There was nothing you could have done for a sick dragon that far gone to Weeping Disease. But the spell is an excellent final ingredient in this cure."

Raven brushed aside the memory of the huge brown dragon she'd watched die on the Ossel property and smiled. "It completely destroyed the fungus. I thought only the Blue Flame spell could do that."

"To eradicate the fungal growth, yes. I don't think the mages who accomplished that a hundred and fifty years ago were particularly concerned about curing the dragons who were still infected by it, unfortunately. But this?" The man's smile widened. "Well, I don't want to put any words in your mouth, Mage Alby. What do you think?"

"I think this looks like a cure. Dr. Welby, you're brilliant."

"Well, it wasn't through sheer brainpower alone."

When she met his gaze again, she grinned at the usually stoic dragon doctor.

"But thank you," he added and inclined his head.

"You should take this to Kauler. He'll clear it, and we can go find whatever infected dragons are still out there and completely heal them. We don't have to lose any more."

Welby's smile faded. "Provided we find them in time before the Weeping Disease has progressed too far. I'm a little concerned about how effective this will be on a dragon who was as far gone as the one you tried to cure on your own."

That caveat certainly dampened her spirits too. "Then we'd better get moving."

"I agree. Would you like to join me?"

"I—"

A heavy beat of wings outside made the canvas walls of the huge tent rustle and flap seconds before a dragon's massive silhouette landed on the grass outside, followed by a low growl.

"Of course we're coming with you," Leander said.

Raven chuckled as his long neck snaked toward the tent's entrance flap.

"Ah. Yes." Welby nodded. "I would expect nothing less from you, Leander. And I understand you're eager to help but I don't think—"

"You need us." The red dragon nipped at the entrance flap, then shoved his huge, scaley muzzle into the tent and snorted. "This isn't a cure only for those working with humans. I know the wild dragons who were infected. They'll listen to me. They followed Raven across the continent from the sea and you need someone they can trust."

The vet looked at her with wide eyes. "They followed you?"

"They followed us both." She smiled sheepishly. "And it was mostly because we had the Origin Seed so we could support magic returning without it getting way too out of control and— You know what? It was a long time ago."

And we don't need to hash out how a seventeen-year-old mage student saved the world's magic. That's over and done with. Why is he still gaping at me like that?

She shrugged. "What?"

Welby laughed in surprise. "I suppose I should have put two and two together at this point."

"If Raven goes," Leander added, "I go. You can't separate us and we're coming with you to cure those dragons."

The vet turned his gaze to the red dragon and regarded him with a blank expression. "You thought I was trying to separate you?"

"I could smell your excuse for leaving me behind, healer." The dragon's yellow eyes widened. "It will not happen."

Another low growl escaped him and reverberated around the tent.

Raven headed around the table and stared at her dragon in warning. *You can't start threatening the guy who found the cure.*

Did you want me to let him finish telling us he didn't think it was a good idea? If he thinks he can separate us simply to get you alone—

"Oh!" Welby laughed.

Raven and Leander both turned their attention to the vet, who simply stared at the dragon and shook his head.

"Perhaps he is a mad dragon doctor," Leander muttered as he lowered his head.

"Leander," she chided.

"I've been called mad before at times." Welby cleared his throat. "But I have never attempted to separate a dragon from his rider and I certainly would never support separating a mage from her familiar." He raised both hands in surrender when Leander growled again. "I do apologize for the misunderstanding, Leander. I was referring to Mage Alby accompanying me to deliver our findings to Primus Kauler. Nothing more. Of course I want both of you to join Gruene and me when we distribute the cure."

The red dragon chuffed. "Good."

He whipped his head out of the tent and the support frames wobbled when the canvas snagged momentarily on the scales of his face.

Raven sucked in a sharp breath and readied herself to throw up a protection spell should the entire tent come down around her and the vet. It didn't help that her familiar chose that moment to launch skyward again to join the other military dragons flying around at the end of a long day. His wingbeats buffeted the tent even more but the canvas walls stabilized quickly before Dr. Welby's private tent turned laboratory fell remarkably silent.

She cleared her throat. "I'm sorry about that."

"Don't be." He chuckled. "I wouldn't have erected this tent on a military base filled with free dragons if I didn't have the necessary safeguards. With the way Gruene enjoys taking off and landing, this structure would have come down five minutes after I set it up."

A slow smile returned to the STAR mage. "Reinforced enchantment?"

"Absolutely."

"You know, it's nice to have another mage around. On base, I mean. The legionaries have a small amount of magic like everyone else, but it's different when someone has…"

"A similar level of experience?" He removed his gloves quickly and placed them neatly on the table. "Or at least a mage's training, now that I think about it. I'm not quite sure anyone has the same level of experience as you, Mage Alby. Although a few do come to mind in terms of reputation and sacrifices made for this kingdom."

She stiffened.

We went from talking about curing dragons to sacrifices for

15

the kingdom in no time flat. I'm not sure I like the way this is going.

"Yeah, I can think of a few too," she said. "It turns out I'm related to two of them."

"Understandable." Welby reached toward the dish of the enchanted potion mixture that had eradicated the black fungus, then paused. "You know, I wouldn't usually bring up such a personal topic at a time like this, but I find it difficult to ignore the implications when I'm standing in my tent, looking at a cure with you beside me."

She swallowed thickly and her cheeks flushed again.

Great. Someone else to talk to me about my long list of accomplishments with breaking the rules and still being so much like my mom. I should simply beat him to it and get this over with.

"I know what you're going to say." She turned toward him and nodded. "My mother left a legacy and some very big shoes to fill. I get it. And no, I don't expect any kind of special treatment because I'm her daughter and ended up following in her footsteps with…a few things."

The vet's eyes widened. "It's still a personal topic for both of us, I see. Would you believe me if I told you I blame my lack of sleep over the last few days for this string of apparent misunderstandings?"

Raven stepped back and regarded him warily. "What?"

"I was referring to my experiences, Mage Alby." He looked away from her to study the interior of his tent and inhaled deeply. "I met her once. When I was a boy."

"You met—"

"War Mage Alby." When he settled his gaze on her again, the man's rich, dark eyes glistened. "She came to my

16

village to help settle a dispute created by some of our officials' more...aggressive tactics when it came to accepting other citizens from neighboring parts of the kingdom. Because of your mother, my family and I were protected and allowed to stay after raiders destroyed our first home."

"Oh." She stared at him in surprise. "Yeah, she was good at that."

"She was." He nodded. "War Mage Alby was a hero to me that day. She has been ever since."

"How..." Trying to collect herself after such an unexpected revelation, she shrugged. "How old were you?"

"Nine. And the youngest of five, if you can believe it."

This is so weird. I'm talking to someone who knew my mom as a kid and remembers her more than I do. And he's not that much older than me. A little older than William. Why am I thinking about William right now? This is nothing like that.

Welby chuckled self-consciously. "And now I'm here at the capital, contracted by the royal military to work alongside her daughter. Mage Alby, elite STAR legionary who seems to have developed as much of a love for dragons as I've always had." He took another deep breath and nodded. "It's an achievement I can't take credit for but I can say I'm incredibly proud all the same."

"I..." The story brought a fresh wave of tears to shimmer briefly in her eyes, but she pushed them back and fought the urge to bolt out of his tent without another word. "We're all simply doing the best we can, right?"

"Some of us more than others, perhaps. But yes."

"Thank you, Dr. Welby. For telling me that."

"You're welcome."

They stared at each other for a moment that seemed to

stretch into forever before the man leaned slightly toward her. Whatever he was about to say next, it was interrupted by a loud screech from the sky a second before Leander's voice entered Raven's mind.

Should I remind you this is not the time to let your emotions get the better of you inside a tent with a dragon doctor?

Raven shook herself out of the strange moment with Welby and gestured toward the front of his tent. "We should go see the primus."

"Yes, of course. After you." He nodded for her to step outside first and walked slowly around the tables to follow her.

We have dragons to cure, she thought to her familiar. *So get ready.*

I am always ready, Raven. You're the one who can't keep human feelings under control.

Well, you're the one who thought Dr. Welby wanted to separate us for a mission. He's been nothing but helpful. What do you have against the vet, Leander?

Nothing. Her dragon uttered another screech and swooped above her head as she approached the Level Zero entrance to the Legion tower. *What do you have against him?*

I don't—

Raven paused at the door and turned. Welby was close behind her and his usual stoic determination had returned to his features now that they were on their way to speak to Kauler about the cure.

You merely don't want to fly with Gruene again. That's what this is about.

That black female is— Her familiar's voice vanished from

her mind as the huge red dragon's form swerved around the curve of the tower walls and disappeared.

It's not fair to judge a mage by their familiar. Or a rider by their dragon.

He didn't reply—most likely because he felt a dragon shouldn't have to answer to any human who implied he couldn't get his human-like emotions under control, especially when it came to a female dragon.

"Allow me." The vet stepped past her toward the door and opened it swiftly before she had a chance to do so herself.

"Thanks." Raven headed inside quickly and they hurried through the winding corridors of the tower's ground level before they entered the staircase to take them to Level One and Primus Kauler's office.

"Fingers crossed now, right?" Welby muttered.

"If the primus can't see the value of your cure and sending us both out to give it to those who need it, having a few sick wild dragons running around and scaring citizens will be the least of his problems."

He stifled a laugh. "Among other things, I imagine he'd find a civilian contractor who isn't obligated to take orders and a Legion mage with a tendency to go rogue on that list as well."

She smirked as they reached the top of the staircase. "Fingers crossed for him, then."

CHAPTER THREE

Primus Kauler stared at the vet and the STAR mage who stood in front of his desk. Raven darted her companion a sidelong glance before she straightened and waited for her commanding officer to say something after the eager, admittedly rushed report Welby had given him.

He has to say something. We have the cure and have waited for this for weeks now.

After he stroked his well-trimmed beard and mustache for far longer than seemed necessary, Kauler nodded and fixed his gaze on the vet. "I appreciate your confidence in this so-called cure of yours, Dr. Welby. And I've come to understand that you don't place your confidence in much of anything unless it's entirely warranted. But I do have one more question for you."

"Hopefully I have an answer, sir."

The primus drew a deep breath. "How confident are you in this cure's viability as a preemptive inoculation?"

Welby rolled his shoulders back and frowned in concentration. "Completely, Primus. I've run several tests,

and this eradicates the fungus and the disease in every possible form I could think of."

"Hmm." Kauler turned his attention to Raven. "What do you think, Mage Alby?"

"I think we need to get out there and find any other dragons with Weeping Disease so we can cure them before they're too far gone to save. Sir."

"And before it spreads." The primus nodded. "Those sick dragons are still contagious, aren't they?"

"It can be spread that way, yes," the vet replied.

"All right." The commanding officer leaned back in his chair and sighed heavily. "I'll send you a team who understands how to handle alchemical production, Dr. Welby. Every dragon in the Airborne must receive a dose of this cure. Then you and Mage Alby will head south to look for the wild dragons who—"

"We don't have that kind of time," Raven blurted.

Kauler pierced her with an intensely warning stare. "You'll make that kind of time, Mage Alby. Understood?"

"The Airborne dragons in Havendom aren't in danger of dying from this disease. But those who already have it need that cure as soon as possible. Otherwise, it'll be too late to save them."

"The dragons of Lomberdoon's Airborne Legion are the top priority in this matter."

"We already destroyed the fungus," she shouted. "It's gone. The wild dragons have been exposed and they aren't coming here to Havendom to spread it around the military. We have to go now to help as many—"

"You are out of line, Legionary!" Kauler thumped a fist on the top of his desk and stood.

She stiffened and glared at him.

The desk beneath his fist creaked when he leaned forward slightly. "I realize there was a slight misunderstanding around my intentions to promote you as STAR's drill instructor, but now I want to make this very clear. I've demoted many ranking officers and enlisted legionaries in this military for far less insubordination than what you've exhibited during this conversation.

"The only reason I'm giving you this warning now, Mage Alby, is because I truly believe your experience and expertise regarding this issue are of more value to us at present than taking disciplinary action. You're no good to any of us in the stockade or pushing parchments for Legate Harper but you will not receive a second warning. Is that clear?"

Raven gritted her teeth and nodded. "Yes, sir."

He's your commanding officer, Raven, not a teacher who doesn't believe what you're saying. Keep your mouth shut and do your job.

"Now, I'm well aware of the threat to wild dragons around this kingdom," the primus continued, his voice far lower now but with an unmistakable level of firm warning as he removed his hand slowly from the desk. "And I'm equally aware of our duty as citizens who've formed an accord with all free dragons, whether they're wild or have chosen to remain in a working relationship with humans and mages. Dr. Welby has confirmed how contagious this disease is and I will place the safety and security of the Legion dragons before all others.

"Airborne mounts who contract this disease jeopardize this military's ability to respond to any and all threats—

including Weeping Disease. It compromises our ability to protect this kingdom, to uphold the safety of its citizens, and most certainly to deploy units with orders to distribute cures to those dragons you say are closer to the source of this entire issue. Whether or not that fungus was eradicated is irrelevant at this point." The primus tapped an index finger on his desk and lowered his head to stare at her like he was waiting for her to argue again.

I won't. Because I want to be a part of this and keep my job.

"Every military dragon will receive inoculation first. Once that process has been completed, Mage Alby, you'll receive your orders to go south again with Dr. Welby to administer the cure to the wild dragons." The primus paused, drew a deep breath as his mustache twitched, and added, "If you have any questions, now would be the appropriate time to voice them."

Careful, Raven. He wants questions, not concerns.

She swallowed and forced her voice to remain steady. "Sir, I'd like to request authorization to go south alone while the inoculations are implemented on base. The wild dragons don't have much time."

Kauler leaned away from his desk. "Those who have enough time will get this cure. The rest will be dealt with in the same effective manner in which both you and Dr. Welby already have sufficient experience. Either way, you'll do what has to be done." He looked from one to the other and nodded. "You're dismissed, Mage Alby."

"Sir."

The man didn't look at her again as he sat behind his desk and entered his trance-like perusal of all the reports and paperwork scattered in front of him.

Her fists clenched, Raven spun and stalked out of the office. She didn't bother to wait for Welby, who muttered a quick, "Primus," before he turned to follow her.

She stalked down the hall, infuriated by her commanding officer's decision and the fact that she couldn't entirely blame him for making it.

He's not wrong. We can't fight anything with sick military dragons, but getting all of them this cure first will take forever.

"Mage Alby," the vet called gently behind her.

"We have our orders," she replied without slowing or turning. "Well, at least I do. You should get started on making a huge batch of that potion."

"Raven."

Hearing him call her by name made her stop short. She hesitated, then turned to look at him. Every muscle in her body was tightened by fury and a level of defeat she hadn't expected to find as a grown mage assigned to Lomberdoon's royal army.

The vet approached her until they stood a mere two feet apart and he lowered his head toward her. "Trust me, I find the primus' priorities as frustrating as you do. Still, he's not—"

"He's not wrong. I know." Her gaze darted around the dark stone corridor until she finally managed to look him in the eyes. "I can't argue his reasoning behind what we're supposed to do next. But I'm—" She sighed.

"Tired of waiting." Welby nodded. "I understand. If I could have moved any faster to find this cure, believe me, I would have."

"I'm not blaming you, Dr. Welby—"

"Please." He smiled. "Call me Chui. And while trying to

place blame where there is none is completely useless, especially in a situation like this, I can promise you we'll have the entire Airborne Legion inoculated against the fungus within the next two days."

Raven shook her head. "That's ambitious. We have hundreds of dragons."

"And skilled mages. Don't worry, I won't commandeer your services and try to pull you away from your division. Havendom has more than enough mages on assignment available to help me here. A few of them are even particularly gifted in alchemy production."

"You mean like a spell for instantly replicating that potion times a few hundred for all these dragons?" She'd meant it as a joke but it sounded far more bitter than she'd intended.

Somehow, Welby was able to overlook the dripping sarcasm and his smile widened instead. "Something like that, yes. Two days. That's all. And I'd say I'd come find you to let you know when it's finished, but I assume Primus Kauler will beat me to it."

"With new orders to escort you south again." As most of her anger dissipated into acceptance and a little more renewed hope, she nodded. "Okay. I can wait two days but I hope most of the sick dragons out there have that long."

"As do I, Mage Alby."

That's weird. He told me to call him Chui, and now he's back to using my formal address as a mage. Was I supposed to say something about the first-name-basis thing?

She continued down the hall toward the stairwell that would take her to the mess hall. Welby was no longer beside her and had turned in the opposite direction to return to the exit to Level Zero. It took her a moment before she realized he wasn't with her.

"You said you haven't been sleeping," she called after him. "Don't tell me you're skipping meals too."

He slowed and looked over his shoulder at her. "I've taken meals in my tent to save time. But if you'd like me to join you in the mess hall once we've finished curing as many dragons as possible, I will gladly accept the invitation."

His crooked smile and brief nod before he turned made her freeze.

What? He thinks I was asking him to have dinner with me? In the mess hall on base? I was only trying to make sure he's not starving himself—

So you asked him on a military date. Leander's voice rang loud and clear in her mind, complete with an inflection that sounded very much like he was laughing at her again, although there was no accompanying rumble from her dragon familiar.

She spun and raced toward the curved tower staircase leading to the mess hall. *That wasn't even close to what I was doing and you know it.*

Raven, I would tell you to come outside so I can see your face, in which case I would only be proven correct once I pointed out yet another silly human flush in your cheeks. Unfortunately for us both, I can feel your feelings. Please don't expect me to join two mages on a date with human food.

The mage rolled her eyes and hurried down the stairs while she tried to ignore the fact that she couldn't hide anything from her dragon given how closely they'd bonded over the last four years. *Then I guess you already know about the plan—*

To cure the Legion dragons before we have a chance to contract the plague, yes. It will make saving the others easier, at least. And safer.

"Right," she muttered as she reached the bottom landing and slipped through the final door into the cacophony of legionaries sharing dinner in the sheltered stone courtyard. "Only two more days before we can finally finish this whole situation and keep everyone safer."

CHAPTER FOUR

Waiting for Dr. Welby and his Havendom mage friends to reproduce the cure and administer it to every dragon of the Airborne Legion felt like one of Raven's most intense lessons in patience—which she wasn't very good at anyway. The vet and his team worked ceaselessly through that first night to create enough potions enchanted with cleansing spells for the military mounts, and the entire next day was spent handing them out to as many of them as they could fit into one day.

That also meant her regular schedule of early waking, a brief formation with the primus on the Level Five platform, and a full day running tactical drills and flight maneuvers with her STAR division was completely disrupted by the primus' orders. Even the cohort who'd taken over kingdom patrol for this rotation was ordered to stay on base and present their dragons for the mandatory and preemptive inoculation.

The orderly line of dragons that stretched away from Welby's tent was a fearsome sight in and of itself.

Hundreds of winged mounts were curious about the sudden and unexplained new dragon medicine being administered by the dragon doctor himself. Most of them were more than willing to take it. A few, however, simply didn't agree with being ordered to ingest a mage-crafted potion, despite the threat of Weeping Disease or the proven efficacy of the cure.

One pale-green dragon from the Second Cohort became particularly aggressive when he demanded to know exactly why this was necessary. He recalled the times when dragon riders—even those in the military—hadn't always made their decisions for the good of the dragons they stabled.

"It's to keep you healthy and safe," Dr. Welby said calmly and held his hands out toward the agitated male who snorted and clawed the grass in front of the tent. "That's all this is."

The male raised his head to the sky and bugled in anger. "I do not need a potion to keep me healthy and safe, doctor. I have always been strong. I do not want this!"

"Dartaine, you know me." The vet spread his arms placatingly. "I set your broken leg and helped those scales at the end of your tail heal correctly instead of leaving them to jut out after they'd practically been torn off. Your safety is my highest concern, and Primus Kauler's orders to inoculate every dragon here against this deadly disease is for your benefit."

"We have never needed magical concoctions before," the dragon roared. He appeared to struggle with the blow to his pride and a certain level of fear around the one and only illness known to kill a dragon with so little effort. The other mounts in line beside him picked up on his irritation quickly and many of them tossed their heads, stamped, and shouted occasionally in agreement as they screeched their protests.

At that point, Raven and Leander tried to get involved, although she hadn't been ordered to do anything but oversee the STAR legionaries and ensure they all got their dragons to the vet. They'd flown above the field to ensure that none of the dragons were already exhibiting signs of infection—even though that was incredibly unlikely—and to see that everyone had a chance to line up at Dr. Welby's tent.

When one of the soldiers in line shouted at the green male's rider to take control of his dragon, all hell broke loose.

"He should not have said that," Leander growled.

"Yeah. That's the complete opposite of progress." The mage leaned forward over the saddle and they dove to land right in front of Welby's tent and the now-terrified pale-green male who was too distressed to think clearly.

She leapt from Leander's back and raised her hands in front of her to show the frustrated dragons she meant no harm. "Dr. Welby's only intention is to protect you," she shouted in an attempt to get their attention. "This is to keep all dragons safe when you're out on patrol where you have to interact with other dragons in the kingdom and even the wild clans. We found the cure and the black fungus has been destroyed, so there's no—"

"Mage Alby." The vet nodded at the angry green male and his rider and excused himself to sidle toward the Legion mage. "I can handle this."

"I don't understand why they're so upset right now. They trust you and they know what could happen if they somehow get infected by this. Why would they have an issue with taking a potion that will save their lives?"

He grimaced, leaned toward her, and lowered his voice. "Dragons have long memories."

"What?" Raven stared at him.

"Many of these dragons are fairly new to the Legion," he muttered and glanced at the line of agitated dragons. "They enlisted with their riders within the last two years. But there are those, like Dartaine, who still remember their…mistreatment."

"Well, it sounded like one or two of the other legionaries remember it too. Telling someone else to get control of their dragon? I thought everyone here knew we no longer tried to control anyone."

"They do. But tensions are high, of course. The stress is bolstered by the fact that dragons have never needed medicines for a malady or a wound they can't see or feel for themselves."

"That's because this is the only cure for the only disease this deadly to them."

"Yes, Mage Alby. I know that and I've repeated it numerous times. Unfortunately, a level of distrust I didn't expect remains. Like I said. Long memories."

With a sigh, Raven gazed at the agitated line of military mounts again. "Well, is there anything I can do to help?"

He shook his head. "Nothing beyond continuing to draw them here to my tent to receive their dose."

One of the Legion mounts screeched again, followed by a roar from the next one in line. "They want to trap us under their control! I will not be forced into anything. We are free!"

She lost the rest of her self-control and stalked toward the dragon line. "That's not true. No one's forcing you into anything and they never will."

Leander raised his head and uttered a rumbling bellow that momentarily settled the other Legion mounts who had reacted to each other's agitation and defiance. "This is to protect you."

He was cut off abruptly by an angry screech overhead that overpowered all the other chaotic noise that issued from the line of dragons waiting to receive the potion.

Raven barely had time to look at the dragon who'd stopped her familiar before Primus Kauler and his gigantic dark-green female swooped into a landing in front of her. Leander's wings extended in agitation as he backed away from the female's massive tail when it whipped toward his face.

"Legionaries!" the primus shouted. His voice carried perfectly well on its own and ricocheted off the walls of both the Legion tower and the stone wall surrounding the base. "Every soldier and mount in the Airborne has received their orders!"

Another sharp screech from his dragon followed to make his point and to ensure that everyone was paying attention. They were now.

"To anyone here who believes they're being forced against their will to uphold the safety of this kingdom and its citizens, human or dragon," Kauler continued, "believe me when I say you are mistaken."

Raven gritted her teeth and watched the startled dragons shift uncomfortably under their primus' attention.

They think they're strong enough to not get infected. Kauler must know how this looks to them. I seriously hope he knows enough about a dragon's pride to not make them think they're right.

"The dragon illness that originated in the southwest mines," the primus continued, "would tear this Airborne Legion apart before it ravaged the rest of Lomberdoon's dragons. You've all been briefed on this. We have dealt with the source and now, we are taking steps to protect every Legion mount against this disease. Fortunately, Dr. Welby is the first man in history to have found a cure and he is stationed here at the Airborne base. I gave the order for every mount to receive this inoculation against a disease that has killed dozens of dragons already. I mean to see that order carried out."

The legionaries who stood beside their mounts had all stiffened to attention when the primus and his mount landed but they now looked as wary as their dragons. Still, no one spoke or attempted to ask questions.

Raven snuck a glance at her commanding officer and couldn't help but feel Leander's wariness mixed with hers.

Yes, dragons are free, but Kauler won't get their support if he issues orders without addressing why they're so upset about this.

"Some of you have served Lomberdoon and this Legion far longer than others, and I realize that memories of the past may still be fresh in your minds. But the last two years have brought extensive and lasting policy changes regarding military mounts and their treatment both on and off this base. Today, ensuring the safety and efficiency of every legionary and their mount is my top priority.

"I shouldn't have to remind any of you why following orders is your top priority, even on base. No free dragon of the Airborne or anywhere within the borders of this kingdom will be punished for making their own decision. You have my word on that. You do not, however, have authorization to confuse free will with permission to abandon your duty as a mount of the Airborne. Any dragon who refuses this and disobeys their direct orders will face immediate discharge. Is that understood?"

"Sir, yes, sir!" the legionaries called sharply in reply.

The primus' mount spread her wings wide and screeched again. Her cry rebounded off all the black stone around them and made Raven grimace.

What surprised her most was that all the other dragons who'd been so close to dissenting stretched their long necks and echoed the screech of the primus' mount in a single call in hundreds of dragon voices.

With that, Kauler and his dragon turned and the primus nodded at Welby from his place in the saddle. "Continue with the line, doctor. We have a schedule to keep."

"Yes, sir." The vet glanced at Raven and looked almost apologetic before he headed toward his tent and the massive supply of the Weeping Disease potion ready in vials for every military dragon on base.

"Mage Alby," Kauler snapped.

"Sir." She raised her chin and only then realized how angry she must have looked. It was impossible to remove her scowl completely.

"You had your orders as well for the next two days." He

raised an eyebrow. "And yet I find you here trying to quell an outbreak of concern among Airborne mounts. Would you care to explain?"

She pressed her lips together and nodded. "I think some of the legionaries here might have forgotten the policy changes around the handling of military mounts, sir."

The primus frowned and gestured with a flick of his hand for her to continue.

"Specifically, telling a fellow legionary to control his dragon. Leander and I touched down in case Dr. Welby needed help to confront the outdated opinion—before the dragons took it personally. Sir."

"Your orders are to ensure that every dragon on this base is directed to Dr. Welby's tent to be inoculated. Not to correct outdated opinions or mediate a surge of wounded dragon pride."

"Yes, sir." It took everything she had to give him the only reply she knew he would accept.

"A mage is not above the chain of command. Even an Alby mage." The warning in Kauler's narrowed eyes as he stared at her was enough to convince her she'd made the right choice in biting her tongue. In the next moment, her commanding officer took her completely by surprise when he asked, "Can you identify the legionary you overheard?"

She recovered quickly, looked over her shoulder, and nodded. "Yes, sir. Third from the front of the line."

The primus' scanned the legionaries and his dark-green dragon snorted violently as she lowered her head.

They're both upset about that part. Maybe even more upset than finding me on the ground when I'm not supposed to be. I hope.

"We've already discussed the implications of non-compliance, Mage Alby. And I did tell you there would be no second warning."

Crap. Why do I keep getting myself into trouble for trying to help and do the right thing? And now I have to face the consequences.

She raised her chin and met his gaze head-on. "You did, sir. I was more concerned about the damage that might've been done within the Airborne after what I heard and... and if it means a demotion, sir, I understand."

At least I can seal my punishment with a little dignity still left.

He studied her intently, then glanced at his mount. She had swiveled her head to gaze at her rider and now uttered a low, short rumble deep in her chest that was barely audible above the noisy commotion of so many other dragons waiting to receive their potions. "I don't believe these particular circumstances warrant that level of disciplinary action."

"You—" Raven glanced from her commanding officer to his mount. "You don't, sir?"

"You clearly have a deep respect for dragons—not only your familiar or the Airborne mounts on base. It's an admirable trait and I appreciate you bringing the issue to my attention, Mage Alby. The legionary in question will be reminded of exactly why this military body has overturned its previous policies, which I frankly find distasteful and always have." He scrutinized her again before he turned his head away slightly. "I trust that the next time you witness such outdated opinions, you'll remember to gauge the situation and report it directly to me instead of ignoring your orders in the heat of the moment."

She squared her shoulders and barely managed to not exhale a sigh of relief. "Yes, sir. I will. Thank you."

"There is no need to thank me, Legionary. Mount up and get back to work."

The mage swallowed thickly and Leander's low rumble —less in amusement and more in gratitude this time—was barely audible above the din of the other dragons reassured enough of their freedom to carry out their orders as well. "Yes, sir."

Without another word, Kauler flicked his dark-green female's harness lightly and they launched skyward.

Raven stood for a moment and tried to pull her confusion and surprise under control. She'd been so sure she was about to lose her place as STAR's drill instructor and maybe even as a legionary altogether.

Leander nudged her shoulder from behind with his snout. "It seems you're finally being appreciated."

"Apparently," she muttered and turned to face him. "It's good to know the primus is dedicated to cutting out the military's bad habits with dragons, right?"

He snorted. "Perhaps things haven't changed enough for everyone yet. But they are changing."

"Right. Let's get back up there, then. The sooner we get Welby's potion to all the dragons here, the sooner we can stop worrying about change not happening as fast as we want."

She accepted his boost into the saddle and as he turned to find a clear path for takeoff, she caught sight of Dr. Welby patting the side of a dragon's neck as he dismissed it in order to deal with the next in line. The vet met her gaze, his lips pressed tightly together, and nodded before he retrieved another glittering potion vial to distribute.

We're all doing the best we can right now but with a whole different way of operating. It's gonna be a long rest of the day but at least it's for the right reasons.

Her familiar spread his wings and launched them smoothly so they could continue to carry out their orders —fly around base to make sure every Airborne mount reported to the vet's tent to receive their only protection against Weeping Disease.

And very soon, that disease will no longer exist. We'll save as many of the sick wild dragons as we can. Then, it's back to regular legionary work.

CHAPTER FIVE

By noon the next day, every Legion dragon had been inoculated with Welby's cure and Raven and Leander received their next set of orders from Kauler. Reporting to the primus' office was almost as frustrating as having to wait for them. The man barely looked at her from the mountain of paperwork on his desk.

"You are to escort Dr. Welby to those mines again," the man said tersely. "Scout the surrounding areas and find the dragons who've been infected. Do what you have to do to contain this disease. I don't want to have to deal with this situation again, so make sure you find every single one of them out there before you return."

"Yes, sir." She stared at him and waited for either the rest of her orders or for her commanding officer to dismiss her.

I won't leave until he tells me to.

It seemed he wasn't in the mood to make either of those easy for her, and she stood there in his silent office for at least another minute while he scribbled on parchment paper with his quill.

"Is there something else, Mage Alby?"

"How much time do we have there?"

That made him finally look at her, and his mustache twitched as he stared at the STAR mage with widening eyes. "As long as it takes. Don't come back until you and Dr. Welby can report one hundred percent success on this mission. So get going."

"Yes, sir."

"And find someone to take over division training while you're gone."

Raven nodded and turned to leave the office. She only let herself smile once she stepped into the hall and headed to the tower's spiral staircase that would take her to her STAR quarters on Level Six.

At least he knows we can't simply assemble all the sick dragons onto a base to distribute the cure. No deadline means we'll find them all and do this right.

An hour later, with both Gruene and Leander's saddlebags filled to bursting with vials of the Weeping Disease potion, Raven and Dr. Welby mounted their dragons and left the Legion base at Havendom to return to the mines in Lomberdoon's southwest region.

The half-day flight was mostly silent and uneventful and the vet looked stoic and not exactly pleased with the situation. This made her nervous.

This is how I prefer to fly, Leander thought to her. *Every dragon keeping their wings and their frost-breath to themselves.*

She snorted a laugh at that and glanced at Gruene, who soared beside them and looked directly ahead. *So you're more comfortable with this weird, silent aggression than a female dragon trying to flirt with you?*

Absolutely. You should be too.

Once they reached the outskirts of Sector Seven, where Raven had first been assigned on patrol before her first encounter with an infected dragon on the Ossel property, she couldn't stay silent about it any longer. Her frustration was mostly because she didn't understand why Welby was so silent, especially after the conversation they'd had in his tent and how eager he'd been to head out on this mission in the first place.

"Have you seen anything?" she called.

The man's head twitched toward her but he didn't reply and didn't look at her. Maybe she hadn't been loud enough for him to hear her over the rush of warm evening air that washed over them and the steady, heavy wingbeats as two dragons soared onward.

"Should we check the mines first?" she shouted.

That caught his attention and he looked briefly at her before he shook his head. "The skirmish we had down there the last time would have been a signal to others to stay away. And I'm not particularly fond of the idea of another run-in with that foreman."

She laughed and he smirked at her before he returned his attention to scouring the landscape beneath them.

Okay, so maybe he's not upset. Only weirdly concentrated for the entire flight.

"We might have better luck searching the outlying

ranches, then," she added. "That was where I found the first one."

"They won't be difficult to find either way. We'll take a slow, methodical approach on this one, Mage Alby. But if you think the ranches are a good place to start, I have no problem beginning there."

Gruene curved her long black neck toward Leander to fix him with a glittering emerald eye. The red dragon snorted and banked away to put more distance between them.

"Okay, Leander. Let's head toward the Ossel land and the other ranches in the area."

You don't have to give me verbal instructions. His words were full of irritation even in her mind.

Yeah, but if I didn't, you'd take off that way and force Gruene to correct her course after you.

If she could even keep up. And now, we'll never know.

The mage shook her head and leaned into the saddle as he banked away from the Brightsbane Mountain range to head toward the outlying ranches at the edge of the kingdom. Gruene fell in line with perfect precision.

It didn't take them long at all before they found three dragons between ranch properties. They were grounded and their wings twitched awkwardly in what was probably an attempt to fly. They no longer could, however, and all three stumbled in circles, tossed their heads, and flung flecks of yellow-brown foam from their noses and mouths. The black sludge oozing from their eyes was also more visible as the two riders approached.

"Leander received his dose of the cure, didn't he?" Welby asked.

Raven nodded. "His was one of the first."

"Right. Of course it was. I've personally seen to more dragons' care in the last two days than in my entire career." He shook his head and checked the satchel across his shoulder for whatever tools and implements were necessary.

Both dragons banked together to sweep in another wide circle around the three grounded creatures on the grass below. Two of them warbled bellows that sounded more like pain than anything else, although that could have been Raven's imagination.

They don't know what's happened to them yet. And by the time they do, it's already too late.

"So what's the plan?" she shouted at the vet.

He retrieved a handful of cure vials from Gruene's saddlebag and lifted them toward her. "Gruene and Leander have been inoculated, but that doesn't mean there's no danger. We go in quickly and take as many passes as necessary. How's your aim, Mage Alby?"

"My aim?"

He gave her a tight smile. "Whatever spells you might have to improve your accuracy, I suggest you use them. I can always make more doses but we don't exactly have an unlimited supply this far south. Get as close as you can but I still highly recommend staying away from jaws and talons to be safe."

She stared at the vials in his hand. "You mean—"

"I don't expect them to stand in line and open their mouths for a cure." With that, he leaned forward in his saddle and Gruene dove out of the two-wing formation toward the infected dragons who circled and stumbled against each other.

Leander's amused rumble vibrated through the saddle as he banked again to swoop toward the infected dragons. "He doubts your aim."

"There's nothing wrong with my aim." She slid her hand into one of her saddlebags and withdrew two small vials of the enchanted cure. "But I honestly thought he had a more...I don't know—a scientific approach to this rather than simply lobbing potions into their mouths."

"Don't worry, mage. My aim is impeccable."

Raven smirked. "I know."

Her familiar straightened out of his wide turn, tucked his wings against his back, and dove toward the infected creatures on the ground.

Welby and Gruene were already on their first pass over the group. The vet's arm drew back as he aimed at the largest of the sick dragons—a dark-brown male with patches of red-flecked scales winking in the sunlight. None of the diseased creatures seemed to notice the two Legion dragons coming toward them.

This meant that none of them looked at the vet and his black female as they swooped into position and so left Welby without an open mouth as an initial target.

Gruene's slightly extended talons brushed within an inch of the largest brown dragon's head and she screeched and wheeled into the sky before she turned again. Her rider scowled in concentration and all three dragons on the ground turned their heads to bellow at those who tried to get their attention.

"I guess that's our cue," Raven muttered.

Leander uttered a loud cry as they initiated their first pass over the infected. The large brown male tossed his head, stretched his wings as if he intended to take off after the new dragons swooping over the valley, and bellowed.

She zeroed in on his huge, gaping mouth and prepared to toss one of the vials into it. At the last second, he reared onto his hind legs with two furious wingbeats and jumped.

Everything else happened like the world moved in slow motion.

The vial flew from her hand. The brown's snapping jaws closed around the shimmering glass, which disintegrated in an instant before he'd even stopped bellowing. A splash of glittering potion—now freed from its nonexistent vial—disappeared into his throat a split second before the deadly teeth cracked against each other with a sharp click.

Horrified, she realized that the enormous mouth had closed inches from the tip of Leander's translucent red wing.

The surprise of being attacked by a dragon who leapt off his hind legs instead of flying made her familiar's speed and his confidence falter momentarily. She shouted in surprise and he tilted almost ninety degrees to avoid having his wing shredded by angry, foam-flecked jaws.

Raven leaned into the unstable, startled turn and tried to press herself against her dragon's neck the way she always did when he performed dangerous last-second maneuvers like that. The pommel of her saddle prevented her from flattening herself against his body and bruised her sternum instead.

For a moment, she thought she was about to fall off her familiar for the first time in years and stared with wide eyes at the other two infected dragons who jerked their heads toward her and lashed out with their snapping jaws.

None of it could have lasted for more than four seconds before Leander corrected his evasive maneuver and straightened again. Raven was whipped upright in the saddle and stared straight ahead with her hair blowing furiously around her face and over her eyes.

"He jumped at me," the red dragon snarled.

"Yep." She swallowed and looked over her shoulder to where the large brown male bumbled around with foam spraying from his mouth. He'd started to turn against the other two in his madness and pounded his tail against their scaley hides to get them away from him. "I didn't know dragons jumped."

"We do not."

"Raven!" Welby shouted as he and Gruene came up quickly behind them. "Did Leander—"

"No," her familiar growled.

"He's fine," she added and met the vet's gaze as Gruene leveled out beside them. "It was close, though."

"It was." His dark eyes were wide as he scrutinized Leander. "I didn't expect that one to try jumping when he can't fly. Did he get the cure?"

She nodded. "The vial disappeared."

A small smile broke through the man's concern. "That was an added enchantment for distribution these to wild dragons. Curing them won't do any good if they have a belly full of glass because of it."

"Right. Smart."

I can't believe I didn't even consider what it would do if crazed dragons ate the entire potion, vial and all.

Both dragons banked again to make another run at the grounded two who had yet to receive their cure. "This will take longer than I thought simply to get all three of them these potions," she commented.

Welby nodded. "We'll have to make a few passes but now that they know we're here, I think we can keep their attention long enough to get their mouths open. Are you ready to go again?"

"Of course."

Gruene swiveled her head toward Leander and fixed him with a challenging look. The bursts of dragon frost that curled around her lips didn't quite reach him as the wind whisked them away behind her, but they left a trail of glittering ice in their wake. "Would you like to dive first this time?"

The red dragon didn't look at her. "I have no preference."

"Suit yourself." She tucked her wings and dove toward the grounded dragons with incredible speed.

Raven tightened her hold on the second vial and readied herself to go in after them. "I hope those other two don't try to jump."

"Now we know what to expect." Leander beat his wings and followed the black dragon.

All three creatures on the ground screeched and bumbled around each other. This time, even with the Weeping Disease raging through them and muddying their minds, they were ready for what they thought was another attack instead of a well-prepared attempt to save them.

It took three more passes over the sick dragons, avoiding teeth, heads, and tails, before they managed to hurl a cure potion into each of the two dragons' open mouths. The vet delivered the last one himself before Gruene pulled away from the infected creatures to land twenty yards away in the field.

Raven and Leander followed them and both mages sat on their mounts to watch the progress of the cure eradicating the Weeping Disease.

The two smaller dragons shook their heads and stumbled for a while but they no longer circled randomly or spewed yellow-brown foam from their mouths. In another two minutes, their eyes had cleared as well. They blinked and looked at each other, then noticed Raven and Welby on their mounts across the field.

Leander uttered a screech of greeting, which was returned warily by the small violet-colored female. She started to head toward them but was cut off by a vengeful roar from the large brown male behind her. The other one turned as well to see the dragon who'd tried to bite Leander's wing off charge toward them.

He was unchanged.

"Oh, no." The mage's heart sank. "Seriously? It worked so quickly on the other two, but he's still—"

"We were too late for him," Welby muttered.

The cured dragons snapped at their infected companion and tried to get him to desist, but the crazed creature couldn't be reasoned with even by other wild dragons. When the other two took to the sky to avoid him, he continued to flail in the grass while he bellowed, stumbled, and lashed out at phantom threats, seemingly unaware that he stood alone.

"It has him." The vet drew his longbow from the side of

Gruene's saddle and produced an arrow with it, which he dipped into his satchel like he had the first time they'd come out together to deal with the situation.

"Wait." Raven looked at him. "Maybe we should give him a little more time."

"There is no more time. We know the cure works. The timing was simply off for that male, and I don't intend to sit here and watch him suffer through the rest of it."

Gruene leapt into the sky and headed toward the poor dragon who couldn't be saved.

The young mage gritted her teeth and stared after them. "We shouldn't have to sit here and watch them put another dragon down. We could have saved him if we'd been cleared to come down here sooner."

Leander swung his neck from side to side as Gruene curved in a sweeping arc around the deranged dragon too affected by Weeping Disease. Welby stood in the saddle to aim with his longbow. "Maybe not. He could have been at the end already."

"We should have tried harder to get out here the second we had the cure."

He growled impatiently. "This is no one's fault, Raven. We're doing what we can."

A piercing cry erupted from the brown male's throat and they both flinched a little before they steeled themselves against what they'd already known was a possibility. The sick dragon toppled with one of Dr. Welby's perfectly aimed arrows protruding from his eye.

Two mournful calls rose above them from the cured wild dragons as they circled the scene. She looked up and wanted to scream with them.

"They know what we've done," Leander muttered as he raised his head to watch them too. "And they're grateful."

"So am I, Leander. I only wish grateful and grieving didn't have to be so closely tied together with this."

"As do I, mage."

When Welby and Gruene circled again and landed beside them, the mood among them was far less celebratory than any of them had expected after seeing visible evidence that the cure worked effectively. The success was offset by the harsh reality that its efficacy carried the condition that the sick dragons weren't too far along in the destructive stages of Weeping Disease.

Gruene swung her head slowly toward Leander and this time, he didn't flinch or try to escape her.

Finally, Welby drew a deep breath. "Thank you for not trying to stop me this time."

Raven grimaced. "We're on the same page about what has to be done. But we shouldn't spend any more time down here. We need to get back to the sky and look for any other dragons who need your cure. Hopefully, we can work as quickly as that potion does."

He nodded. "Agreed."

Without another word from either of their mages, Gruene and Leander became airborne and the small team of dragon healers went out in search of others to save before it was too late.

CHAPTER SIX

After that first day, she and Welby had agreed it was in everyone's best interest for them to stay somewhere within the region to avoid the cost of all the time it would take to fly to and from the southwest.

Raven had immediately offered the use of Alby Ranch to house two dragons and two mages. He accepted gratefully and only then did she realize how strange it was that the second dragon and mage who would return to her home every night for the foreseeable future weren't Connor Alby and his newest dragon Calista.

They're still missing without a single word about either of them. And now I invited a vet contracted by the military to stay in Connor's old bed while we're here. Leander and Gruene are gonna end up fighting over his favorite hill.

Fortunately, sharing the space at the ranch after long days patrolling Lomberdoon's southern region was much easier than the actual patrol work itself—and the number of infected dragons the team found as the days progressed.

For the next week, the small team scoured Lomberdoon's southwest region for more dragons infected by the black fungus. Most of those they found were lone dragons who stumbled in circles in the middle of nowhere, suffering from the infection and all too easy to identify from a distance. They encountered a few other larger groups of dragons and performed the same distraction techniques to get them the cure—one dragon familiar swooped to catch the tiny clan's attention and the other came in behind so their rider could aim the vial at snapping jaws and bellowing throats.

The majority of the wild dragons who'd caught Weeping Disease were completely cured of all their symptoms and their suffering within minutes. Welby kept count in a small journal in his satchel of the numbers they helped as well as the number of those they hadn't acted quickly enough to save.

By the end of the week, a fifth of the wild dragons they'd encountered had to be put down by the precision of the vet's longbow, which only made Raven and her small unit all the more frustrated by their helplessness in those situations. They didn't give up, however, and there were more wild dragons to administer a cure to than any of them had realized.

Finally, the numbers who exhibited the odd telltale behavior of hyper-aggressive, confused, and black-teared victims foaming at the mouth dwindled into maybe two or three a day. They had widened their patrol route to include the neighboring towns and villages, although they'd only found two dragons who'd ventured anywhere close to human settlements. They were incredibly lucky that both of them responded quickly to the cure before any real damage was done to citizens, livestock, or property.

When their route grew again to encompass Harpertown, Welby suggested the next step of their plan. "When we go two days without seeing another infected dragon, I'll feel confident enough to return to base and report to Primus Kauler."

"One hundred percent success on the mission," Raven muttered.

"What was that?"

She shook her head. "That's what he said. Don't report unless we've been one hundred percent successful." When she looked at the vet as they soared on dragonback across the top of the forest stretching north past Brighton, his disturbed scowl looked exactly how she felt. "I know. It leaves a bad taste in my mouth too, trust me. With how many of them we haven't been able to cure…"

"No. I wouldn't call it a complete success either." He nodded gravely. "But however it has to be done, we're eradicating Weeping Disease from the entire dragon population. That's better than the alternative."

Right. The alternative being this disease spreading through every single dragon until it wipes them off the continent altogether.

"That will not happen," Leander growled.

Gruene screeched in agreement. "Not if we have anything to do with it."

They only found two other dragons in the northern part of their patrol that day and by early afternoon, Raven wondered if they'd find two or three every day for months. The team soared over the northern road for the third time before the rooftops of Harpertown came into view.

A burst of golden light erupted from the chimney of a large stone building at the end of the town's central avenue, followed by a loud crack and burst of high-pitched cackling. Gruene faltered slightly in her flight path and snarled at the unexpected intrusion into their airspace.

Welby scowled at the building and leaned slightly over the side of his saddle to get a better look. "What in the world was that?"

Raven grinned. "A friend."

"I'm sorry?"

"We haven't taken many breaks at all in the last week, Dr. Welby." She pointed at the building being coated with glittering golden sparks like slow-motion fireworks. "I've heard Harpertown is a great place for lunch. And they have added a few extra perks recently."

The man shrugged. "I am hungry."

"Great. Come on."

Leander dove toward the outskirts of the town's central square. Gruene followed without her usual enthusiasm for trying to race the huge male dragon to every new destination.

The mage couldn't get to the ground and the front doors of the building fast enough.

Of course, the locals of Harpertown had already cleared the end of the avenue once they'd caught sight of two dragons swooping from the sky into their town center.

When they landed beside the stone building, the humans brave and curious enough to stay where they were stepped into storefronts, hopped into their supply carts, or tugged each other farther down the avenue.

"Like they've never seen a dragon before," Leander muttered.

"Maybe not two as huge and regal-looking as you and Gruene," she replied as she patted his massive shoulder.

The black female chuffed and swung her head toward the STAR mage. "I like you, Mage Alby."

"Huh. I like you too, Gruene."

Her familiar shifted his head to settle it over his mage's shoulder and lowered his voice. "Any dragon who hands out compliments to strangers has altogether hidden motives."

"I wouldn't exactly call us strangers at this point." Raven glanced at him in exasperation and decided it was best to not finish the conversation out loud. *Maybe she assumes that if I like her, my dragon familiar might be a little more open to being friends. With her.*

He snorted. "I wouldn't call us friends either."

The black dragon showed no sign that she'd heard the conversation, although Raven knew the eerie capabilities of a dragon's honed senses full well.

Welby, on the other hand, stood in front of the stone building's entrance with his arms folded and frowned at the massive painted sign hung above the door. "Magical Madness. What is this?"

She approached him and stopped to admire the signage as well. "Only the best magical toyshop and purveyor of enchanted jokes in Lomberdoon. Then again, I'm very sure it's the only one."

"With a winged unicorn and a frog as its emblem?" His frown eased into wary amusement. "I can see why there's only one."

"I'm sure that's supposed to be a toad—his familiar Maxwell."

"I see."

Raven snorted a laugh. "My best friend opened this a few weeks ago. His newest creation, I guess. You don't have to come in with me but I promise it'll be worth it."

"A novelty among toyshops, I'm sure." He darted her a sidelong glance and chuckled. "I have to admit I'm a little curious."

"Trust me. With Henry Derks, a little curiosity goes a long way. Leander, we won't be very long. So—"

"I won't go anywhere," her dragon muttered and glowered at Gruene as she pranced in the small patch of grass in the shade of two large trees beside the shop. "And I speak only for myself."

"Well, you're in very good company," Welby added.

The red dragon didn't seem to think that was worth a response, but he stared at the patch of grass like he either wanted to curl on it or swat the black female out of it to take the entire area for himself.

Be nice, Raven thought to him.

I will be civil. Nice is taking it too far.

She shook her head, opened the front door of Magical Madness, and held it wide for Welby. "You know, I can't help but wonder if something happened between them and I missed it completely."

The vet stepped into the small square room that separated the exterior doors from a set of interior doors and shrugged. "Gruene likes him. You know how these things work. The harder he tries to hold her at bay, the more interested she'll be."

"Wait." The first set of doors closed behind her. "How what things work, exactly?"

He paused with his hand around the door handle in front of him and looked at her over his shoulder. "Dragon courtship, for lack of a better word."

She pressed her lips together and didn't know if she should laugh or fake her way through this entirely new set of lessons in How to Have a Dragon Familiar. "I'm not sure he knows how these things work."

His small, closed-lipped smile returned. "I think it's best to let them work it out for themselves. No matter how it turns out."

"Right." Raven gestured toward the door he was about to open and tried to hide her surprise with a not-quite-genuine smile. "Shall we?"

"If you insist." He opened the door and they stepped into the main room of Henry Derks' Magical Madness.

It was everything she had expected after listening to her best friend lay out his plans for the venture countless times over the last year and a half. And it was so much more.

Rows of brightly colored candy in every shape, size, and color filled the back wall of the shop behind the large green desk. Glittering gold bubbles floated through the air and bounced against shelves and walls without popping. When they merged with each other, they formed entirely new shapes before they burst and very real-looking trinkets dropped onto the floor. Most of them were renditions of the same mythological creatures Henry had constructed in his illusion display at Fowler Academy's Robing Ceremony.

Flying rocking horses the size of apples whinnied and moved between the bubbles, although they stayed well away from the giant chocolate fountain at the far end of the shop that somehow ran backward and tossed silver sparks into the air every thirty seconds.

A fleet of toy wagons rolled across the wooden floors, drawn by absolutely nothing, while the five-inch-tall horses darted between customers' legs to chase the conveyances.

Raven stared at the odd collection and wrinkled her nose.

Cart before the horse, huh? That'll be lost on every kid.

A life-sized dog inside the door opened and closed its mechanical mouth and occasionally barked realistically. Between those barks, however, it made sounds like every other animal under the sun, which was what produced the floating golden bubbles.

The rest of the inventions that filled the shop seemed like regular toys with odd magical twists—spinning tops that flung sparks and drops of water, floating play swords that jerked the wielder in complicated moves, and an entire shelf dedicated to slingshots of every imaginable shape and size. One section was completely devoted to joke items—cups and plates that cleared themselves instantly, boots that changed colors to clash with the rest of the wearer's outfit, "Stink 'Em Out" smoke bombs, and a full kit with instructions on "being in two places at once."

Raven grasped one of the carved wooden boxes, examined it, and read a portion of the description on the thick card tied to the handle with a piece of twine.

Have you ever wished you could be in two places at once? You don't have to clone yourself but they won't know that. This kit includes everything you need to enchant a stuffed double of yourself, complete with realistic eye movements. Boring work meetings. School assemblies. Having to go to bed early when you wanted a night out on the town. Merely enchant, and poof! The Double Trouble Twin Maker will take your place in any situation where no one expects you to move or speak for yourself.

She laughed when she read the fine print beneath:

"For realistic-breathing add-ons, speak to management."

"Derks..." She set the box gently on the shelf, then ducked when one of the flying horses uttered a high-pitched whinny and almost collided with her head.

"That one seems a little different than the others." Welby pointed at the flying animal that had almost careened into her and tilted his head. "Is it a Pegasus or a unicorn?"

"It's a Pegacorn."

"What?"

No matter how hard she tried, she couldn't force back a sharp laugh. "You know, from the sign out front. I think he's trying to make that his—"

"Wait, wait, wait! Hold the show!" Henry Derks vaulted over the large green desk in the back as an entire armada of toy Pegacorns leapt off their various positions on the shelves toward the visitors. The vet swatted at a few of them and his scowl returned. She laughed when one of the Pegacorns' wings caught in her hair and it struggled to free itself. "No, no. Hey! Leave the mage alone. And you—you break it, you buy it. So go gentle on the Pegacorns, huh?"

"Excuse me?" Welby turned from trying to bat the toy nuisances out of orbit and Henry stopped to study the man warily.

"Uh...ha. Sorry. I thought you were someone else."

"Is that a frequent misunderstanding in your store?"

"Well, no. But I recognized Alby, and I assumed you were—"

Raven widened her eyes at her best friend and tried to shake her head subtly.

Of course, he thought I wouldn't walk into his store with anyone other than William. They don't even look the same from behind.

"That you were, uh..." The wizard scratched his head vigorously and his mop of dirty-brown hair stood up in all directions. "Someone else. Someone I knew. I mean, someone we all know. Except for you, obviously."

Please stop right there, Derks. Or this will turn into the kind of awkward we can't back out of.

He chuckled nervously. "But you're not, so—"

"Dr. Chui Welby." The man held out his hand toward Henry, who took it and pumped it up and down with enthusiastic gratitude for being rescued from his tongue-tied confusion.

"Henry. Henry Derks." He looked at Raven with raised eyebrows and she cursed herself for not having stopped her friend sooner.

"Dr. Welby and I work together," she said. "And Henry and I have been friends since before we could walk."

"That's what happens when your only neighbor is a

good one." Henry released the man's hand, snatched a wayward Pegacorn out of the air, and tickled its belly until the toy went limp in his hand. "I still have a few bugs to work out with these guys. Who knew they'd try to form an army, right?"

Welby's eyes widened before the wizard placed the toy on the closest shelf. "Indeed."

"So. You're a Legion doc, huh? You know, I put a few requests in after graduation for a Lifebringer assignment, but I guess we healed all the people who needed healing when magic returned and the whole kingdom flocked to Fowler for—"

"Not that kind of doctor, Mr. Derks," the vet corrected with a patient smile. "I'm a veterinarian."

"Oh, yeah? Cool. Hey, so if I hypothetically wanted someone to take a look at one or two of Maxwell's weirder-looking warts, I could bring him to Havendom and know he's in the right hands."

Right on cue, Maxwell poked his head out of the breast pocket sewn into Henry's tunic and croaked.

Welby chuckled. "Well, I suppose I could take a look. Mostly, I specialize in dragon care."

"Oh." The young wizard frowned. "Oh, a dragon doctor. That's…" He studied the man with renewed interest. "That makes much more sense. Welcome to Magical Madness!"

Raven's friend spread his arms in an expansive gesture and grinned.

"It's incredible, Derks," she added when her companion took too long to offer any praise. "You did it."

"I told you I would. Come on. Let me give you the tour."

The vet started to protest, but Henry grasped her hand

and dragged her through the shop while he pointed out all the inventions he'd spent the last year and a half imagining before he finally brought them to fruition. Welby sighed, dodged another diving Pegacorn, and followed the young mages to experience a tour of Magical Madness with the owner himself.

"Over there, we got your Living Blocks."

"Those look like regular wooden blocks, Derks. Probably the least exciting thing in here."

"Ah." Henry thrust a finger in the air and wiggled his eyebrows. "You'd think that, wouldn't you?" He snatched two blocks up and made a small figure that looked something like a rabbit before he took a small vial off the display. His face scrunched in concentration, he uncorked it and poured two glowing silver drops onto his creation. "Add only a little animating potion, and…viola!"

The blocks erupted with thick gray smoke and a few sparkles, but when it cleared, it left behind a white rabbit that twitched its nose and took two small, tentative hops forward.

"Living Blocks! Make your family pet, and the best thing about this one is you'll never have to feed it or clean up after it. It's merely cute."

Welby chuckled. "And what about a rabbit's reproductive tendencies?"

Henry sputtered, scratched the side of his head, and shrugged. "I didn't think about that one, honestly. But hey. Trust a vet to ask that kinda question, huh? Thanks. I'll look into it. Maybe I should make a list of approved animals only."

Raven laughed and hurried after him as he took them

down the rows of toys and stopped now and then at displays at the end of most aisles to give a brief demonstration.

"And this one. This one's good right here. Sentient Slime."

A small blob of luminous green sludge moved on the display table. It bounced between the raised walls of its makeshift pen, hiccupped every few seconds, and made wet, squelching noises like an animal sniffing with a runny nose.

"What's that for?" she asked.

"For fun, Alby. Come on, that's the whole point of this place. Everything is fun. Look, this is a cute, squishy eradicator of anything you don't want lying around. Sometimes things you do want, though. It's a little—hey, hey. No, kid. Put that back on the shelf."

A little boy was tugged along by his mother—who either hadn't heard Henry's protests or wanted to get out the store as quickly as possible—and he stared at the Sentient Slime before he dropped an animated Cyclops figurine into the sludge pen. He barely had enough time to see the result before his mother ushered him away from the display, but Raven, Henry, and Welby watched the green pile of slime streak toward the toy and devour it in two seconds.

Now, it was a pile of moving, hiccupping slime with a perfectly visible Cyclops inside its body. It seemed completely unaffected by the smaller enchanted toy that kicked and punched in an attempt to free itself from the inside.

"Oh." Curious, Raven reached toward the slime. "And how do you get the stuff back again once it—"

Her friend's urgent grasp on her wrist made her stop, and he shook his head before he released her quickly. "I, uh… Yeah, I haven't worked that part out yet." He darted Welby a sidelong glance, took an empty wooden crate off the top shelf beside him, and turned it over the Sentient Slime. "I should probably find a better way to keep that safe."

"And away from wayward fingers, I imagine," Welby muttered.

"Anyway. Those are the highlights. Well, all the ones I can think of now. You caught me off guard, Alby. I didn't think I'd see you here again any time soon."

"I know. I got your letter about the grand opening but couldn't get away. Work, you know."

"Tell me about it." When the young wizard looked at Welby again, he cleared his throat. "I guess it's a little different than what you guys do all day long. By the way, what are you guys doing? Havendom's a long—"

"Raven?" From behind the green desk—which was now close enough to see the front had been painted with a warped, desk-shaped likeness of Maxwell—Anne Marie Murphy emerged from a door in the wall decorated with moving, shimmering murals that changed by the minute.

"Hey, Murphy." She laughed and turned to Welby for another introduction. "This is…well, her last name is—"

"Murphy, and that's what everyone calls me." The brown-haired witch who used to be so shy and hesitant to talk to anyone stepped forward and proffered her hand.

"Dr. Chui Welby. It's a pleasure to meet you."

"The Legion sends doctors out with dragon mages?"

"We're working on something down here," Raven clarified. "And Dr. Welby's a civilian contractor."

"He's a dragon doctor," Henry muttered, leaned toward Murphy, and widened his eyes.

"Oh. That's cool. So the red leather outfit is only for mages then, right?"

"It's the division uniform." Raven looked at her ensemble and shrugged. "I'm so used to it."

Welby cleared his throat and now looked more uncomfortable than he had when he stood in Kauler's office while the primus reprimanded Raven for speaking out against him. "The three of you have some catching up to do. Mage Alby, I think I'll head out to take another pass on my own. If I see anything, I know where to find you. Otherwise, I imagine I'll see you at the ranch."

"Okay. Are you sure?"

"Yes." He scowled at four flying Pegacorns that converged on each other at the center of the shop beneath the ceiling. "And I don't like the idea of having to explain any surface injuries potentially incurred in a toyshop."

The wizard laughed. "They're harmless. Mostly."

"It was nice to meet you both." The vet nodded at Henry and Murphy, who returned the farewell as he hurried through the shop toward the front door.

CHAPTER SEVEN

"Huh." Henry cocked his head and stared after the retreating veterinarian. "You know, I can't quite work it out. Every kid who walks into this place completely loses it over the awesomeness in here. And way more adults than I expected take one look at what's going on and run outta here like they remembered their barn was on fire. It doesn't make sense."

Murphy smirked at him. "Some people don't appreciate an overactive imagination."

"Aw... Thank you!" He slung his arm around her shoulders and pulled her in to peck her on the cheek. Then, he paused. "Wait, you're not talking about you, right?"

She rolled her eyes and pretended to shove him away.

Raven grinned at her friends.

It doesn't look like anything has changed for them since mage school. Except for Magical Madness.

"Raven." Murphy looked at her and nodded. "Who is he?"

"Who?"

"Your…doctor friend." The other witch leaned sideways to get another look at the front door, but Welby was already well gone. "He doesn't look like a doctor."

"Yeah, I second that." Henry wiggled his eyebrows. "There's no way he's simply a vet. Did you see the arms on that guy? And he's, like, eight feet tall."

"Henry, no one's eight feet tall."

He gaped at Murphy in mock insult. "Oh, but you aren't gonna argue with me about his hulking muscles?"

"They're a little hard to ignore." She squeezed his bicep. "So are yours."

Of all things, that was what rendered Henry Derks momentarily speechless, and he fixed his girlfriend with one of his signature goofy grins.

"We work together," Raven said. "That's it."

"Uh-huh. Right." Murphy folded her arms. "Because the military started sending infamous war mages and surprisingly muscular dragon doctors into toyshops as part of their secret missions."

The young wizard threw his head back and burst out laughing. Raven couldn't help but join him, although her laughter was much more subdued.

"No, Murphy. We happened to be out this way and saw the fireworks display from the sky. I thought we deserved a little break, and it was a great chance to see Henry's new business. Which is incredible, by the way."

"Thank you, thank you." He kicked up one heel to perform an exaggerated bow. "I do what I—wait. What fireworks?"

He and Murphy turned slowly to look at each other and their smiles morphed into almost terror before a loud bang, a high-pitched squeal, and a short string of sharp staccato cracks came from the very end of the shop. Blue and yellow smoke ballooned from that area, and boys' uproarious laughter rang out and momentarily made all the other customers stop what they were doing.

"Are you kidding me?" Henry cried.

His girlfriend put a hand on his shoulder. "I'll handle this." She stalked toward the smoke still rising thickly from the group of laughing boys and shouted, "You know the rules! Mature kids, right? That's what you said. If you wanna test the Sky-High Explosion section, you need a staff member with you to supervise. Get away from there."

Henry stared at Raven until she met his gaze, then he laughed nervously and shook his head. "Yeah. I had to make something that would appeal to the...older crowd. Not old enough, though, I guess."

"It looks like Murphy has a good handle on it, though."

"Yeah, I'd be dead without her, Alby. For real. You know, maybe I should have let her bring that battle-ax with her, but I kept thinking about all the complaints we'd get from parents."

"Well, she's always been good for you. Ax or no ax."

"And she still is." He puffed his chest out and nodded toward Murphy and the Sky-High Explosion section. "We're kind of a thing. I mean still. I mean... Hell. She finally dropped the job she never wanted as a seamstress with her mom to come help me, and I didn't even have to ask. I think..." He leaned slightly toward her and let the anticipation build with his knowing smile. "I think I might even end up popping the question. You know, to Murphy."

She laughed. "Good, 'cause I would have told you no."

"Ha! Don't tell her I said anything. But if she doesn't kill me after the next few months of running this place with me, then yeah. I might."

She clapped a hand on her best friend's shoulder and gave him a little shake. "It's about time, Derks."

"That I get married?"

"That you found someone who appreciates your over-active imagination. Besides me, of course."

"Of course."

"I'm very happy for you."

"Thanks, Raven," he muttered and his face reddened a little. He cleared his throat and nudged her toward the back. "Come on. It's a little quieter at the desk."

Trying not to laugh, Raven followed him to the toad-painted desk, where Murphy's instructions were now muffled by the thick blue and yellow smoke she cleared quickly. She didn't leave the group of boys to their own devices again, however.

When Henry stopped to look over his store, he drew a deep breath, nodded, and placed a hand protectively on the desk. "It's real, Alby. This place is finally here. And it works."

"It sure does." She laughed when a group of small children raced after the Living Blocks bunny, which now hopped away from a giant frog made of enchanted sticks. The smoke and lights from the "mature toys and explosions" section at the far end of the shop had completely settled, and Murphy kept a vigilant eye on the older and slightly more destructive boys who'd come into Harpertown to test Henry Derks' Magical Madness.

Raven caught the girl's eye for a moment and grinned.

"You know, I wonder if there's anything at that end of the shop that would work in a military context. Or maybe a new invention of yours. Something your brain could cook up in a few days, probably."

"What? Are you serious, Alby?" Henry scowled at her. "This is a toyshop, not an arsenal. Toys are supposed to be fun. To bring joy. Not…war."

She snorted. "Hey, even if it's a giant stink bomb. We could clear out any enemy with a super-sized version of what you pulled at the Robing Ceremony."

He sniggered, then a thoughtful frown wiped every other expression from his face. "You know, maybe I'll think about it." Maxwell uttered another croak from his breast pocket. "Yeah, Maxwell. You're right. It might turn into something."

She regarded her friend's toad familiar with amusement. "It's always good when you can see what's in front of you, right?"

Maxwell croaked again and Henry looked across the shop before he nodded at the front door. "Same to you, Alby."

"What?"

At his raised eyebrow, she turned and froze as a knot of discomfort tightened in her gut.

William Moss had stepped through the second set of doors into the shop and now walked quickly toward the toad-painted desk, his smile growing.

We're not in Brighton. What's he doing here?

"Alby?" Henry leaned toward her and lowered his voice. "You look like you're about to be sick. Hey, wanna try one of these candies? Technically, they were supposed to fake cold symptoms. I think. But it kinda turned out that they do the opposite, so they're not that much of a bestseller at this point."

"I don't think candy's gonna help, Derks." Raven tried to plaster a smile on as William approached them. "But thanks."

"Hey, guys." William reached the desk as another Pegacorn swooped, lowered its head, and aimed its single horn at the center of the dragon trainer's forehead.

The wizard snatched it out of the air at the last second and tickled its enchanted belly until it went slack. "Seriously. These are worse than a simple hex. Not that I know anything about the dark magical arts. You know, in case anyone was wondering." He put the toy on the desk and turned to shake hands with William. "How are you doing, man?"

"All right, Henry. Look at this place." The guys smiled and nodded and surveyed the surrounding toyshop filled with children screaming in enjoyment and their parents who merely looked like they wanted to scream. "You finally pulled this together, huh?"

"With a little help from my Uncle Marv and a few friends." Henry darted Raven a sidelong glance.

"I don't see any toy dragons in here, though." William smirked. "They didn't fit the bill?"

"Oh, trust me. I wanted to do something with dragons." Henry nodded toward Murphy. "But then my better half reminded me it's probably a little too soon to start handing out miniature versions to kids when half the kingdom still...you know, has a few trust issues."

"Your better half, huh?"

The young wizard shrugged. "Honestly, she's just better. Period."

Raven watched their exchange with growing apprehension.

William won't even look at me. I don't know if that's better or worse.

But the conversation had died down and it was now impossible to ignore the awkward silence around them beside the frog-painted desk. "What are you doing in Harpertown?"

The dragon trainer fixed her with a tight smile. "Teo and I had a few errands to run. Easy stuff for some of the other southern dragon ranches. Then we saw Leander outside and thought we'd come say hi."

Her mind reached out immediately to her dragon's. *You didn't think it would be a good idea to give me a little warning?*

Flyboy isn't a threat. And Teo's here. Why would I want to warn you about either of them?

She tried to not roll her eyes.

"Raven…" He cleared his throat and glanced at Henry, who still stood with his arms folded close to both of them in their odd circle of three.

The wizard grinned like he was watching a complicated drama play out and no one else would notice his presence. Maxwell blinked slowly and his eyes sank momentarily into his head as he stared at them as well.

William leaned closer to her instead. "I know we're not exactly in Brighton, but since you're more or less in town and Teo and I are done for the day, I wanted to see if you'd like to get dinner with me."

She gaped at him. "Dinner? I, uh… I mean, that's—"

A group of very young children laughed and screamed when two of the golden bubbles overhead converged and popped to drop half a dozen goldfish onto the floor. William turned to look at the commotion, and Henry widened his eyes at her.

Oh, sure. I have my best friend telling me to have dinner with someone who used to be my...something.

When the dragon trainer turned again, Henry snatched the toy Pegacorn up and pretended to inspect it thoroughly. "Does that happen a lot? Goldfish?"

The wizard feigned surprise to be asked a question. "Yeah. All the time. They'll turn into fish-shaped fudge in about five minutes. Then it'll get crazy in here."

William wrinkled his nose in confusion. "They're all over the floor."

"Huh. Right. Yeah, I guess I can't leave them there and expect a horde of kids to eat floor fudge." The way he said it made it sound like he was excusing himself from the still-awkward conversation, but he didn't budge. Instead, he looked pointedly at Raven.

"So?" William looked hopefully at her and rubbed the back of his neck. "Dinner?"

"Yeah, okay." No one moved until he gestured toward the front door of the shop. "Oh. You mean now?"

"Yeah, Raven." He laughed. "While we're both here. Otherwise, some kind of mission or unexpected battle will probably get in the way."

Henry snorted. "That's happened often."

"I know." The dragon trainer looked particularly uncomfortable now, but he placed a hand on her elbow and guided her gently with him. "I know a good place in Harpertown. You'll like it."

"Okay."

"See you later, guys," Henry called after them. "And don't stay away too long, Alby. You don't wanna miss what I'm coming up with next."

"I have no doubt." She gave her best friend a hesitant wave and plastered a smile on her face as William held the door open for her.

The sound of squealing children, animated toys, and grumbling parents followed them outside onto Harpertown's main avenue.

I did not expect to go on a date in the middle of a mission to cure sick dragons with Welby. But now, I don't have the mission as an excuse when William found me in a toyshop.

They stepped into the early-evening sunlight to where Leander and Teo pranced in the grass beneath the huge, shady trees. Teo stopped and stretched his long neck toward them. "Raven. It is good to see you."

"You too, Teo." She frowned at Leander in disapproval, and her dragon familiar stretched his wings beside his shimmering green friend.

William turned to scan the end of the town square's avenue and the crowd of people who'd tentatively gathered to watch two dragons they didn't know playing in the grass. "You two are good to stay here for a while, right?"

"For as long as you need, William," Teo replied with a soft purr.

"Well, it won't be too long," Raven said. "It's only dinner."

The dragon trainer darted her a sidelong glance and

pressed his lips together. "Yep. We'll be…back. Come on, it's right down here."

"Have fun," Leander called after them.

She looked over her shoulder at her dragon familiar's red scales winking in the dappled sunlight through the trees. *You're not helping.*

I'm very helpful. You're simply letting your human feelings get the better of you, mage. Again.

She swallowed and continued down the cobbled streets beside the first real crush she'd ever had. Maybe the first person responsible for breaking her heart in some ways.

Not broken. Merely bruised a little. And I don't know if things can ever go back to the way they were. Dinner's probably not gonna change that.

CHAPTER EIGHT

As it turned out, the "good place" William knew in Harper-town was the back porch of Mr. and Mrs. Narshdale, who ran the town's inn and the bakery next door. They were thrilled to see him, incredibly happy to meet Raven, and confused as to why their frequent dragon-trainer patron walked into their establishment with a redheaded mage in Airborne Legion uniform.

"Your usual table, Mr. Moss?" Mrs. Narshdale asked with a grin.

"It's my favorite for a reason." William nodded. "That would be great, thank you."

"Right this way. Samuel, open the cask from Blueridge for Mr. Moss and his guest, would you?"

"Yes, dear." Mr. Narshdale nodded and smiled as he finished drying tin cups with a rag at the bar.

"You'll love what we got in from North Willbrook," the woman told the young couple as she ushered them through the back door of the inn's main room and along multiple hallways. "They've had a fantastic summer harvest, and we had first rights to almost everything after the alderman of North Willbrook heard of our bakery. All the way down here, can you believe it? I haven't even been as far north as Havendom in my life, and here we have the alderman of North Willbrook asking specifically for my pies. My pies! I didn't know anyone that far north even knew we existed."

"Raven's stationed in Havendom," William said.

"Oh?" Mrs. Narshdale opened a final door that led onto a small, private back porch with a beautifully and meticulously tended garden. "What are you doing here?"

"Well, I'm in Brighton for a short while."

"A true southerner! You know Mr. Moss owns the Moss Dragon Ranch in Brighton, don't you?"

"We used to live down the road from each other," he replied.

"You don't say!" The woman pulled a chair out at one of the two small, two-person tables on the private porch and grinned at her. "Last time I checked, there were only the Derks property and the Alby Ranch out that way. It's been a while, though."

Raven tried to hide her discomfort at being in such close proximity with someone who knew of the Alby family but had no idea who she was speaking to in the moment. "No, it hasn't changed that much. My grandfather's had Alby Ranch all my life."

"Really? So that makes you…" Mrs. Narshdale paused, cocked her head, then laughed as her face flushed a little. "Well, I'll be. Mr. Moss, if I'd known you were bringing Sarah Alby's daughter into my inn, I would have spruced up a little."

"It was last-minute," William replied with a shrug. "But

I did tell her I knew the best place in Harpertown for dinner."

"Best place in..." She batted his arm playfully and chuckled. "You're too much. And we have the best pies. Oh, you wait, Miss Alby. I'll bring you one of my famous calliberry pies—the same kind the alderman of North Will-brook sank his fork into and can't get enough of."

"It sounds amazing," she replied.

"Yes, it is. But I'll let you judge for yourself. Not until after dinner, of course. Now, you two sit back, relax, and enjoy yourselves out here. It won't take me but a minute."

"Thank you, Mrs. Narshdale." The dragon trainer nodded and she bustled away from them, glanced once over her shoulder, and grinned before she slipped through the door.

"Your usual table, huh?" Raven turned toward him with a playful smile, but he was already behind her to draw the chair out a little more so she could sit. That surprised her enough to let him slide the chair under her.

He's pulling chairs out for me. This is a date, then.

"I come through Harpertown more often these days. It saves Teo and me a few hours when we're heading back from Nadine or any of the other ranches where we've been...uh, training the trainers, I guess."

"It's nice out here. I can see why you like it."

White-painted latticework closed the porch in on two sides and thick, lush vines covered in bright-purple blossoms had grown in and through the siding. Potted plants lined the edge of the porch and exploded with every other color of flowers, and lit candles in small jars hung from the ceiling. The section that wasn't walled gave them an incredible view of the open fields that stretched north away from Harpertown.

The highest peaks of the farthest Brightsbane Mountain ranges rose like purple silhouettes in the distance as the sun made its descent toward them. Their shadow fell over the edge of another forest along Lomberdoon's westernmost border that stretched as far north as Raven could see.

"And it's incredible as a usual table."

William's eyes crinkled at the corners as he scanned the gorgeous landscape in front of them. "The first time Teo and I came here, Mr. and Mrs. Narshdale didn't quite know what to do with a dragon but they didn't want to lose the patronage. It was a challenge but they were very accommodating. Yes, there are two tables here but honestly, I think I'm the only one who knows about this patio."

"A private patio because you had a dragon."

"Well, he could hang out back here, I could keep an eye on him, and the innkeepers didn't have to worry so much about local gossip that would result if I parked my ride out front."

Raven pressed her lips together but couldn't hide a smile. "That's a smart arrangement for everyone."

"It is. Hopefully, one day, I won't feel like I have to sit out back behind any inn at all simply to keep a dragon out of sight. The people here know Teo fairly well by now. Leander's something of a novelty."

"Ha. That's an understatement."

"They'll be fine at Henry's store."

"Oh, I know." She clasped her hands in her lap and

couldn't look away from the perfect view in what would she would otherwise have considered a perfect setting for a perfect date.

It's not like much has changed. We're still talking about Leander and Teo and how people feel about dragons. And after that? Who am I kidding? Everything's changed.

The silence between them should have been easy and comfortable like it used to be, but it wasn't. William drew a deep breath and leaned forward slightly. "Raven, I—"

The back door opened, and Mr. Narshdale came out this time carrying a large tray. "Now this is a special vintage, Mr. Moss. Exactly as the missus said." He took two glasses filled with a light, slightly yellow liquid off the tray and placed one in front of each of his dinner guests. "It's from Blueridge. Some of the best I've had, and you know we save it for our best patrons."

"Thank you." Raven stared at the glass as the man set the small table with plates, cutlery, and two rolled cloth napkins.

"My wife told me we have an Alby gracing our inn tonight." Mr. Narshdale chuckled. "Who'd have thought? It's a pleasure to have you here, Miss Alby. And Mr. Moss, as always. Only a pleasure. Dinner will be out soon. If you two need anything—anything at all—you come let us know."

"I'm very sure you and Mrs. Narshdale already have everything covered," William said. "You always do. Thank you."

"You bet." The man looked from one to the other, grinned, and finally realized he was intruding in some type of private moment. He rapped his knuckles on the corner of the table. "Well. You enjoy that. If you like it, I'll bring out some more."

"That sounds good."

The man hurried away and the back door swung closed with a gentle creak and a thump.

"Well." William lifted his glass and studied the light, cool liquid. "It looks like we're getting the special treatment."

"You mean they're not like this every time you stop here?"

He laughed. "No, they're a little more...excited, I guess. That tends to happen when I'm with you."

"It's the Alby name that does it." She sniffed her drink and pursed her lips. "This is wine."

"Special vintage from Blueridge. In case you hadn't heard."

"I'm not much of a wine drinker—"

"Raven, if you don't want it, we can send it back—"

"And crush their souls? I don't think I can do that." They both laughed and she sipped tentatively. "That's...not bad."

He smirked over the rim of his glass. "You're not a wine drinker because you haven't ever had wine, have you?"

She took another sip and put the glass down. "I went straight from mage school to the Airborne. There wasn't much time for sampling special vintages."

The unspoken part of her sentence hung between them as they stared at each other.

Straight from graduating and a Robing Ceremony he couldn't make it to. And right into Havendom to start my first mage assignment after that last seriously awkward visit to Moss Ranch.

William looked away from her and put his cup down. "I didn't think the military had an issue with alcohol."

She shrugged. "I don't think they do. But drinking and flying probably don't mix well."

"Ha. That's one way to look at it. We can stick to one glass, then." Another tense moment of silence surrounded them before he glanced at the porch's back door into the inn. "I noticed you didn't try to correct either of them when they called you Miss Alby."

"Hey, feel free to let them known I'm a mage too. If they haven't already heard of me by now, I don't wanna send the wrong message by clearing that up while we're on their porch."

"Why not? It's Mage Alby now." He frowned teasingly at her. "You've worked hard to come this far."

"Well, I didn't go to Fowler so everyone could call me Mage Alby. That's merely an extra perk."

"A perk you've probably earned five times over at this point." He held her gaze for a moment longer, then looked away to take another sip of wine.

This is going about as well as I expected. And not nearly as well as he'd hoped, I guess.

Raven sipped her wine as well and looked over the fields north of Harpertown and the changing colors as the late-summer sunset filled the sky with pinks and oranges.

"It's nice to have a little time alone with you again," William said. "Without dragons around or a ranch to run. Without all the constant interruptions when we least—"

The door opened again, and his instant scowl as both

Mr. and Mrs. Narshdale stepped through with a serving cart carrying their guests' dinner made his companion burst out laughing. He turned his scowl onto her instead with more surprise now, and she laughed even harder.

Why is this so funny? He's right. We're always interrupted. And now I'm laughing at him.

As the cart rolled toward them with a soft, repetitive squeak, he chuckled, then laughed with her.

"It sounds like you two are having quite a time out here already," Mrs. Narshdale said jovially. "And you haven't even started the meal yet."

"Oh, we're very much looking forward to it, Mrs. Narshdale. This was perfect timing."

William snorted and shook his head before he sipped his wine. Raven did the same and watched him over the rim of her glass as the innkeepers set down a massive bowl of summer salad with strawberries and crumbled cheese, a whole roasted chicken with lemon, buttered and seasoned green beans, and a basket of rolls with whipped butter.

"Is there anything else we can get for you, Mr. Moss?" Mr. Narshdale asked and wiped his hands on a rag before he shoved it into his bar apron.

"This is fantastic. Thank you."

"You make sure to save room for that calliberry pie, now." Mrs. Narshdale nodded vigorously. "That's not something you want to miss out on."

"Absolutely not." Raven's cheeks flushed for seemingly no reason and she stared at her wineglass.

Okay, not for no reason. I'm drinking. With William. It's probably not the best idea right now, but neither was this date.

The innkeepers hurried inside to attend to their other

patrons seated in the front room, and the young couple was finally left alone for at least a little longer than they had been to enjoy their dinner in peace.

They talked a little about Raven's work with the Airborne, although she mostly kept the conversation to her training regimen with STAR and the fact that Primus Kauler had promoted her to oversee tactical maneuvers for the entire division. She assumed the topic of sick dragons and black fungus in the old Swarm-tunnel mines and Weeping Disease cures was off-limits. Mostly because it was still Legion business and then a little because she didn't want to have to explain to William that she'd spent the last week with Dr. Chui Welby—another mage with a dragon familiar who happened to be a vet contracted by the royal military.

The young trainer listened intently, entertained by her stories of the other legionaries in the STAR division and night rides and the things she was slowly but surely learning about military life after coming in with no training whatsoever to be a Legion mage. He shared what was happening at Moss Ranch with her, how the dragons were doing, and all the things he was getting used to in his own way now that his father had passed and he was completely responsible for all of it.

He did mention the message she had left with his ranch hand Kyle weeks before.

"To be on the safe side," she said and avoided his gaze. "You never know when one little thing might make a huge difference for everyone."

That seemed to break the momentary spell of ease and

comfort in each other's presence, and Raven realized at that point that she'd almost finished her glass of wine.

Mrs. Narshdale appeared with two massive slices of her allegedly famous calliberry pie. This time, however, with the sunlight almost completely gone behind the mountains and two young people enjoying their meal on her patio together, she left quickly and didn't try to start more conversation.

The young mage cut into her slice of pie and glanced at William.

He frowned at his dessert and tried to cut into it but wasn't paying attention. After a few moments, he put his fork down and sighed. "Okay, I've been trying to find the right time for this, but I'm not sure the right time exists and dinner's almost over. So I simply have to say it."

She met his gaze with wide eyes and a twinge of guilt and sadness in her heart.

It looked like there were tears in his eyes, but that could have been the candlelight from the jars hanging above them.

William swallowed and blinked quickly. "Raven, I'm sorry."

"For what?" She took the first bite of pie without looking away from him and wanted to hit herself.

This might be the best pie I've ever tasted, and he's sitting there trying to have the serious conversation I don't want to have.

Raven put her fork down and gave him her full attention.

"For leaving when I did. The way I did."

"William—"

"No, I am. I know I could have handled it better. I should have handled it better, and I know that's what's been...I don't know. Pulling us apart."

"You had so much going on. I understand."

"Raven." He stared at her for a moment, then shifted his chair and leaned closer to her. "Since the day you arrived at Moss Ranch wanting to learn about dragons and how to make one your familiar, you've always had a lot going on. More than most people, honestly, and you would never have run away from me like that."

"You didn't run away." Without thinking about it, she took his hand and gave it a little squeeze. "You had to go. You had to take care of the ranch and your dad at the very end. You're more committed to dragons than most people I know, even trainers and riders, and going to Nadine was the best way you could do both of those things. Even if it meant you weren't in Brighton anymore. You keep your word, William. No matter what. It's what you do."

He laughed bitterly and looked away again, but he squeezed her hand in return before he drew a deep breath. "I didn't with you. I left you waiting for a letter or a message or something. Now, you've set up a whole new life for yourself. You're a Legion mage in Havendom and are doing what you wanted to do, and I'm so happy for you, Raven. Truly.

"I only... You know, I thought that when I came back, I'd be able to explain what was going on. That I wasn't in a good place when I left and I never meant to push you away like that. But I can't get rid of this feeling that it's already way too late to make up for the awful way I handled everything."

They both looked at their clasped hands resting on his knee and she couldn't bring herself to pull her hand away.

This is the talk I didn't want to have with him, and it's not as bad as I thought it would be. Go figure.

William nodded. "I know you don't think of it as me abandoning you or anything, but—"

"It's not too late," she blurted.

"What?" He looked at her in surprise and his hand went slack in hers.

"It's never too late to fix anything," she added. "Or to at least try. If I didn't believe that, I would have given up a long time ago."

His wary, crooked smile almost made it feel like they were the same people they had been two years ago—or even one year ago. Before his world had been turned upside down with all the work that went into being a dragon trainer in a kingdom where all dragons were now free. Before Ernie Moss had finally passed away. And yes, before she had felt a little betrayed and a little abandoned by the way he'd so brusquely left without saying goodbye and without sending anything but one short, terse letter saying he couldn't return to Brighton and he didn't know when he would.

It almost felt like she could tell him anything in the world the way she used to and know that William Moss would be there for her every time, happy to cheer her on because they believed in the same things and he believed in her.

"I can't imagine Raven Alby giving up on anything," he muttered.

"Well, it would have made things much easier in some

ways. And I did sometimes. Especially when things didn't turn out the way I expected or even hoped they would. But it's never too late to keep trying."

"Do you…" He shifted in his chair to face her more directly and caught her hand with both of his this time. "Do you think it's too late for us?"

Raven swallowed thickly and studied his blue eyes that glistened under the candlelight. "I honestly don't know. I mean…I'm in Havendom, for one thing. And I don't know if things have settled enough for either of us to know what's coming—"

"No, you're right." He nodded slowly. "I know that. And I'm not trying to make you decide anything now. I only…" A heavy sigh escaped him. "If you tell me it's not too late, Raven, that's all I need to hear. And right now, sitting here on the back porch of an inn with calliberry pie in front of us…"

They both laughed.

"This is probably more than I deserve and I don't want to ruin it."

Raven shook her head slightly. "You haven't so far."

"Good."

She didn't know what she'd expected after that, but it wasn't for William to lean even closer, cup her cheek, and pull her in for a kiss. She certainly didn't expect to kiss him in return—or to kiss him at all after their very few tense and awkward moments together in the last year where kissing hadn't even remotely been an option.

But it felt like it always had been.

Beneath the admittedly romantic setting, the single glass of wine, and her brief reprieve from patrolling the kingdom's southern region for sick dragons to cure, that was what scared her—that being with William felt the same as it always had but everything else in both their lives had changed.

When he pulled away, he chuckled and pressed his forehead against hers. "I've missed you."

"Me too."

She meant it but in a different way she didn't quite understand.

Not the same way he means it. I think that's the problem.

Eventually, they pulled away from each other completely. The dragon trainer smiled with his dimples on full display and the Legion mage darted him occasional sidelong glances as they dug into their pie.

"This is so good," he said through a mouthful.

"At least we know Mrs. Narshdale wasn't blowing anything out of proportion."

CHAPTER NINE

Saying their goodbyes after dinner didn't carry the same hopeful, content-for-now feeling they had managed to capture on the back porch of the inn. That might have had something to do with both their dragons staring at them and listening to their entire conversation as they walked to the side of Henry's toyshop, which was amusingly still open for late-night business.

Fortunately, Leander didn't say a word—either aloud or in his mage's mind—until they were airborne and on the way to Alby Ranch. "So you finally got them out of your system, did you?"

"Them?" Raven looked over her shoulder at the last few lit lanterns along Harpertown's main avenue. She could barely make out the outline of William climbing into Teo's saddle, although the two seemed to be having a private conversation and waiting a while before they took to the skies. "I don't know what you're—"

"Your feelings, Raven. They make you indecisive. And it seems you were wrong about what they meant."

"No, I wasn't wrong. I'm not wrong." She closed her eyes and let the cooling night air wash over her as they headed south for the very short ride to the ranch.

"That conversation wasn't as terrible as you expected," Leander muttered. "Or have I mistaken the meaning behind two humans smashing their lips together for exceedingly long amounts of time?"

"Oh, great. So you were spying on my thoughts during dinner, huh?"

"No, Raven. I felt your response."

"Well then, you would have also felt that my feelings weren't wrong." Her red dragon didn't say anything to that and she sighed heavily. "I don't know what's going on with William. I couldn't tell him I don't care about him—"

"Because you do."

"Yes, dragon. Thank you."

A low rumble rose from his throat as they passed over Moss Dragon Ranch and continued south toward her grandfather's property.

"And yes, it was nice to spend some time with him. Relatively uninterrupted and where being with him felt like it used to. Or mostly, at least."

"You don't want it to feel the same." It wasn't a question because he could discern her thoughts and emotions as if they were pellets of dragon feed in a trough. But after four years of sharing everything with her dragon familiar, this had become a part of their process, no matter which one of them had to do the majority of the processing.

"I don't want it to feel the same," Raven replied. "That's the problem. I'm comfortable with William. Most of the time. But over the last year…"

"You think you have changed too much," Leander finished for her.

"Hmm. Maybe. Honestly, I think it's that I haven't changed much. I'm still doing what I do. With you, of course."

"Of course."

She laughed. "But I'm not so sure the William we knew two or three or even four years ago is the same one taking on all these new responsibilities. And that's okay. I merely expected…I don't know what I expected, honestly."

Another low rumble issued from her dragon's throat as they circled the Alby Ranch property. "You expected his leaving when he did and the way he did to have changed him more. If he was sorry and didn't want to hurt you again, it would have changed him enough to feel different. If he returned to Brighton and didn't want the same relationship with you, it would have changed him enough to feel different."

"Okay…well now, you're running me around in circles. I don't follow."

On silent wings, her familiar alighted at the top of the hill, snorted, and tucked his wings against his back before he swiveled his head around to regard his mage calmly. "Everything else has changed. William has not. You're afraid he will do it again."

"Do what?"

His only reply was to blink slowly at her before he resumed his knowing stare.

I'm afraid William will get up and leave like that all over again. When I least expect it and exactly like the first time.

"Fine. You're right."

"I know."

With a wry laugh, Raven leapt off her dragon and landed on the grass with a thud. "But thank you, as always, for helping me to get to the bottom of it."

"You're welcome. Now you can stop thinking about him and brush all these pesky human emotions out of the way?"

She unstrapped the girdle of his saddle and removed his flying tack to turn him loose for the night. "I don't think that's how this works. At least not this time."

He snorted. "Why not?"

"Well, because knowing what I'm afraid of doesn't exactly tell me what I'm supposed to do next."

"Whatever you want, Raven. It isn't difficult."

The mage stroked his scaley muzzle and shook her head. "It is, though. It's difficult when I don't know what I want either. Not with William."

"You know what you're afraid of. So what you want is naturally the opposite of that."

"Oh, boy…" She pressed her forehead against the soft patch of flat scales between his eye ridges and sighed. "Dragons are some of the most complex and complicated creatures in the world, and here you are telling me something so incredibly simple that it seems impossible."

"Yes, being a dragon is straightforward. You would not make a very good dragon right now, little girl."

"Oh, because I don't know exactly what I want?"

"Among other reasons." Leander lowered his head to nudge her shoulder, then froze and stared over it instead.

A swell of anxiety and anger flowed through her, and it all came from her dragon familiar. When she turned, she realized that Gruene lay at the base of the hill, her wings curled around her and a tendril of dragon frost issuing from her nostrils. She stared at Leander and her eyes glowed green in the darkness.

"Yep." Raven patted her dragon's neck. "Maybe you should decide what you want too. After we cure the rest of the sick dragons."

He spun in a slow circle on the top of the hill beside the ranch house, uttered a low growl, and curled into his usual tight ball of red scales in preparation for sleep. Although she waited for a few moments, he didn't say anything else.

This is weird for all of us in so many ways. We're all trying to find out how everything works now that the whole world has changed this much in the last two years.

The ranch hands had all turned in for the night, but a few lanterns were still lit inside the house that belonged to her and her grandfather—the man who still hadn't been seen or heard from in months. Again.

I'll focus on hearing from him next once we finish administering these dragon cures. And Bella's looking for him too. If anyone can find Connor Alby at this point, it would be Bella Chase.

She stepped as quietly as she could into the main house, surprised to find that the glow of one of the still-lit lanterns came from Connor's bedroom—now Dr. Chui Welby's temporary room for the duration of their stay in southern Lomberdoon. The floorboards creaked under her flight boots as she crept toward her room across the hall.

Welby's voice made her pause. "I'm awake, Mage Alby."

She grimaced and turned to face the open door. The vet had made himself rather comfortable in the room in the last week, and he now sat at Connor's small writing desk along the wall, consumed by whatever he'd been writing in his journal with an array of cure vials spread in front of him on the desk.

This is way too weird. I feel like I'm eleven again, only it's not my grandfather behind that desk. And I'm not eleven.

"Well, I wasn't sure. I guess this means you didn't find any other sick dragons after you left Harpertown."

He raised a finger while he continued to write in his journal with the other hand as if telling her to wait a little longer until he was finished.

"Right. Sorry to interrupt your work. We'll head out again in the morning—"

"Only one."

"What?"

"One more dragon." He put his quill down and stood from the chair to face her head-on. "I realize the ambiguity of having expressed that by counting silently on my fingers. I apologize for that."

"Oh." She laughed. "No, that's okay. You looked very focused on…whatever you're working on."

"Simply my personal accounts." Welby walked slowly toward the door and cast his journal a lingering glance. "I find it difficult to sleep without releasing my thoughts for the day on a piece of parchment paper. Sometimes, it's useful to look back on but mostly, it's for my sanity."

"That seems to be a common pastime with mages. My grandfather kept a journal too. I never saw him write in it but I was able to read it eventually. Of course, he was more focused on chronicling the deeds and triumphs of War

Mage and Dragon Rider orders than dumping his thoughts out of his head."

"It's a little different." The vet braced a hand against the doorframe, and Raven had no idea if she should move out of his way to let him into the hall, turn and go to her room, or stand there and continue to compare the handsome civilian veterinarian to her rebel dragon rider of a grandfather.

I don't think any of those options is better than the other.

"I'm sorry I never had the chance to meet him," Welby added with a sympathetic half-smile. "I've heard stories, though. Do you mind if I ask what happened?"

She frowned in confusion. "What do you mean?"

"To your grandfather. I'm merely curious, but you don't have to tell me a thing if you don't want to—"

"No. No, that's fine. You can ask." She nodded and backed away a little because his massive frame and broad, muscular shoulders took up more of Connor Alby's bedroom doorway than her grandfather ever had.

"All right. So what happened?" His sympathetic frown made her pause only for a moment.

He's curious and we're in Connor's house. It makes sense.

She shrugged. "Which time?"

"I..." Welby set his other hand on the opposite side of the doorframe and tilted his head. "Well, I suppose it would have to be the last time."

"Ah. Right. I'm still trying to find answers for that one. Trust me, if I knew where to look and if I had the time, I would have scoured the kingdom for that old dragon rider by now. But I have someone looking into it. When I find him, though..." She shook her head and scowled at the hallway wall. "I don't think I'll be able to hold back at that point."

The vet frowned and looked genuinely sorry to hear everything she'd said. "That must be hard, Mage Alby. When you haven't even found the body yet."

"Wait, the body?" She pulled away from him again with wide eyes. "What do you mean by body? Do you know where he is?"

"No. I—"

"Then why would you talk about finding his body?"

"I merely assumed that was what you were referring to. After losing him."

"I didn't lose my grandfather, Dr. Welby. He disappeared like he always does, but this is the longest he's been away without sending a single word to me about whatever giant mess he's gotten himself into this time, and I—" Raven stopped herself quickly and realized how much she was dumping on her military-assigned mission partner and a man she hardly even knew. Then she recognized where the conversation had completely lost them both. "Wait, you think he's dead?"

The vet frowned, shook his head, and lowered his hands from the doorframe to take one step back into Connor's bedroom. "It certainly sounded like you did."

"No. No, no, no. I—" She laughed. "He was completely alive and healthy and as unpredictable as ever the last time I saw him. But it's been over six months and… Wow. I guess I should have led with the part about Connor Alby disappearing off the face of the Earth as a force of habit."

He responded with a small smile. "So your grandfather is still alive."

"Like I said, I honestly don't know. But I sure hope he is." Her face warmed again in the presence of this man who was only seven years older than her but acted like he'd been around so much longer—a man who'd met her mother when he was nine. He was old enough to remember Sarah Alby but not nearly as involved in the world of Lomberdoon's mage orders to understand that Dragon Rider Connor Alby was always like this and probably always would be.

"But none of that has anything to do with why we're here right now. In the south. So…it's probably better for everyone if we don't talk about this."

"I'm sorry, Mage Alby. I assumed too much and I certainly didn't mean to—"

"Can we please drop the Mage Alby thing?" She couldn't help but laugh. "We're standing in my house and you've spent the night writing at my grandfather's desk. Call me Raven—at least when no one else is watching."

In no way did she expect the dark-haired vet to flash her a beaming grin after that. "Only if you call me Chui."

"Deal."

"Wonderful."

She stood in the hall and drew a deep breath while her gaze roamed the walls and ceiling.

This is way too personal. And I'll never call him Chui so I won't call him anything.

"Well, I guess we better get some sleep. We'll be back at it tomorrow, right?"

"With the sun, yes." He wouldn't stop grinning at her, and that made her strange discomfort even worse.

"Right. And sorry for dropping all that on you about my grandfather."

"You have nothing to apologize for."

"Okay." She turned stiffly toward her room and headed to the door she'd elected to close every time she entered and left, although he'd kept the door to Connor's room open at all times.

Her bedroom door creaked open under her hand.

"Good night, Raven."

She paused, turned over her shoulder to shoot him a glance, and nodded. "Good night."

The young mage hurried into her room and closed the door behind her. Only then did she let herself draw a massively deep breath before she blew it out again in an extended sigh.

That was so weird. This whole situation is weird. Why did I suggest we stay here? The Legion would have paid for a couple of rooms at an inn. Then again, the closest inn is in Harpertown, and that would have been so much worse. Staying at a place with Chui Welby when William decides to fly through and take me out to dinner on a private back porch.

Raven spun and flopped backward onto her twin-sized childhood bed. The wooden frame creaked beneath her weight as she bounced a few times, her arms spread at her sides, and stared at the ceiling.

I need to quit thinking about all of this. We have dragons to cure and Weeping Disease to stop. And I'm in here counting my issues with Connor, Welby, and William.

She closed her eyes and drew another deep breath. It hadn't been this hard over the last week to consider getting a good night's sleep before a day of patrolling the region again, even with Welby sleeping across the hall. Then again, it was the first day she'd been on a date with William and had almost spilled her guts about family problems to her partner on this mission. Another mage with a dragon familiar—another professional who cared about the future of both the kingdom they protected and the dragons living in it.

Her thoughts swirled in her head like they would never stop until she realized how insanely quiet it was.

Why hasn't Leander pitched in with his dragonish wisdom and told me to quit overthinking everything? There's no way he's already asleep. Not with Gruene camped at the bottom of his favorite hill.

In an instant, she bolted upright in her bed. At the same second, she caught a wave of overpowering emotion from her dragon familiar—fear, agitation, restlessness, and rage.

It was stronger than anything she'd felt from Leander in a long time.

She focused on his mind—which hadn't picked up her thoughts and feelings because he'd been so preoccupied with his own—and reached out to him. *What's going on?*

Something is very wrong, Raven.

His voice in her head was alarmingly weak and she bounded to her feet. *What do you mean? Are you sick? Is it Gruene?*

A piercing screech cut through the silence of Alby Ranch, joined by a second a moment later. Leander and Gruene continued to cry to the night sky and heavy boot-steps thumped down the hallway outside her room. Raven was already at the door when it banged with a fervent knock.

"Raven? I think we—"

She jerked the door open to see a wide-eyed Welby on the other side. "I know. What did Gruene say?"

Her door remained completely open and forgotten as they both raced down the hall, across the main living area of her home, and out onto the porch.

"Not much," he muttered. "Or at least not much I can make out. She's too distraught."

"Leander too."

The porch's screen door creaked violently and clapped shut again behind them before the mages sprinted across the dew-studded grass toward the top of the hill. Gruene had joined Leander there and they pawed the ground, tossed their heads, and stretched their wings wide. Both dragons screeched continuously, and Raven couldn't climb that hill fast enough.

"Leander! What is it? What's wrong?"

"We do not know." He stamped back away from her, swung his powerful tail from side to side, and snorted thick clouds of smoke.

"Are you sick?"

"That's impossible," Welby snapped. "They were both inoculated before we came down here."

"Well, it's not like we tested how effective it was at preventing them from getting sick after the fact!" Raven dropped to her knees beside Leander's saddle and saddle-bags that she'd left out for the night and snatched up two potion vials of the Weeping Disease cure. "So we'll take care of it right now and everything should be fine."

"No!" Gruene bellowed. "Save them."

A streak of blisteringly cold dragon frost spewed from

the black female's mouth and cracked into the ground mere inches from Raven's foot.

Leander roared in anger and turned toward the black, his fire breath brewing in the deepest pit of his belly and lighting his open mouth.

"Hey!" Welby darted toward his dragon and caught hold of her face. "Raven is with us."

"Leander, don't you dare!" Raven shouted.

The rumble of his dragon fire continued for another second as he beat his wings. Then, he clamped his mouth shut with a terrifyingly powerful snap, stepped away from Gruene, and belched a massive cloud of black smoke.

His mage raced toward him with the vials in one hand and used the other to stroke the side of his neck. "Here. Take this, okay? Then you'll be fine."

"It is not for us, Raven." With a snort, he swiveled his head toward her and fixed her with his glowing yellow eyes. "We are fine."

"You don't seem fine."

"They aren't sick." Welby finished studying his familiar's eyes and muzzle before he stroked the side of her face. "The potion works, Raven."

"Then what's going on?"

"The others," the red dragon growled.

"Wild," Gruene added and more frost curled from her nostrils in an icy spray.

The two mages studied the dark night sky but there was no sign of any other dragons moving through the area. If it hadn't been for these two, she would have called it a silent, peaceful, perfectly normal night.

"Okay." She continued to stroke her familiar's neck and

he began to settle second by second. "So it's something wrong with wild dragons."

"Yes," the black dragon whispered.

Leander closed his eyes. "Very wrong, Raven. We can feel it."

"Where are they?" Welby asked.

Both dragons turned slowly away from their mages and raised their heads to the west, where the stark ridges of the Brightsbane Mountains cut into the sky and drowned out the starlight.

"Across the mountains." Raven nodded. "Close enough to reach in a night?"

"With as strongly as I feel their pain, yes. I can make it."

"It is an easy flight to make at this time of year." Gruene pawed the ground. "I would rather leave now."

"I'm right there with you. Let's go."

Welby stared at Raven as she hurried toward Leander's flying tack and saddlebags. "Right now?"

"I don't know about you, but I believe what Leander can feel. What they both can." She slung the saddle over one shoulder. "And I won't stick around for a few hours sleep when we could be there saving those wild dragons whatever precious time they might not have left."

"I understand the urgency, Raven. But I don't believe any of us can go forever without the necessary rest."

Crouched under Leander's belly to cinch his saddle tighter, Raven looked at the vet and grinned. "I've been flying at night since Leander and I first took to the sky together. And you've had more than enough practice not getting the kind of sleep most people need simply to function."

"Are you sure?"

"Well, there's no way I'll sleep now so we might as well."
She slipped the harness over Leander's head and accepted
his boost onto her back. "Are you coming?"

"I suppose it paints me in a rather negative light if I
say no."

"Good point."

CHAPTER TEN

They took to the sky and immediately headed west toward the wild-dragon disturbance in the Brightsbane Mountains. What should have been a relatively straight flight to pinpoint the source of the agitation Leander and Gruene had felt, however, was anything but. They traveled in sporadic patterns and banked left and then right without any real reason other than they'd felt something unusual in that direction before it disappeared.

After a few hours of this, Raven leaned forward over her saddle to stroke her dragon's long neck. "Leander, if we need to take a break, we can—"

"No. We will find them. We must."

She glanced at Welby, who rode with his back perfectly straight and a deep scowl of concentration on his face as he searched the mountains.

He's probably having a silent conversation with Gruene anyway. Why is it so hard for these dragons to decide where they're going? That's never been an issue before.

After another twenty minutes and no change to the

erratic weaving and dipping of two dragons trying to find their agitated brethren, she began to wonder if they might have been better off staying at the ranch until daylight when they could see.

"There!" Leander shouted before he screeched in greeting. His cry echoed around them in the canyon above which they soared before the sound of another dragon's response call carried to them on the wind. It was faint but very clearly a dragon.

"Where?" Raven scanned the skyline.

Welby pointed. "A little south."

It was hard to see anything but the jagged outline of mountain peaks all around them, but a single wild dragon raced through the sky to position herself against the moonlight. In the next moment, the young mage saw what was impossible to ignore.

The poor thing beat her wings wildly, faltered, and wobbled as she struggled to stay aloft. One of her wings buckled for seemingly no reason and she dropped like a stone with a gut-wrenching scream.

Raven's heart leapt into her throat even before Leander tucked his wings and dove after the fallen female, who'd quickly disappeared into the darkness of the forest lining the other side of the canyon.

She fell out of the sky. Is that how the others were grounded too when they were infected?

Gruene screeched and dove with them, keeping close to Leander's side. Welby leaned forward with his mount, his gloved hands tight on the harness and his eyes narrowed against the wind. It took them less than five minutes to find the location where the wild female had crash-landed.

Even if they hadn't seen her stumbling on the forest floor while she tossed her head and thumped her tail against the trees, they would have found her. Most of the surrounding pines had already been splintered by her landing.

The two dragons landed with a spray of dirt and pine needles, and the infected female snarled at their arrival.

Welby pulled a potion vial out of his single saddlebag and his mount held her ground as the wild dragon charged toward them, foam flying from her mouth. Gruene spread her wings and lowered her head. At the last second before the wild female prepared to lash out with the bone-crushing force of her jaws, the black dragon rose on her hind legs and beat her wings furiously. The potion vial found its target in the wild female's open mouth before Welby and his mount launched back from the edge of the canyon.

Raven shielded her eyes from the spray of underbrush and dirt that flurried against her and Leander, but the outraged cry she'd expected from an infected dragon didn't come.

The wild female—it was too dark to tell her color—hacked and sputtered against the cure potion that had made its way down her throat. She spun in tight circles and shook her head, and her wings expanded with a heavy thump. Her sides heaved violently and she stared at her rescuers with wide, clear eyes that glowed silver in the dark forest.

"Explain this," she growled.

"How do you feel?" Welby asked as Gruene settled lightly on the forest floor again.

"I want answers, mage," the wild female snapped. She

swung her head toward Leander and her eyes narrowed. "You."

"You are lucky tonight," the red dragon muttered. "What about the others?"

"You told us we would be safe!" The wild dragon beat her wings and took two lurching steps toward Raven and her familiar. "You said to get as far away from the other side of the mountains as we could to protect ourselves. You were wrong."

"Do you know her?" Welby asked.

Leander didn't break away from the angry gaze. "She was among those I'd warned of the sickness. Those who believed my words and took heed."

"Wait a minute." Raven studied the creature who looked only too ready to attack another trained mount, this time without the excuse of being consumed by Weeping Disease. "You went out west to the other side of the mountains?"

"That is what I said."

"Leander, that was before we found the fungus in the mines."

Her dragon lowered his head again. "Yes."

"What's your name?"

The wild female tilted her head and studied the young mage. "Ayal."

"My name's Raven. You know Leander already. We can help you and we can still help the other wild dragons you were with, Ayal, but I need you to tell me as much as you can remember about when you started getting sick—not feeling like yourself. Do you remember how long it's been?"

Ayal's blue eyes narrowed again and darted across the darkness. "I do not."

"Had you flown to any new locations recently?" Welby asked. "Dark, damp places with black fungus growing in or around it?"

"Dragons want bright, dry sunshine, mage. Why would I—" She froze, snorted, and uttered a low, terrifying growl. "We saw movement—large numbers swarming across the plains toward our new nest in the mountains. My clan drew closer to investigate, and we were...attacked."

"Attacked." Raven's stomach clenched. "By what, Ayal? Was it other infected dragons?"

"No." The wild female stepped back and her eyes widened as she seemed to retreat into the apparent safety of the forest. "Strange humans. And black stones."

"Black stones." Welby searched the trees behind the wild female. "Dusty black stones?"

Ayal growled again. "I saw no dust but they glowed."

"Oh, no." Raven met the vet's gaze. "That sounds like the ore deposits we found at the end of the Orion tunnel."

"Those miners were only concerned about payment for their work and the price of the Smithheart ore, and I didn't see any of the fungus on their haul before we entered the tunnels. Why in the world would they use such a rare metal to attack wild dragons? Or any dragons?"

"It was not the miners," Leander said. "Not those in Lomberdoon, at any rate."

"The abandoned camp." Raven nodded. "We found what they left behind before we eradicated the fungus. If they mined that ore and left the tunnels before we even had a clue..."

"There's still more fungus out there." Welby hissed in frustration. "We need to find them."

"Take us to your clan." Gruene's voice was gentle enough but the command in it was clear.

Ayal was too overwhelmed by having been so recently taken by Weeping Disease and efficiently cured of it by these strangers to argue against such an idea. But she was distraught, nonetheless. She stretched her wings experimentally and snorted. "The others are not themselves. And I fell." Her long neck stretched toward the tree branches and the stars that dotted the black expanse above her. "From the sky…"

"You have your wings," Leander reassured her. "And the dragon healer to thank for it."

Welby blinked in surprise at being both addressed and thanked that way by Raven's familiar.

"Dragon healer?" Ayal tilted her head.

"Yes." The vet lowered his head toward her. "Dr. Welby. And this is Gruene."

Raven was equally surprised by Leander's gracious explanation and impressed with her dragon.

Giving credit where it's due. Good work, Leander.

It won't be unless we cure the rest of her clan and stop the strange humans with glowing black stone.

"Right." She nodded. "Ayal, you don't need to worry about flying. And the cure Dr. Welby gave you will keep you safe."

"How do you know this?" the female asked and narrowed her eyes.

"We have seen it," Leander assured her. "Many times."

"And we need you to take us to the place where you and

your clan were attacked so we can heal them like we healed you and find the humans who did this to you. Can you do that?"

The wild female straightened her spine and expanded her wings to their fullest. She seemed to regain the pride her kind always carried with them. "If a dragon can fly, she can do anything."

Welby nodded. "We'll follow you."

Ayal ambled past both dragons and their riders to escape the thickest part of the forest. Once she had enough space, she launched into the sky with a screech and darted toward the stars.

Raven and Welby had enough time to meet each other's gaze and share a determined nod before Leander and Gruene took off in tandem to follow their wild guide.

At least they finally found something they can both agree on. We have to stop this before it gets any more out of hand. And whoever's been attacking wild dragons with fungus-covered ore is seriously gonna get it if they can't explain why they're doing something so incredibly stupid.

───────

Ayal led them across the thinnest of the Brightsbane Mountain ranges along Lomberdoon's western border. The wild female flew with complete confidence again as if she remembered her entire mind-altered passage across the mountains before Weeping Disease had taken her ability to fly and left her stranded in the forest.

She probably does remember.

Of course she does. Leander's voice in Raven's mind was

filled with a determination bordering on rage. *A dragon never forgets, Raven. Even though her mind was taken from her, it has now returned. We will find them.*

Another hour of silent, expectant flight followed during which Raven and Welby scanned the mountain passes as well as they could in the darkness for any sign of "strange humans" or other infected dragons. They finally reached the edge of the mountains and the open expanse of the unclaimed lands between kingdoms.

In the first valley they crossed out of the foothills, they found Ayal's wild clan. Eleven of them stumbled awkwardly in the open grass, clawed the earth, and tossed their heads while sprays of yellow-brown foam spewed in all directions.

A short fight broke out between three of them who'd collided with each other while the rest staggered around in circles. The scuffle was quickly settled when it seemed the most aggressive of the three could barely see her mistaken opponents through the black sludge oozing from her eyes that had almost coated her entire face with black streaks.

Ayal screeched a desperate greeting, but her clanmates didn't even seem to notice her or her two escorts from the Airborne Legion, let alone that one of their own had returned to them completely healed.

The wild female swiveled her head to look at Leander and Gruene. "They are not likely to listen to reason. Or to take your mages' healing."

"We know," he replied.

"We have done this before," the black dragon added. She met Leander's gaze without any trace of the usual teasing, flirtatious glint in her emerald eyes. "We will do it again.

Despite what you may see, Ayal, know that we are here to help them."

"We will help them." Leander snorted. "Leave us to do it on our own."

Ayal stared at the dragons a moment longer, then banked sharply to the south to make a wide circle around the sloping valley and left the rest of her clan suffering in confusion and agony below.

"Eleven." Raven turned toward Welby to gauge his reaction. "That's more than we've taken on at once."

He nodded. "We'll aim for the most aggressive first—that large female who tried to take on two of her own. If we can separate the more troublesome ones, the others might be easier to target after that. Do you think you can manage it?"

She frowned and returned her attention to the bumbling wild clan that quickly drew closer. "Please tell me that wasn't a real question."

"Raven, we have to be—"

"That means yes, healer," Leander growled. "Do not ask us again."

The vet widened his eyes at the red dragon who flew beside him and inclined his head. "My apologies."

"Apologize later."

Raven nodded. "After we get them this cure."

She didn't have to tell her dragon to head toward the infected clan. At this point, the mage and her familiar thought and felt as one, exactly as they always had when faced with a threat that required them to be perfectly in sync with one another. Raven lurched forward over the saddle at the precise moment that he tucked his wings and they plummeted toward the wild clan.

The sound of Gruene's wingbeats close behind them as she and Welby dove on his tail was all the proof they needed that the doctor and his familiar were on the same page.

Leander uttered a violent, furious bellow seconds before his first pass over the clan to make several of them look up with blackened eyes at the two dragons who swooped toward them. He'd aimed his descent toward the largest female who'd become the most aggressive under the hold of Weeping Disease, but she paid him no attention at all.

Instead, she turned and lashed out at her closest clan-mate with a vicious swipe of her forepaw. It caught the other wild dragon completely unaware and he stumbled sideways as he screamed and tossed his head. His wings flapped uselessly and at awkward angles against his back.

"Get her attention!" Welby shouted behind them, both hands filled with potion vials ready to be flung. They only needed to get the wild dragons to open their mouths.

The red dragon banked sharply to turn and approach the clan for a second pass. He shook his head like a dog shaking water off its fur and snorted. "I know how this works."

"Welby knows that too. We'll have to find something they can't ignore," Raven told him.

"Fine."

They both had the same idea in mind and didn't even need to think it to one another. As he dove again at the aggressive wild female, he opened his mouth and the rumble and hiss of his fire breath warming in his belly sizzled. She felt the heat of it even beneath the cool night wind that buffeted through her hair and against her leather uniform.

As soon as they reached the three dragons still fighting each other at the edge of the confused clan, the night sky illuminated with a brilliant burst of flame from Leander's open mouth. He launched it at the largest female who caused most of the trouble, although through no real fault of her own.

"*Sequantur flamma!*" Raven shouted. She felt the tug of her magic latch onto her dragon's fire and direct the flames. Instead of pounding into the infected female's side, the fire lurched away at the last second to strike the ground at the aggressive female's feet.

The pseudo attack was enough to finally make her look up and she snarled at the massive red male and his red-haired mage bearing down on her.

From the other side of the valley, Ayal uttered an angry cry and surged toward the mages intent on healing her clan. "You gave your word to help them!" she bellowed.

Neither Leander and his mage nor Gruene and hers had the time to respond to the healed wild female and her misconception of having been betrayed.

Leander darted over the insanely aggressive wild female who'd been their first target. Now that they had her attention, she seemed determined to turn her destructive inclination toward the newcomers.

She hammered her head against another one of her clanmates to get him out of the way, reared her head back, and opened her mouth. The roar and hiss of her fire breath building inside her came a second before the red-hot glow at the back of her throat.

Crap. They can still attack with everything they have, even if they can't fly.

Leander spread his wings again to catch the air and raced over the fiery female's outstretched head.

Raven braced herself for another spell to control the fire of a dragon she'd never met and turned in the saddle.

Gruene and Welby were so incredibly close behind them. The vet lobbed a potion vial into the female's gaping maw, the enchanted glass disappeared, and the glittering liquid cure splashed against the back of the wild female's throat with a violent hiss.

She choked, snorted, and belched a cloud of noxious black smoke before she uttered a gurgled scream of rage.

"Watch your clanmate!" Leander roared as Ayal hurtled toward him. He veered out of the way at the last second and the small wild dragon pulled back to stare at the aggressive female on the ground with wide eyes.

The change was almost instantaneous, and she beat her wings furiously to dart out of the way and avoid Gruene and Welby.

With a heavy sigh, the vet stared after Ayal as she darted wildly above her clan while she screeched and tried to get their attention, but to no avail. "This would be far easier if we could garner the full trust of those we're trying to help."

"She saw what happened," Gruene told him. "We have that trust."

"Not a moment too soon, either. *Eatenus exstinxisti!*" A gust of wind burst from Welby's outstretched hand and morphed into a gush of water a second before it splashed the ground beside the aggressive female, where the grass and sparse wildflowers of the valley had already caught flame beneath Leander's fire breath. He looked at Raven in front of him who had turned fully in her saddle and shouted, "May I recommend healing this clan without burning the entire valley to cinders?"

She smirked. "You said to get her attention."

"Then I'll be more specific next time." Despite the dire situation and the fact that they still had ten more wild dragons to administer cures to, Welby's crooked, closed-lipped smile betrayed his wry amusement with the tactics of the STAR mage and her dragon. "We'll take lead on the next pass."

"It sounds good to me." Raven dug into Leander's saddlebags and retrieved two vials in each hand.

The dragons banked again and red and black flew side by side until they swung to face the rest of the clan.

CHAPTER ELEVEN

Once the aggressive female was under control, she'd taken off the second her awareness had returned to her and now joined Ayal to circle over them in the sky. With her out the way, it was easy enough for the mages and their familiars to deliver the cure to the rest of the infected wild dragons below. Easy in comparison, at least, although they had to make twice as many passes as there were dragons to be healed.

The infected clan was too unpredictable in such large numbers and couldn't be reasoned with or told to stay put and open their mouths. To Raven's surprise, Welby's usually perfect aim with his longbow that she'd witnessed so many times before didn't fully translate to his throwing aim and he missed an open mouth twice before he finally found his targets on the next pass.

I can't say mine are all that better. I think we got lucky. It's not like anyone's ever done this before, but maybe we should find a precision spell or something.

When every dragon had inadvertently swallowed

Welby's cure in their attempts to attack their unexpected rescuers, Leander and Gruene took to the sky again to circle the clan and watch for signs that any of them had been too far gone to Weeping Disease and were beyond the mages' ability to heal.

Raven heaved a sigh of relief when every single wild dragon eventually stopped circling, clawing, and tossing their heads. The foaming spray at their mouths and nostrils dried up, as did the blackened tears that oozed from their eyes. "We weren't too late for them."

"This would most certainly fall under my assessment of one hundred percent success," Welby replied with a satisfied smile. "But it's not the end for them."

"No." The short-lived moment of triumph faded beneath the knowledge that these wild dragons had been deliberately attacked by humans who'd mined that ore and now used it to infect any dragons within reach. "We need to speak to them."

"Agreed."

As Leander and Gruene swooped toward the wild clan again—this time to hold council with them instead of to deliver their cure—both dragons uttered piercing screeches.

The entire clan looked up and responded with cries, although they sounded weak and uncertain.

Of course they do. They've been through hell.

Ayal and the large female they'd healed first darted toward their clan to land between them and the mages' familiars. Wingbeats, startled snorts, and the scrape of dragon claws through the soil filled the air. For a moment, Raven wondered if Ayal's misplaced anger at thinking she'd been lied to would lead them all into another battle, which was the last thing any of them wanted.

But the wild female who'd led them there regarded Leander and Gruene solemnly as she lowered her head slowly. After a moment, she turned to address the others. "These mages have done more for us tonight than you know."

The agitated shuffling of her clan settled a little. "We were sick—"

"We were attacked!" one of them snarled.

"By a fungus. It grows on ore mined from the mountains," Gruene interjected.

"By humans!"

Leander bellowed and spread his wings. He didn't exactly rear on his hind legs, but both forepaws left the ground before he stamped them down in a puff of loose dirt and dry grass ripped from the earth. "Let your clanmate speak!"

Raven grunted when she thumped onto the saddle after he'd bucked beneath her.

Anything could happen at this point. And I'm simply extra weight, I guess.

The wild dragons glanced at each other and shifted uncomfortably again, none of them willing to anger the massive red male who'd come to warn them of this danger weeks before.

Ayal's long, low growl drew all their attention to her. "This is the disease Leander warned us of. We fled and still, we caught it."

"Then he was wrong."

"He came to our aid."

"Leander spoke the truth," Gruene snapped. "But the threat remains in a different form. Tell us of the attack."

Wary and angry, the wild clan studied the dragons bearing mage riders in their midst. Raven and Welby looked at each other but neither of them said a word.

He knows this isn't a conversation we're supposed to be a part of but we're here. And now we have to let them work this out on their own or this whole thing could blow up in ways I don't even want to think about.

The vet nodded to her but she couldn't tell if it was in agreement with her thoughts he couldn't possibly hear or in an attempt to reassure her that they would be fine.

He thinks I've never been in the middle of a wild-dragon conference before. It's probably better to let him think that than go through the story of everything I've done.

Finally, a young, smaller male raised his head above the backs and twitching wings of his clanmates and spoke. "Humans."

"We heard they were strange," Leander said. "Not of the kingdom to the east beyond the mountains."

"Not of any kingdom I have seen," the young male replied. "They almost smelled of dragons."

"What?" Raven whispered, then realized her mistake in saying anything during a meeting meant only for dragons and pressed her lips together.

"Explain this," Gruene prompted.

"I cannot."

"They smelled of dragons," Ayal added. "Or something like dragons. And of the sea."

Dragons hate the water. Anyone who spends enough time

with them would know that. These people can't be working with dragons and the open water at the same time.

"We were curious," the young male continued. "That was our only purpose but it was transgression enough for the strange humans to attack us."

"They launched black stones into the air," another added.

The valley erupted with shouts from the dragon clan all at once.

"They meant to strike us out of the sky!"

"Relentless!"

"We could not stop them!"

"Humans immune to fire breath!"

"Wait." Raven's gut churned at that last one and she didn't hear anything else shouted by the angry creatures.

Did he say immune to fire breath?

He did. Leander curved his long neck to look at Gruene, who glanced at him before she returned her focus to the clan.

Raven tightened her hold on the harness she didn't need to ride her dragon and gritted her teeth. *That's impossible.*

A dragon does not lie. But they can misunderstand what they have seen.

The massive female who was slightly larger than both Leander and Gruene beat her wings and roared so loudly that the sound echoed off the mountain range behind them even after her wild brethren had settled. She snorted and looked at each of the dragon familiars. "What does this mean?"

Neither had an answer for that but Raven did.

"It means we have more work to do," she said and raised her voice so everyone could hear despite knowing that every dragon in this valley could have heard her whisper. "Dr. Welby and I destroyed the fungus that infected you. It appears that it grew in the same cavern where these strange humans mined the ore. Mining is one thing, but using it to attack any dragon, no matter what kingdom they're in, is another. We will find them and we will stop them."

"Humans attacked us," the large female replied. "They will never stop, no matter how many promises of freedom you have given us."

Leander lowered his head and growled but said nothing.

"Yes." The large female narrowed her eyes at Raven. "We remember you, mage. And we have thanked you for the opportunity of peace you offered when you rallied us from the north. But that does not change what has been done to us."

"The people of Threndor did not do this to you," the mage replied curtly. She had no idea how she knew that was true but she couldn't conceive of any kingdom on this continent that would order an attack on wild dragons with fungus-covered ore mined from the Brightsbane Mountains. They'd all seen what had happened when the wild dragons arrived from the north with the return of magic for everyone, mage or otherwise.

The large female snorted. "It seems you are alone in your promises to our kind, mage."

"She most certainly is not," Welby interjected. Gruene snorted and tossed her head. "Every dragon we've found over the last few months who was infected with this disease—wild or trained but all of them free—has found allies in Mage Alby and myself. We brought you the cure without any expectation of receiving repayment for our efforts but because we mean to keep that promise of peace and cooperation between humans and dragons. The entire force of Lomberdoon's military and—"

"You speak of peace and warring armies in the same breath!" the large female bellowed. "This does not gain our trust."

"The military is on your side!" Raven shouted. "On every dragon's side. If peace between us means war with someone else, so be it."

Welby choked and tried to cover it with a cough behind a tightly clenched fist.

Without any knowledge of human politics or the chain of command, the wild clan was completely oblivious to his surprise or his reasons for it.

She, however, knew perfectly well that she'd spoken out of turn on behalf of Lomberdoon's military—maybe even on behalf of all humans on the continent—and didn't care. Even when she felt Welby's disbelieving stare on her in the semi-darkness of the valley, she couldn't look at him.

They need to hear this from someone they know will keep their word. If I have to answer for it later, fine. But I won't stop before whoever is doing this pays for the damage they've already done.

The valley grew quiet again as the wild dragons stared at the mage who'd spoken for all humans two years before and had now spoken for at least the citizens of Lomberdoon, if not the entire continent of Threndor. Leander raised his head. "How many of these strange humans were there?"

"Hundreds," Ayal replied gravely. "At least those we saw."

"They attacked you on this side of the mountains?" Gruene asked.

"Yes."

Raven finally spared a glance at Welby, who seemed to have dropped the issue of her promising war in the name of the Airborne Legion. Now, his jaw was set in grim determination as he listened to the dragons continue their conversation.

"What of the others?" a wild dragon asked.

Leander scanned the sky. "What others?"

"We were fourteen when we left the valley," Ayal said. "After you warned us of the dragon plague. We came west."

"Where are the other two?" Welby asked urgently.

The wild clan shifted and their wings twitched in agitation.

"We do not know." Ayal lowered her head and turned it slightly away from the Lomberdoon dragons to speak in a low tone. "They were with me when we tried to cross the mountains tonight. Before my wings...betrayed me."

Two more infected dragons are stranded somewhere in the mountains. Alone.

"Could you find them again?" Gruene asked.

The clan paused and every dragon became perfectly still until they looked more like statues in the night than living, breathing creatures. Finally, the young male who'd described their attack pawed the ground. "One is silent. He could be anywhere. The other—"

His head jerked toward the sky and he uttered a keening screech that sounded more like a howl than anything else.

One by one, the rest of the clan joined him. A dozen dragon voices filled the night, although it wasn't anything like the joyous shrieks of greeting and recognition Raven had heard so many times before. Nor was it the dangerous, warning cry of winged creatures angered and prepared to fight.

A shiver triggered by their song of mourning skittered down her spine despite the warmth of her riding leathers.

The other one is dead. I had no idea they could feel it in their clanmates.

When the grieving howls faded again, she realized both Leander and Gruene had lowered their heads almost to the ground. Neither of them had joined the heartbroken cry for a lost wild dragon as this wasn't their clan. But that didn't make Leander's sadness any less potent as it seeped from the red dragon and into his familiar's heart to mix with her own.

"You must leave the mountains," he muttered. "Fly east across the kingdom to the rocky pass on the other side. Windroot Pass, the humans call it. We have brethren there."

Ayal lowered her head slowly from the sky to fix him with glowing blue eyes. "The ancient ones."

"Tell any dragon you see along the way to venture there," Gruene added, "and to move as far east as possible from these mountains. Except for those behaving strangely, if any have ventured into the kingdom. They are caught by this disease."

"Take note of those you see." Leander snorted. "We will do what we can for them."

"Will it be enough?" the large female asked.

"For some."

Without another word, all twelve of the wild dragons who'd been cured but had lost two of their clan launched into the night sky. The massive gusts of air from their wingbeats buffeted the ground and flurries of grass and dirt sprayed toward Leander, Gruene, and their riders. In seconds, the valley was empty.

Raven looked up to watch the clan race across the night sky before they disappeared over the high peaks separating the foothills from the highest Brightsbane passes this far south. Even after they were gone, it was hard to break the silence but she had to.

"We have to find the humans who did this to them."

Welby sighed heavily. "You promised wild dragons a war in the name of Lomberdoon's Legion."

Leander rumbled softly in amusement despite the gravity of what they'd witnessed, and she instantly knew why he found it so funny.

I guess I'm gonna have to tell him at least one part of the story most people haven't heard.

She looked at the vet mage on his familiar's back beside her and shrugged. "I promised them freedom and safety in the name of the entire human race. That was two years ago when I was still at Fowler."

His eyes widened as he looked from her to Leander in astonishment.

"If my promise means even less now that I'm a Legion mage, I'll simply have to find another way to keep it."

With that, the red dragon launched himself skyward and caught the breeze that gusted down from the mountains.

That'll only create more questions than I want to answer right now.

Leander curved his neck to fix her with one yellow eye and winked. "Let him ask his questions, Mage Alby. You are who you are."

CHAPTER TWELVE

Welby and Gruene quickly caught up to Raven and Leander as they streaked north over the no-man's land between kingdoms. The STAR mage focused on scanning the foothills for sick dragons and now, of course, for any sign of the "strange humans" who'd attacked a wild clan with black fungus.

"Raven." The vet and his mount drew beside them until the two dragons flew neck-and-neck. "I think we should call it a night."

"Are you tired already?" The bitterness in her voice surprised her, but she couldn't argue against common sense.

"It won't do anyone any good if we push ourselves through the rest of the night. We won't get to your ranch before sunrise and we all need at least a little sleep."

"Why would we go to my ranch?"

He gestured to the east in the general direction of Lomberdoon. "To return to the mines. If there are other caverns with more fungus—"

"There's no way hundreds of men attacking dragons crawled out of the mining tunnels without being seen before they crossed the mountains to get here." She shook her head. "Not since we destroyed the fungus."

"And you think they're still here."

"They have to be. At the very least, we need to find out where they are and how they're infecting so many dragons simply by throwing rocks at them."

Welby bit his bottom lip in frustration. "We can't take on an unknown force of hundreds on our own. We have to report this."

"With what? That one clan of wild dragons told us they were attacked by strange humans with black rocks? I've been chewed out by him enough as it is. Reporting hearsay won't make the Legion pay attention to this."

Leander snorted.

The vet glowered at the sky while he struggled with his inability to change the STAR mage's mind, but he finally relented. "Okay. I'll make my report tonight and we'll investigate further in the morning. After we get the rest we all need."

"Fine." She stared directly ahead and forced herself to maintain a straight face even though she wanted to grin.

He knows I'm right. And while we're here, I'm the Legion mage calling the shots on this mission.

Don't let it go to your head, mage.

She nudged her familiar's flank with the heel of her boot. *You're as much a part of this as I am, dragon. And don't think I can't feel how satisfied you are about this too.*

Why would I try to hide it?

They hadn't packed any gear to set up a camp beyond the borders of all three kingdoms on Threndor. Nor did they have the time to cross the Brightsbane Mountains again to sleep at Alby Ranch as they had been. As a result, the prospect of where they could settle for what few hours remained in the night was a little daunting.

Fortunately, however, roaming groups of citizens from all three of those kingdoms had begun to push into the unclaimed lands over the past four years since the last of the Swarm had been eradicated for good. Tiny villages and small outposts had been erected along the base of the mountains this far south, and the team found the first in less than half an hour after they'd left the valley where they'd met the wild clan.

"This looks big enough to hold an inn," Welby said. "Or at least something similar."

"Let's take a look."

The dragons dove and landed a little beyond the wide, ten-foot stone wall that had been built as a barrier against raiders and traveling bands and whatever other threat might still have existed where no kingdom could protect the outpost.

Both mages dismounted, and she immediately began to remove Leander's harness and saddle. "I hope whoever runs this inn is a relatively light sleeper. Will you two be okay out here until the morning?"

Gruene stared after her mage as Welby walked a few paces in the opposite direction of the outpost's border walls. "We'll manage."

Leander chuffed and nudged his mage's shoulder with his snout as she pulled the saddle off his back. "Define okay."

She frowned and slung the saddle and harness over one shoulder before she hauled the saddlebags over the other. "I know it's not ideal but you saw how tiny this place is. There isn't room for one dragon inside those walls, let alone two."

The rest of it, she didn't exactly want to voice aloud. *And I thought you two had come to some kind of agreement after everything we've done tonight.*

He growled softly and turned away from Gruene. *That remains to be seen.*

Raven stroked his face when he lowered it in front of her chest and nodded. "It's only for a few hours until the morning. And if anything approaches before then, it'll be much easier for you to see it and let us know. Strange humans or dragons or anything—"

"*Loquimi magus,*" Welby said from yards away.

She turned to stare at the window of light that opened in front of the vet's outstretched hands. The angle was sharp enough that she couldn't get a good look at the mage on the other side of the Full Appearance spell, and their voices were too low for her to pick up more than a few words.

"He's making his report," Leander muttered.

"To a mage and not Kauler?"

"I believe that is how the spell works."

She rolled her eyes at her dragon and ignored his soft hissing laughter.

I guess I never thought about other mages I hardly know

using the Full Appearance spell. It's not like it's owned exclusively by War Mages or anything.

Welby's spellcast report was quick and efficient. He broke off the connection of the Full Appearance and returned to Gruene to remove her riding tack.

"Who was that?" Raven asked.

"My advisory friend in the king's fortress." He stooped to unstrap the girdle, then pulled Gruene's saddle and harness off. "I believe I told you of the other mages I know in Havendom."

"You did. I'm merely wondering how giving a Legion report to another mage who isn't military is the next best step."

The vet stood and swung the saddle over his shoulder before he met her gaze. "Delivering updates on our mission in the only way available to us is not the same as making promises on behalf of an entire kingdom, Mage Alby."

"And you don't have orders to not talk about Legion business with anyone who isn't in the Legion?"

"I'm not in the Legion." He nodded toward the high stone wall surrounding the outpost in the middle of nowhere, and she glanced at her dragon.

She gritted her teeth and stared at the man and her grasp on Leander's riding tack tightened with a creak of leather beneath her fingers.

So he thinks he's better than a military mage, huh?

"Good night, Mage Alby," Leander muttered behind her with an annoying level of amusement in his voice.

Keep an eye out, she thought to him. *And don't do anything without telling me first.*

I could say the same to you.

Meaning what, exactly?

Her dragon stepped around her and nudged her forward with a forceful thump of his muzzle against her lower back. *Meaning don't kill the dragon doctor. Not yet, anyway.*

Yeah. Don't kill his familiar, either.

He snorted and stepped away from Gruene, who'd already curled in a tight ball of black scales yards away from him. Despite her sleek head resting on the grass, she stared at the red male with shimmering emerald eyes.

Raven stalked after Welby to catch up with him and finish the conversation she was suddenly too indignant to let go. "Did I strike a nerve, Dr. Welby?"

He paused six feet from the wall, where there were no entrance gates or a way for them to get into the outpost and turned halfway to frown at her. "I'm sorry?"

"About mages not in the Legion." She caught up to him as he traversed the outside of the wall in search of an entrance. "Listen, I'm not trying to tell you how to do your job while we're out here, but we both know how the military works. Even if neither one of us is exactly following protocol right now."

"It sounds as if you believe sending word to the primus through a mage already serving the king—the man to whom your commanding officer answers—falls under that category."

"Yes." She readjusted her grip on Leander's riding tack and the saddlebags. "I do."

"I fail to see why we're having this conversation. Especially now."

"Why? Mostly because I'm not a fan of hypocrisy."

They finally reached two wooden doors that served as the entrance gates to the outpost, although they weren't locked or guarded and swung inward to reveal an interior comprised of trampled dirt and multiple short, squat buildings. It was as big as some of Lomberdoon's smaller villages but had been maintained with a purpose, mainly survival beyond any kingdom's walls.

"Hypocrisy." Welby stopped at the entrance as the wooden gates finished swinging open on their softly creaking hinges and turned to look at her and meet her gaze. He seemed to realize then that she was completely serious, and his jaws worked a few times before he sighed. "Speak your mind, Raven."

She cocked her head, studied his dark gaze, and felt a little silly now that he'd abandoned the stoic air he'd adopted the first time she'd escorted him to find sick dragons. But it wasn't enough to make her drop the conversation. "You have an issue with me promising the wild dragons we would fix this before the Legion even knows what's going on. I get it. I'm the one who said it, not you, so whatever fallout there is for the promises I've made, I have no problem taking responsibility for it. I've done it before."

His eyebrows twitched up in surprise but he didn't look away from her or try to interrupt.

"But if we're going to work together like this on our own," she continued, "out here, away from the Legion, to finish this mission that's already more complicated than we expected, I need to know I'm not working with someone who has a grudge against military mages. Even if we're on the same page about how important this is."

The man stared at her for a long moment, pressed his

lips together, then nodded. "While I prefer to not discuss my personal preferences in a professional capacity, you make a fair point."

Raven hadn't expected that at all, but she hid her surprise and returned his nod. "Thank you."

He gestured for her to step through the gates and once she did, he stopped to shove the large wooden doors closed again behind them. His lips pursed, he scanned the outpost settlement built along the base of the southern Brights-banes. "May we discuss this while searching for the inn?"

"Sure." She pointed toward the tallest building within the circular wall and hoped it was at least close to something resembling an inn if not the actual building with available lodging for the night. They walked slowly in that direction and he lowered his gaze to the trampled dirt that would have been a cobbled courtyard in any other town or city in Lomberdoon.

"The Legion contracted my skills to serve the ranks of their dragons. It's an opportunity I would have been foolish to pass up. I enjoy it as much as I do because I know I'm making a difference for the dragons within the capital where their treatment and training was so obviously lacking until magic returned."

She nodded and waited for him to continue.

"That being said, I can openly admit that I am not a fan of the military itself—the inner workings, the chain of command, and all the red tape. It keeps some of us who know we can do more from fully exercising the extent of our capabilities and our passion to utilize them."

Her head tilted, she adjusted the saddle over her shoulder and remained silent.

It sounds like he knows the Legion, all right.

"I believe it's safe to assume you understand the sentiment," Welby added.

Raven laughed wryly. "Absolutely."

They reached the tallest building in the settlement and a fresh wave of fatigue swept through her when the starlight illuminated the wooden sign hanging above the door and the name of the establishment painted across it —*The Long Road Inn.*

"So yes." The vet turned to face her. "I suppose I do hold a certain resentment against the Legion for my personal reasons. And I want to apologize."

She looked away from the sign above the inn's front door and met his gaze, completely taken off guard by that last statement. "For what?"

"For having given you the wrong impression. I may not agree with any number of Primus Kauler's decisions or the way the Legion operates as an entity in and of itself. But after the last few months of dealing with this Weeping Disease matter, I'm well aware that even a military assignment doesn't define an individual mage. I have nothing but the utmost respect for you, Raven."

"Oh." She almost dropped her riding gear then and there.

"And Leander, of course," he added. "Although I imagine that goes without saying at this point."

"I…" Thankfully, it was too dark for anyone to have seen yet another flush creeping into her cheeks.

Now I have a whole new appreciation for what Murphy must have gone through during school.

"Thank you." She nodded and couldn't quite manage to meet his gaze. "I wasn't fishing for—"

"I didn't think you were. But you're right. If we're going to work together like this here, then yes. A certain level of respect is the least we can offer each other. I'm sorry I haven't made that clear enough until now."

"Well, now we're on the same page."

"I hope so." A small smile flickered at the corner of his mouth as he studied her intently.

What am I supposed to say now? I respect you too, Dr. Welby, but I'm not gonna call you Chui?

Clearing her throat, Raven turned toward the door of the inn and nodded. "How hard do you think we'll have to knock before someone realizes they have travelers on their doorstep in the middle of the night?"

"There's only one way to find out."

CHAPTER THIRTEEN

Welby stepped toward the door of the inn and knocked firmly three times. They waited for any sign of light through the shuttered windows or the sound of groggy, shuffling footsteps. After a few seconds, the man clenched his jaw and extended his hand to try again.

Before his knuckles met the wood, a massive, heavy-sounding metal lock slid away on the other side, followed by the rattling of multiple small chains and more metallic clicks. The door opened inward and creaked in the almost complete silence that hung over the rest of the settlement.

The woman who stood on the other side smiled wearily at them and blinked against the wavering light from the lantern above her head. It swung from side to side as if she'd only just mounted it on the hook attached to a long chain dangling from the ceiling. She was still in her night-gown but had at least tried to cover it with a light house-coat she'd forgotten to fasten in her haste. "Welcome to Midway Outpost."

Welby nodded. "I'm sorry to wake you, ma'am—"

"But it's the middle of the night, you found yourselves here in No one's Business between kingdoms, and you're looking for a room."

"Yes," Raven said.

"There's no need to apologize. I was already awake. That's the business of keeping an inn in the ungoverned lands. Come in. Come in. I have a room."

The woman withdrew from the illuminated doorway and held the door open for her newest patrons to enter.

The mages exchanged a glance before he gestured for her to step inside first. He cleared his throat. "We would prefer two rooms, if at all possible."

"Oh? Well, sure. I've got two rooms. I fixed up the available ones this evening. But don't expect a discounted rate for taking the extra space. Believe it or not, we don't get many folks passing through out here. Which I'm sure you might have guessed." She chuckled as she pushed against the heavy front door of her establishment with both hands.

"We're happy to meet your price for both of them," Welby replied.

Raven plastered a tight smile onto her lips.

Three cheers for Legion wages.

"Then I'm happy to accommodate you. As long as you don't ask me for a pint of ale and a hot meal before you turn in." All the metal locks, bolts, and sliding chains slipped heavily into place beneath the woman's sleep-dulled fingers.

"Only the rooms, thank you," Raven assured her.

"Good. I don't stoke the fires until the sun's up, anyway. But once it is, if you're hungry, this front room is as close to a tavern as you're likely to get in Midway Outpost." The innkeeper retrieved the lantern still swaying from the hook and raised it in front of her. "This way."

Instead of leading them through the darkness of her inn, the woman squinted at her guests and lifted the lantern a little higher before she moved it toward them. "Giant saddles like those...I can't imagine you rode into our little independent haven on horseback."

"Dragonback." Welby had to lower his chin almost to his chest just to meet the short innkeeper's gaze. "We've left them outside the settlement walls for the night. They won't disturb anyone."

"No, of course not. Dragons fly free all over Threndor, even the ones with riders." With a shrug, she turned and finally led her midnight guests across the completely dark front room of her inn toward the narrow staircase on the far-right wall. "Trust me, we've seen our fair share of them around here these days. More than ever in the last few weeks especially. And boy, can they kick up a ruckus. I didn't know they flew in numbers like that, but if you folks only brought the two, I'm willing to take you at your word they won't be any trouble for us out here."

Raven frowned at the staircase before she followed their host first and struggled to maneuver her bulky riding gear through the narrow space lit only by a single halo of light from the lantern. "It sounds like you've had a few wild dragons passing through the valley."

"Wild? Ha. If you ask me, all of 'em are wild. It's in their nature, isn't it?"

"Have they caused any trouble for Midway Outpost?" Welby asked.

"Not other than the noise. It gets the worst late in the

evening and through most of the night. All that roaring and screeching, and it's so hard to tell how far away they are. The only time they don't make a peep is when they're flying over. But who knows with wild creatures like that, right?"

The woman grunted when she reached the top of the stairs and lifted the lantern in front of her before she turned left down the next hall. "Now, I haven't had anything against dragons as a whole. Not when I was farming in Heatherwood and not when I left to take my chances out here beyond the kingdom walls. But I tell you what. Listening to all that squabbling and screeching ring through this valley almost every night sure does make you appreciate those who come through with their riders. It's hard to not notice the difference in behavior, you know? At least with other humans around. And the silence."

Raven stopped short in the hallway.

Other dragons with riders have been out here? I haven't heard anything about patrols going beyond the kingdom borders.

She jumped when Welby cleared his throat behind her and muttered, "Sorry."

"No need. I'm tired too."

That wasn't even remotely why she'd stopped walking so suddenly but she didn't consider correcting him before she hurried after the innkeeper again. "How many other dragons and their riders have you seen pass through here?"

"Only the one. That was...oh, three weeks ago at the most. The rest of them are out there doing whatever they're doing without humans to help show them the way, I suppose. And acting real strange, if you ask me."

The vet's sharp breath seemed to confirm that he'd caught onto Raven's line of thinking as well. Or most of it.

"What do you mean by acting strangely?" he asked.

The woman stopped at two doors at the end of the hall and took a massive iron keyring from the pocket of her housecoat. "Well, I'm no expert, of course. Not like someone getting up and riding one of them like the two of you. But stumbling in circles and flapping their wings all wrong when they get particularly loud? That's something I've never seen. It must be a wild thing. Put a feral wolf and well-trained hound side by side, you'll see that wolf do things no hound would ever do. As long as those dragons don't bring their scuffling and roaring to Midway Outpost's walls, they can do whatever they like out there. Free lands, free dragons. Yes, sir."

The whole time she babbled on, the innkeeper searched halfheartedly for the right keys on her keyring to unlock the last two doors in the hall.

Raven didn't dare to turn and look at Welby. Even if the hallway had been brightly lit during the day, trying to share a knowing look like the one they would have shared in that moment would only give their host reason to suspect something was wrong.

And it certainly was.

How many wild dragons out here have already been infected? If this has been going on for weeks, we haven't even made a dent with the cure.

The woman finally unlocked one door, then fiddled with a second key to unlock the room next to it.

The young mage's pulse raced faster as she mulled the implications in stunned silence.

And how many of them have already made it close enough to Lomberdoon to infect the dragons there we thought were already safe?

Both doors creaked open and the innkeeper sighed. "Oh, for crying out loud. I didn't expect to light two rooms. Wait here for a moment, and I'll—"

"That won't be necessary, ma'am," Welby said. "Thank you."

Although Raven could hear him whispering the spell that conjured an orb of white light from the tip of his finger, their host hadn't. The woman stared with wide eyes at the magical light bobbing toward the closest open door of their lodgings for the night.

"Well, I'll be. A bonified mage right here in my inn."

"And we're very grateful you answered the door," Raven added and tried to keep her voice level. "How much do we owe you for the rooms?"

"I'm too half-asleep to work with numbers, miss." She chuckled. "I say we all get to our beds for the night and we can settle that in the morning. If you need anything else, that'll have to wait for morning too. But then you ask for Mrs. T and I'll see what I can do to get you whatever it is."

Before either of the guests had a chance to say anything more or even thank her again, Mrs. T bustled past them down the hall toward her room and the lantern light bobbed against the walls as it swung from her hand.

"*Circum inlustro*," Raven whispered and an orb of glowing white light bloomed at her fingertip before she sent it into the room beside Welby's. The mages stared at each other. "Many wild dragons acting strangely."

"Indeed." He turned to study the other doors of the

rooms around them in the hall. "I think it's best if we discuss this in the morning once we've set out again. Alone."

"Right. Good night, then."

With a stiff nod, he stood in the hall and watched as she entered her room. His door closed immediately after hers. It sounded way too loud in the silence of the inn this late at night, as did the soft thump of his boots on the floor as he headed to his bed.

She trudged to hers with a heavy sigh and sat on the mattress.

We have to find out what's happening with these dragons out here—who these humans are attacking with fungus and ore, of all things. And why.

But the more she tried to focus only on that one major problem, the more difficult it became to ignore the underlying surprise in Mrs. T's late-night chatter that begged for her attention. And it had nothing to do with her mission to handle Weeping Disease in Lomberdoon and beyond.

Only one dragon with a rider. It wasn't a military patrol and we're the only kingdom that even has dragons right now.

You think it's him, Leander said in her mind.

I don't know what to think. But if Connor and Calista came out here to investigate whatever's going on, this could be way bigger than we thought. And so much worse.

I have seen no sign of Calista. But I'll keep searching.

Get some rest too, Leander. I have a feeling tomorrow's gonna be even rougher.

Good night, mage.

CHAPTER FOURTEEN

Raven tossed and turned in her bed at the Long Road Inn. Strange images flashed through her mind as she dreamed —men in loose, foreign clothing with darkly painted eyes and curved swords, powerful magic she didn't recognize with symbols and flashes of light far different than her own experience with magic, and voices calling out as one in an indecipherable language.

She tried to push through it to find rest, but the voices began to call her name in hundreds of dark voices.

In the next moment, only one voice filled her dream.

Raven. Wake up.

Her eyes snapped open and she recognized Leander's presence in her mind instantly.

What's going on?

The courtyard at the east end of the settlement. Something's happening.

Raven sat with a tired groan and rubbed her face. *You'll have to be a little more specific.*

Men disappearing into the ground.

What?

They certainly look like strange humans to me. He sent her an image of what he'd seen and despite the fact that this was real in her waking life and coming directly from her familiar, she knew he'd tried to wake her with these images.

He'd seen the strange humans she'd dreamed about.

We have to check that.

I agree. Hurry.

She tossed the light covers off, leapt out of bed, and hurried as fast as she could to pull her riding leathers on and thrust her feet into her boots. *How long did I sleep?*

A few hours, he replied. *It's almost dawn.*

Her dragon's agitation grew within her as they shared the same urgency to follow this unexpected trail. When she was finally dressed, she opened her door as swiftly and silently as she could in the early hours of the morning and went next door to Welby's room. She only knocked twice before the door opened. The vet stood there with wide eyes and all traces of sleep eradicated from his expression. He was already fully dressed as well.

"Gruene told me," he muttered and poked his head through the doorway to scan the still-empty hall.

"This might be who we're looking for. Maybe even the same people who left that camp we found in the cavern."

"I agree." He grasped his dragon's saddle from the floor beside the door and nodded. "If they reached the surface on this side of the mountains before we burned the fungus, that would explain how the fungus reached the dragons out here."

"They went underground," Raven whispered.

"Yes." He thought for a moment, then reached for his bulging satchel already strapped over his head and shoulder and retrieved a coin purse. "Either a new base they've made for themselves, or—"

"Some of the tunnels go all the way through the mountain and out the other side."

Welby poured a number of silver coins into his hand, paused, then looked up to meet her gaze. "I can't say which of those options I'd prefer."

"I know."

"Here." He handed her half the coins and nodded toward her open door. "Leave this in your room."

"I have coin, but thanks."

"Have you left it already?"

"Well, no. But it's all in my saddlebags—"

"We need to leave." He gave her a tight smile that held little amusement under the circumstances. "I have no doubt you're good for it."

"Fine." She took the silver coins from his hand and headed into her room to collect her gear. The coins plinked on the nightstand beside the bed and she hauled Leander's saddle, harness, and saddlebags with her before she closed the door behind her.

Welby was already waiting for her in the hall with another floating orb of white light to softly illuminate the way out of the inn. Without another word, the mages hurried down the stairs and headed across the main front room.

Mrs. T's gonna think someone broke in here if we have to open all those locks again and let ourselves out.

When they reached the front door, though, all the heavy

security measures their host had in place on the inside of the massive wooden door had already been removed. She heard the sound of pots and pans clanking in the kitchen in the back and the splash of water.

Of course. Anyone running a place like this would be up before dawn too. Exactly like the ranch, only she's getting up to feed paying guests instead of dwarf goats.

The vet pushed through the front door first and held it open for her before they raced across the trampled dirt that served as the main avenue through the Midway Outpost settlement.

"There's another courtyard on the east end," Raven muttered and searched the sky for Leander. "That's where they went."

He frowned at her and nodded.

They had to cut around the densest collection of buildings within the center of Midway Outpost's protective stone wall, and as they approached the eastern edge of the settlement, the alleys and building walls seemed to look more like the larger cities of Lomberdoon she'd seen throughout her travels across the kingdom.

They're still working on building this to Lomberdoon's standards. That would make the perfect opportunity to dig tunnels into the mountains if there's still ongoing construction.

The walls of the buildings around them grew taller and the dirt beneath their boots became cobbled stone. Now, it seemed they were moving through a maze without any real idea of exactly where they were going.

Wingbeats cut through the air and Raven looked up where Leander swooped toward them before he banked sharply to lead the way. He almost knocked against the closest building but caught himself at the last second. "This way."

Ahead of them, Gruene wheeled in tight circles over the courtyard their mages were meant to find.

They increased the pace and hastened through the narrow alleys still dark beneath the first gray-blue light of morning twilight. Finally, they spilled out into what certainly looked like a courtyard.

It was empty, and the cobbled stones stretched across the mostly circular space until they reached the barrier wall around the edge of the settlement. Gruene caught sight of her mage and darted toward the courtyard to land gracefully in the clear circle with a sharp scratch of claws on stone.

In his agitation, Leander wasn't quite as elegant. He dropped onto the top of Midway Outpost's barrier wall and grasped the edges with all four sets of claws as his wings beat furiously to keep him aloft. Some of the stone crumbled away beneath his weight to clatter over the cobblestones beneath him. The sound was deafening with nothing in the space to dampen the echoes.

Raven grimaced. "Come on down here."

"They smell like the sea," he muttered where he clung to his precarious perch above them.

"And something like dragons," Gruene added. She swung her head toward Welby and fixed him with her glowing emerald eyes. "This is who attacked the wild clan."

The vet headed toward his familiar, who lowered herself so he could sling her saddle onto her back. As the black female stood so he could fasten the girdle under her belly and pull it tight, he glanced around the abandoned, mostly finished courtyard. "We have to go after them."

"Not on dragonback," Raven said and scanned the cobblestones.

Welby paused. "So where did they go?"

"Underground," Leander growled.

"Under—" The man looked at Gruene again as she lowered her head to accept the leather loop of the harness over her neck. "All of them? I thought we were looking for a tunnel."

"We are," she muttered as she walked slowly around the courtyard and searched for anything that might be a secret entrance beneath the stones. "You don't have to saddle her."

"And risk wasting the time to do it should we need to make an escape?"

"Leander and I don't need a saddle if we have to make an escape."

"Well, you and Leander are the exception that proves the rule—"

"Forget tacking the dragons," she snapped. "We have to find the—"

"Mage Alby." That made her stop and look at him as he finished pulling the straps of Gruene's gear taut. "Your saddlebags hold dozens of cure doses. At this point, I'm less inclined to worry about the repercussions of our reckless decision to follow this lead on our own without backup than I am about leaving that cure and kicking ourselves should we need it in the immediate future. Please."

We're wasting time now. But he's right.

"Okay. Come on, Leander."

Her dragon growled again from his perch on the wall,

shifted his weight, and sent more chunks of stone down around him. *I want nothing to do with those men.*

Well, you won't go into those tunnels. If that's what's even down there. But we're still out here to help infected dragons and we can't do that if we leave everything. What if one of those men finds it and traces it back to us?

For a moment, the STAR mage and her familiar stared at each other. Leander narrowed his eyes, then snorted and spread his wings again to take off from the top of the wall and land with a reverberating crack and crunch on the cobblestones. His claws threw up a shower of sparks as even more stone crumbled and echoed madly around the courtyard.

Raven scowled at him. "This is why we're here."

"Then tack your mount, mage." Leander made no move to approach her and make it easier on her, so she hauled their gear toward the massive red dragon to get him ready for a hopefully unnecessary quick escape.

Welby and Gruene shared a knowing glance before he cleared his throat. "Is everything all right?"

The red dragon snarled as Raven positioned the saddle over his back. "Save your concern for the dragons who need your help, healer."

"Leander." Raven shook her head as he stood so she could tighten the straps. "He's only trying to—"

"It's all right." Welby nodded. "Perhaps I overstepped."

Leander snorted as she finished cinching the girth and straps.

What's gotten into you?

Those humans are responsible for infecting my kin. And for some of their deaths.

And we're going to find them, okay?

You have to.

She turned away from her dragon to tell Welby they were ready, but Leander nipped the lapel of her red leather riding jacket and pulled her back.

"Raven," he said over another low, warning growl. His yellow eyes widened. "You must."

As she stroked the side of his face, she searched the one eye trained urgently on her. "We will."

"Ready?" Welby asked.

"Yes." She looked over her shoulder and nodded.

"Where did they go?"

"I already told you," the red dragon snapped. "Underground."

"Yes, I heard that odd report the first time." The vet stepped back and spread his arms to indicate the entirety of the courtyard cobbled with freshly hewed stones compared to the other streets and courtyards like this within Lomberdoon's borders. "And yet there seems to be a lack of visible entrances."

Leander's jaws cracked together when he snapped in irritation. "That did not stop them."

Raven glanced warningly at him, then forced herself to move on from her familiar's irritation and admittedly rude behavior to study the stones instead. "Okay, we're looking for something that could easily be removed. A loose stone. Something that doesn't look quite right."

"Gruene, did you see anything?" Welby asked.

The black female lowered her head and held his gaze. "No."

"It was here." Leander stormed forward across the

courtyard. If anyone else had seen the red dragon moving like this, they would have thought he was prancing in some kind of spirited show. He stamped on the cobblestones and lifted both forepaws to pound them against one large, flat-laid rock after another. His hind paws kicked up the rubble he'd knocked loose during his landing, and his tail thumped against the wall to crack even more huge chunks away.

"Leander, stop." The young mage turned to search the opening to the courtyard through which she and Welby had arrived. "We told the innkeeper our dragons wouldn't cause any problems—"

"The problem is already here. Right here!" He pounded his forepaws into the ground again and snorted. "Find it."

"Hold on." Welby extended a hand and tried to signal for Raven's familiar to stop. "Leander, I think—"

A burst of dragon frost sprayed from Gruene's mouth in a concentrated stream and struck the side of Leander's neck before he could rear again for another mighty assault against the stone. He stumbled back, shook his head and neck fiercely to dislodge the ice crystals, and snorted. His yellow eyes found Gruene and narrowed as he growled. "That was unnecessary."

Her wings twitched away from her back and she raised her head toward him. "Was it?"

"Leander, back up." Raven waved him away and he fixed the same indignant glare on his mage but did as she said. She pointed at a large stone in front of him that was barely distinguishable from all the others. "That one there looks a little loose, doesn't it?"

"So does the wall," Welby muttered.

She turned to face him and spread her arms. "I trust my dragon, Dr. Welby. Even if he saw something yours didn't. We're standing in the middle of an empty courtyard with two saddled dragons ready to go, so unless you can find the exact location of these men some other way in the next five seconds, this is all we have."

Welby frowned, but the STAR mage turned toward the stone she'd indicated and stepped on the edge to put her full weight on it. It wobbled noticeably.

Leander snorted in exasperation. *Thank you.*

He's a military contractor who spends his time tending to sick dragons, not investigating foreign threats inside or outside the kingdom. When Welby realizes we know what we're doing, he'll stop questioning it.

Like everyone else?

Raven settled into a crouch in front of the loose stone and felt for a space she could slide her fingers into. She also felt Gruene's appraising stare on her back and Welby's frustration. Unless she was imagining all of it.

You're not imagining it.

She ignored her familiar's insistence on reading her mind all the time and focused on the rest of their conversation. *Yes. Anyone else who's seen what we can do stopped questioning us. Or at least they stopped telling us it couldn't be done and finally started asking the questions that matter.*

CHAPTER FIFTEEN

Welby's footsteps moved toward her and to her surprise, the man hunkered down on the other side of the stone and began to feel around the edge of it with her. His lips were pressed tightly together as he slid his fingers slowly along the cracks and he didn't look up at her when he muttered, "I let my frustration get the better of me."

She pressed on her side of the slightly wobbly stone and moved her fingers around the side to check for a widening crack in the dark. "It happens to everyone."

The vet paused, then turned slightly in his crouch to look at Leander, who'd stepped away and now glared across the courtyard at Gruene. "And I doubted your certainty, Leander. Will you accept my apology?"

The red dragon took two more steps back until the end of his powerful tail bumped against the wall, this time without dislodging any of the supporting stones from it. He tilted his head and held Welby's gaze. "Only if my mage accepts as well," he growled.

"I'm sorry, Raven."

She sighed and dug her fingers deeper beneath the edges of the jagged rock. "As long as you help me get this stone out of the ground, we'll call it even."

Welby looked at Leander again, who snorted and lowered his head. "If you trust us, then trust us, healer."

"I've never intended anything else." Finally, Welby returned to examining the heavy stone with Raven.

When she looked at him, his deepening frown told her he hadn't quite received what he'd wanted out of the exchange. "Apology accepted," she muttered with a small smile. He met her gaze with the barest hint of hope behind his dark eyes. "From both of us."

With a nod, he returned to the task at hand and wobbled the stone from his side while Raven did the same from hers.

You're too easy on him, Raven.

She shook her head, knowing it would come across to their mission partners as nothing more than frustration with a loose stone that hadn't yielded to either of them. *He went easy on me when I attacked him for putting down a dragon too sick to be healed. I was new to that then. He's new to this. And right now, we could all use a little break before things get worse. I can't shake the feeling they will.*

Leander growled and tried to pace across his side of the courtyard, but he barely had the room to turn and take the half dozen steps in the opposite direction. Gruene watched him with her head lowered. The only parts of her that moved were her emerald eyes as her gaze followed the large red male.

"I hate to say it," Welby muttered. "But I don't believe this particular—"

"Stand back."

"I'm sorry?"

Raven leapt to her feet and shooed the vet away from the stone. He complied quickly and almost bumped into Leander pacing behind him again before the dragon lurched away to avoid touching him.

She extended an open hand toward the wobbly cobblestone and muttered, "*Verecundia*."

A streak of opalescent light burst from her palm, struck the cobblestone dead-center, and cracked it cleanly in two. The sound echoed against all the stonework rising around them, but if the people of Midway Outpost hadn't heard two dragons in their eastern courtyard behind all the buildings stamping and blowing dragon frost, they probably wouldn't hear this either.

Gruene stepped away and her wings twitched outward in surprise and agitation.

Welby stared at the jagged crack running down the center of the cobblestone and stroked his hairless chin. "Battle magic."

"Used by the Order of War Mage, yeah." She dropped to her knees again and grasped the closest half of the stone to try to wiggle it free.

"I haven't heard of that order taking on a new addition in years."

"Not officially, no." She yanked on the jagged piece and felt it give way even more. "I wouldn't expect Alessandra to go around the kingdom talking about everyone she trains. A few of them in particular."

He looked sharply at her. "I'm sorry, did you say Alessandra?"

"Mm-hmm."

"As in…"

"War Mage Barnasis, yeah." Finally, Raven had a much better hold on the edge of her half and managed to pry her fingers into the large split. With a grunt, she heaved the massive stone toward her and it slid away by an inch. "Look at that."

"Raven, I was under the impression you'd only recently received your mage's robes."

She stopped tugging on the split rock and sighed before she looked at him. "Everyone likes to talk about a mage still in school, but after the robes, it's like people forget about what happened before then."

"War Mage Barnasis trained you to use that spell?"

"Yes. And so many more than that. But I thought if it kept giant dragons from eating me in their cave, it might as well be a little useful to break rocks."

His head jerked up so he could meet Gruene's emerald eyes. His familiar shifted from side to side on the cobblestones and sparks flurried beneath her claws as she shook her head and snorted.

Leander's rumble of amusement sounded like spiteful enjoyment at the surprise in both their dragon and mage mission partners.

Don't say anything, Raven warned as she pulled the stone aside again. Loose pebbles beneath it toppled into the darkness beneath the courtyard and echoed as they clinked against the walls of the massive hole she was slowly uncovering.

The vet cleared his throat. "I'm afraid I don't quite understand—"

"Now isn't the time to talk about what Leander and I did and didn't do before we got to the Legion, okay? I need you to help me move the rest of this giant rock out of the way."

Her familiar's rumbling grew even louder, and the man looked at the broken stone. His bafflement over the few nuggets of her past she had shared with him seemed to have completely blocked the sound of her half as it slid or the fact that they now stared into a widening hole.

"Of course. We can return to this conversation at a later time."

"Yeah, maybe." She tried not to frown and focused on pulling her half of the ridiculously heavy stone toward her while he shifted his from side to side.

I'm not into talking about all the things we did two years ago that make people stare at me like that, but if it's motivation for him, fine.

They heaved the slabs of rock apart and Welby rose to his feet after he'd moved his half completely aside to help her with the other. It seemed that when he focused, he found the task considerably easier.

Raven moved aside to give him more space as stone ground against stone and the last piece clattered on the courtyard. "Wow. I should have had you move all of it."

"It's far easier in pieces, Mage Alby. So thank you for that." He tried to smile at her, but it didn't come across as much more than slight embarrassment on his part.

She returned her attention to the gaping hole beneath the stone they'd cleared. "This looks big enough to fit… well, you, for one."

"I'm not sure whether to take that as a compliment or something else."

"It's merely an observation."

Great. Now I'm talking out loud about his strength and observing him and judging his size by a hole in the ground. Less talk, more jumping into tunnels, Raven. Come on.

"I'll go first," the vet offered.

Raven stood and dusted her hands off. "I can—"

"Before you argue against it, the suggestion was made merely in reference to my size." His half-hearted, closed-lipped smile returned. "Should I be waylaid by a tunnel far too narrow for me to pass, you won't have to continue alone without me."

"Do you think I'd leave you stuck in a tunnel?"

Welby laughed. "I don't want to assume but there is a remote possibility, and that's an idea I'm not particularly fond of."

Despite two agitated dragons waiting for them and the gaping pit they'd uncovered beneath the cobbled courtyard of a settlement in the middle of nowhere along the Brightsbane Mountains, Raven smirked. "I'd come back for you."

"I'm sure you would. *Circum inlustro.*" An orb of soft white light illuminated in the vet's hand and he tossed it into the hole without breaking her gaze. "It's a slight consolation."

"Good to know."

They stared at each other as the orb sank slowly into the tunnel.

Leander snorted. "We'll wait for you here."

"Unless, of course, you've changed your minds," Gruene added.

That made the vet chuckle. "We're going in, Gruene. The two of you are our eyes and ears aboveground. Assuming I don't get stuck."

With a final nod at Raven, he crouched in front of the hole and lifted out the top of a frayed, dirt-stained rope.

"A rope into a black hole," she quipped.

"I assume this was intended to be as difficult to enter as possible. Except by those meant to use this particular entrance."

She looked at the sky and bit her bottom lip. "The sun will come up at any minute. We'd better hurry."

Without a word, Welby lowered himself into the vertical tunnel beneath Midway Outpost and descended slowly.

Be careful, Raven, Leander thought to her. *I can't follow you.*

But you can keep an eye on things up here, and that's as important. Let me know if anything happens.

I don't like it.

Neither do I, Leander, but we can't stop now.

CHAPTER SIXTEEN

Connor Alby pressed his back against the wall of the massive underground chamber. For weeks now, he'd been all but trapped inside this series of tunnels stretching from the open lands west of Lomberdoon and into the Brightsbane Mountains.

The contingent of Malendesh forces was relentless as they scouted through the tunnels and chambers lined with thick veins of Smithheart ore covered by the strange black fungus. Every time he'd tried to extricate himself quietly from what these foreigners had turned into their apparent base of operations on Threndor, a Malendesh man was somehow there and oftentimes, more than one.

The force was surprisingly well-organized and kept a tight watch on every exit point around the massive chamber in which they'd set up their encampment—including the tunnel through which he'd followed the three men from Malenspire out of Midway Outpost.

Even when he'd attempted to explore the other branching tunnels in the hopes of finding an alternate escape route, he'd been pushed back at every turn. He'd known better than to try to confront these men with their loose, flowing attire, darkly painted eyes, oiled mustaches, and vicious-looking weapons hanging from their belts and hidden among the folds of their clothing.

It was a miracle he'd lasted this long down there without being discovered.

That was mostly due to the cloaking illusion he'd cast on himself during his first night there when he'd been foolish enough to think he could take a look around and still get back to the surface once the initial investigation was finished.

He'd been so very wrong.

The Malendesh continuously cut him off and he found it a constant necessity to maintain the cloaking illusion in a near-desperate attempt to extricate himself from the den of foreign invaders upon which he'd stumbled.

And now I'm sagging against an earthen wall beneath the open lands, waiting for them to show their weakness. You should have told someone where you were headed, old man. If Calista hasn't found someone to help by now, you may very well die down here.

The Fade was a powerful illusion, to be sure, and most useful when those around the caster were nowhere near as familiar or skilled with the use of magic as every man in this Malendesh force. But after seeing how powerful their combined magic had become during their numerous gatherings—where every man in the camp stopped what he was doing to perform some multiplied spell that almost looked like a ritual ceremony—Connor was convinced that these foreigners understood the intricacies of magic on a level he didn't dare to access on his own.

They would have found him had he lowered his defenses enough to keep the Fade from draining him of his strength.

Magic always has a cost. You've known this from the very beginning, old man.

His options had been clear from the start. He could have chosen to preserve his strength and risk these invaders catching the trail of his illusion. But that would have landed him in even more dire circumstances. He had no desire to be caught by a foreign Malendesh party during an unsanctioned and unannounced visit to Threndor.

Instead, he'd opted to use every last ounce of strength within him to mute the trail his magic left behind. It had proven incredibly useful and quite successful. He hadn't been detected.

But after weeks of keeping this spell up at all hours— counting the days and nights once he'd learned the patterns and schedule of the Malendesh scouts and the various tunnels they marched through at any given time— his decision had taken its toll.

Connor Alby grew weaker by the minute and he still hadn't found a way to escape these tunnels without being detected.

Who am I kidding? These men wouldn't simply detect me. They'd capture me, hold me prisoner, and most likely interrogate me with the type of tactics Lomberdoon abandoned centuries ago. Now, I'm wasting away beneath the ground. By the Source, Alby. Curiosity and experience are not a remedy for caution.

He could have kicked himself for his recklessness—for

how confident he'd been that he, Dragon Rider Alby, could simply climb into a hole after three strange-looking men and investigate a massive operation like this without any real consequences.

If I don't find a way out soon, they'll find me. Only because my last breath will break the illusion.

The mage sagged against the wall and let himself slide slowly to the dirt floor beneath him to sit in silence. Even then, he listened.

That was what he'd done this whole time because there was nothing else to do once he'd fully realized and accepted his predicament. Over the last few weeks of hearing nothing but the Malendesh language of Spirgul, his isolation had forced his memory to pick up on his basic understanding of the language—plus a few additional layers of the foreign tongue along the way.

It was too difficult to catch all the new words he'd heard and piece them together exactly, but the context made it clear enough.

Now, one of the scouts who patrolled the tunnel where Connor had entered as well as the two branching off on either side hurried out of the right-hand passage toward the group of strangely clad men huddled in the cavern's center.

"Chief Gamahr!"

The man he had come to recognize as the leader of this force—distinguishable only by the two massive rubies embedded in his left ear and a vicious burn scar covering his left arm down to his fingers—turned toward the scout. His eyes narrowed.

"More stone-cutters?"

"No, Chief. Threndoren hold great fear of blackened weapon. There is a cut in our hiding."

Connor frowned.

That can't be right. A cut? No, he means a hole. Maybe a breach?

"Where is it?" the chief muttered and stepped away from the others he'd been in conversation with to pull his scout to a more private area of the cavern.

"*Augende sonus,*" the dragon rider muttered and barely let any breath escape his mouth so he wouldn't be overheard. The spell worked perfectly and the Malendesh chief's voice echoed in his ears while the rest of the noise in the cavern faded into the background. Unfortunately, it siphoned even more of the little strength he had left. He closed his eyes and the men's magically enhanced conversation washed over him.

"The winged eeskri came again," the scout said urgently. "Too close to the stone above." He pointed toward the original tunnel Connor had entered, where three other Malendesh sat with their packs and food rations, laughing and drinking from oddly shaped vessels he could only assume were wineskins. "We fight them daily now."

"Winged eeskri. Too much love for the sky. No respect for the sea. Our ships will not wait forever."

"We cannot wait forever, Chief." The scout lowered his head. "Another cut must be filled."

"Then fill it." The chief thumped a fist against his chest, his scout returned the gesture, and they both nodded.

Not a cut. They are talking about a breach. Connor opened his eyes and blinked wearily against his utter exhaustion. *A breach must be filled? They're talking about caving in more tunnels. The one that leads to the stone above.* He lifted his head away from the wall to get a better view of the passage he'd entered through but hadn't been able to exit. *The only tunnel I know will lead me out!*

His mind reeled as the Malendesh chief issued orders and his men carried the command across the cavern. The old mage could barely make out the words or the intention behind them. He had to stand and get out.

Move your old bones, Rider Alby. If you get caught down here without finding a different escape route, this is the end of you. Move!

"Winged eeskri by the stone!" the men shouted. They ran to collect chunks of Smithheart ore they'd mined and stacked in various piles around the cavern. Then they passed them from man to man until those at the end of the line had gathered armfuls for themselves. By the time the ore chunks coated in black fungus reached the last few, they glowed brighter than they ever had within the stone walls of the chamber or in their previous piles.

Connor stared at the men who gazed at their armfuls of ore in rapturous delight. Greedy sneers captured their mouths.

"Threndoren." The chief snickered and shook his head. "Listen to me, Malandesh! We move our ground now. The strangers to their land will never see us here. They do not see the power of their earth beneath them, all around us now. Stop the winged eeskri, stop the Threndoren. Their magic will be ours on Malenspire to fuel our *maktor!*"

"*Maktor!*" the foreigners shouted as one.

A shiver raced down Connor's spine and gooseflesh prickled over his skin.

Maktor. That's what they've been talking about over and over again, and I have no idea what it means. But winged eeskri? That has to be the dragons. And if they have ships... By the Source, if they have ships on Threndor, they must be powering a concealing illusion the likes of which make mine a complete and utter joke in the face of all of this. Get out!

He pushed away from the wall and stumbled toward the tunnel he knew led to the surface and the stone courtyard in Midway Outpost. His old body had been incredibly spry even in his later years, but all his strength and agility failed him as his attempt to maintain the Fade illusion and remain invisible to these foreigners sapped everything from him.

His limbs almost failed him and he staggered and braced himself against the wall. Although he pushed himself as hard and as fast as he could, he didn't think it would be anywhere near enough.

An intensely bright blue light illuminated the cavern behind him. The Malendesh force began yet another chant and their voices roared through the chamber. Connor couldn't tell if it was the incredible blue glow of the Smith-heart ore fueling the power in those voices or the other way around, but it didn't matter.

They will collapse that tunnel, move to another camp, and do this over and over again until they have everything they want from the heart of these mountains. And I'll be finished before I can ever get word to Havendom about what I've seen.

The old mage lurched forward as the three men with piles of blindingly bright ore in their arms walked slowly toward the entrance they meant to destroy. His eyes watered and his teeth ground noisily in his skull, but he pushed himself to keep moving.

It was through luck alone that he managed to slip through the opening into the tunnel before the three Malendesh converged in front of it. If he'd been any slower, they would have cut him off—or bumped into an invisible body, which would surely have triggered a search for the source of the disturbance.

Thus far, though, it seemed the power of the magic they summoned together—so much power—kept them ignorant to his presence.

Keep moving. Get out before this entire thing comes down on you.

Whatever the Malendesh chanted, Connor could feel the intensity of magic in those words. A high-pitched hum filled the air behind him, followed by an agonizing tingle as the strong magic washed over his back and legs.

The floor of the tunnel shuddered and the walls trembled. Small stones squeezed out of their settings and rained on him like hail. Huge cracks shattered both the Smith-heart ore lining the passage and the thick mountain walls behind them. They raced along the tunnel much faster than he could ever have been able to move, cracked violently, and made his ears ring.

I have enough strength for one more spell. At least enough to avoid being buried alive in here. After that, it's my foolish desperation against a Malendesh army that seems to have no weakness.

He frowned when he saw a light. It didn't come from behind with the blue blaze of the foreigners combined magic but from up ahead. Voices echoed toward him. They were faint at first but the shouting started when the tunnel walls threatened to shatter and collapse.

And they would. He knew they would and any second from now.

I'm the only one who's allowed to be this reckless in the face of a threat like this. Well, if it's the last good thing I do for Threndor and Lomberdoon, whoever you are, I hope you use your second chance better than I did.

Instead of the magical shield he'd been prepared to cast around himself, Connor extended both hands and stumbled forward over the falling chunks of stone. "*Commonitionem!*"

His spell was almost entirely invisible, swallowed by the ceiling of the tunnel when it broke away in front of him. The bright flashes of surging opalescent light swirled up the tunnel toward the strangers who'd found this entrance. It rolled past the rain of dirt, cracking walls, and the surge of Malendesh magic that hurled him off his feet from behind.

The old dragon rider didn't have any strength left to pick himself up and try to raise at least a cushioning shield around himself. Even if he did, he wouldn't have had the time.

Connor Alby shielded his head reflexively with both arms and waited for the inevitable.

A massive slab of rock and a shower of dirt falling free from the tunnel ceiling did come down on top of him but not before the floor gave way beneath his feet.

His stomach lurched and he began to fall. He tumbled for what seemed like forever even deeper into the heart of the mountains so far below the land and the freedom he'd been so confident he would always have. The blazing blue magic of the foreigners' spell, powerful enough to reduce old, stable tunnels like these into nothing but rubble, winked above him and faded as he moved farther away.

Finally, the mage landed with a grunted oath at the sudden impact. Debris fell with him and the deafening roar made it impossible to know what had happened above him now that he couldn't see a thing.

Pain speared through his left ankle and the pile of rubble grew larger around him.

When it eventually stopped and the last few pebbles bounced down the mountain of broken rock and ore that had encapsulated him at the bottom of whatever new pit he'd fallen into, he expected the end to take him at any minute.

It didn't, not the way he'd expected although he knew the end was inevitable.

All he could hear was his racing heartbeat and the heavy breath that wheezed in and out of him in complete darkness.

I'm not dead. How am I not dead?

His ankle burned ferociously but he couldn't move.

Not dead and not entirely trapped. Merely too drained of strength and magic to get out again. At least I left them a warning. I wonder who they were.

His eyelids fluttered and even the sound of his breath faded as if it fled from him down another long tunnel he couldn't traverse himself. Despite the need to remain aware, Connor Alby lost consciousness.

CHAPTER SEVENTEEN

Raven clenched her jaw as she and Welby moved quickly down the tunnel. Since they'd first entered, they'd found more branching tunnels and large caverns filled with glowing plants, glittering stalactites, and shimmering pools than she'd thought could ever exist.

A good number of the passages they'd thought would open into something else had already collapsed. Through the stones piled in huge blockages beside the main passage they walked through now, she noticed the same glow of the Smithheart ore veins winking in the darkness through the cracks.

"This doesn't feel right."

Her companion flicked his fingers toward his glowing orb of light and directed it another ten feet in front of them. "Which part?"

"All of it. Mostly these collapsed tunnels. Why would the caverns that don't lead anywhere still be standing while all the branches on our right have been cut off? It couldn't have been natural."

"I'd considered an earthquake as a possibility as well." He looked at her in the semi-darkness and shook his head. "But that would have collapsed the caverns too."

"I know. And there's still Smithheart ore down here behind the cave-ins. If they were caused by miners, we would have seen some kind of sign that they'd been here. Wouldn't we?"

"The miners in Lomberdoon certainly left an easily discernible trail. Perhaps mining in the outer lands is conducted differently."

She frowned at him. "Inside or outside kingdom borders, I don't think anyone trying to run a successful mining operation would hide their single entrance under a giant slab of stone in a courtyard."

"Hmm. Most likely not." They walked on in silence and Welby brushed his fingers against the right-hand wall. "I can't say I'm particularly familiar with orienting myself underground, but I believe this passage has curved north for the last half mile at least."

"You're not imagining things." She turned to look back the way they'd come, but the vet's light orb illuminated so much less of the path they'd already taken. "We certainly aren't going east into the mountains." She stopped when she registered the pieces she'd already found and only now put them together. "But if we're heading north, all the collapsed tunnels we've already passed are."

"Are what?" Welby stopped and turned to raise an eyebrow at her.

"Heading east. Into the mountains."

"Toward Lomberdoon."

Raven's heartbeat lurched into an incredible pace, but

she forced aside all the urgency that threatened to grow into panic and swallowed. "We shouldn't jump to any conclusions."

The vet nodded. "Agreed."

"But if these tunnels are somehow connected to the cavern we found at the end of the Orion tunnel…"

"That's a very large if, Raven."

"I know, but hear me out. It looks…" She turned again reflexively and felt ridiculous when she lowered her voice. No one else was there. "It looks like someone might have collapsed any tunnels that lead directly into Lomberdoon. If they're connected. I know it's all hypothetical but it makes sense."

"Putting aside all logic and reason to jump to the same conclusions we've agreed were useless—"

"But think about it. Strange humans who smell like the sea. That's what the wild clan said. They had ore covered in that fungus, right? And we found the remains of a camp before we burned all that fungus with the Blue Flame. Whoever attacked the clan and infected them with Weeping Disease must have been down here. They had to come from the cavern with the fungus and maybe they filled all those tunnels behind them to cover their tracks."

"If that's the case, it was a poor attempt." He nodded for them to continue walking, but both mages stepped far more carefully and listened more intently for any sound that might travel through the tunnel toward them. "Anyone thorough enough to collapse that many tunnels to hide their true motives wouldn't have left a rope dangling from the top of a hole in the center of a courtyard."

"Right. This tunnel isn't collapsed, either." Raven bit her

lip. "Maybe they didn't want anyone else who might have been mining the mountains to stumble on what they'd already found."

"There are too many variables." He shook his head again and grimaced at his floating orb. "It's safer to stay away from conjecture and work with the facts we already have. Once we glean more—"

"I get it. Speculation doesn't prove anything. I guess I was simply thinking out loud." She steeled herself to continue through the long, winding passage that left more foreboding evidence by the minute and decided it was best to keep her mouth shut and the rest of her senses on high alert.

Speculation is way different than knowing something I can't prove. I knew what the wild dragons needed and what had to be done with magic up north before we could fix it in Lomberdoon. I knew it like I know the back of my hand or like I know Leander. But this? It's merely a scattering of random clues I'm trying to force together to prove something because I want it to be true.

That thought made her stomach churn.

No. That's not what I want. Because if we do prove this, it means this is bigger than strange humans fighting wild dragons and launching ore into the sky. It would be a focused operation. For what? An invasion? But why block the tunnels heading toward Lomberdoon if someone is trying to attack the kingdom? It doesn't make sense.

"Hold on." Welby stopped and raised a finger.

"What?"

"Shh." He cocked his head and touched his fingertips to the tunnel wall again. "Do you feel that?"

"I don't feel—" Raven cut the words short because she

could feel something. A low, steady vibration rose through the floor of the tunnel and into her boots. It felt like a miniature version of Leander's soft rumbling beneath her whenever he laughed as they flew.

If I can feel it here, even a little like this, that means—

"There's something down there," the vet muttered.

"Yep. We can't call that conjecture, right?"

"I don't believe so." They looked at each other with wide eyes, and because neither mage was ready to admit defeat or fear now that they'd come this far, they continued steadily. "We have to be very careful now."

"Whatever we find, I'm ready."

He chuckled wryly. "That doesn't surprise me in the least."

The mages proceeded with renewed purpose and much more cautious awareness. After a short distance, the end of the tunnel curved slightly away from them to the right and was illuminated by a faint blue glow.

"What's that?" she muttered.

"I haven't the slightest." Welby sent his floating orb farther ahead of them. "But I think—"

What happened next was hard for either of them to follow, although by now, both mages were accustomed to acting quickly.

Raven thought she saw a shadow of movement block the blue light that approached through the tunnel. It could have belonged to a man or a beast given how awkwardly it shuffled and staggered against the walls. Chips of stone began to break away from the passage walls around them and plummet from the ceiling. The roar of crumbling stone drowned out almost every other sound, but she thought she could hear voices.

"It's another cave-in," Welby shouted. "Turn back!"

"There's someone in there!"

He caught her hand and tried to yank her back. "And we'll be in there too if we don't—"

"Stop! We have to help them."

"Raven!"

She darted toward the shadows that moved along the walls while the blue light grew brighter by the second behind the staggering figure.

As she opened her mouth to call out to whoever it was, a massive chunk of stone splintered from the ceiling and thick pieces fell in a deluge of dust and dirt and pebbles.

"*Clypeus corporis!*" the vet shouted to raise the yellow glow of personal shields around both of them.

At the same time, she stretched her hand out and yelled, "*Adsulto protentia!*"

She'd meant to use the forceful spell to move the falling ceiling aside, at least for a moment so whoever staggered toward them might have a chance to escape safely. Before her spell even reached the slabs of hard mountain and veins of ore that plunged and shifted around them, someone else's spell hurtled toward her and Welby down the tunnel.

It spiraled down the passage like a bright, opalescent vortex, unstopped by the falling rubble or the trembling walls or anything else between whoever had cast it and the two mages investigating the tunnels. It even breached Welby's magical shields that glittered around them both and struck her outstretched hands.

Her focus on her magic disappeared—even the sound of the collapsing walls and the dark, deep voices that sounded like chanting vanished—as the wave of light surged into her and made her gasp.

Warning. Turn back. Save yourself.

That was the instant message she received from the powerful blast of opalescent light a split second before the tunnel collapsed around them. Something about that magic and the message it carried felt so incredibly familiar but she didn't have the time to place it.

Then, the entire world tipped and she began to fall.

The vet shouted something incoherent and the pulsing yellow light of his shields intensified around them. She flailed and tried to grasp something to hold onto but found nothing.

After so many times of having fallen off her dragon—some of them arguably more deadly than falling through a tunnel floor that gave way beneath her—her instincts kicked in. She tumbled downward and shrieked, *"Descendere incolumes!"*

It was almost too late but she managed to cast the spell around her and Welby that probably saved them both when they reached the floor of another cavern beneath them. It was no more painful than rolling out of her bed in the middle of the night and toppling onto the bedroom floor—although it was far more startling.

Raven's stomach leapt into her throat, the wind momentarily knocked out of her as her companion landed beside her with a grunt.

His spell was the final advantage that saved them a second time when the rubble of the cave-in avalanched around them and bounced off his shields. Every time something struck them, it pinged off his magic with deafening clarity and threw up even more dust as the pieces clattered across the stone floor.

He snarled in concentration and effort as he focused on maintaining those shields until finally, it was over.

CHAPTER EIGHTEEN

The new cavern where they'd landed was incredibly silent but for the whisper of more dust clouds that flurried from the hole above them and the clack of a few last pebbles as they bounced off the domes of yellow light.

When it seemed there would be no aftershock of more falling stone and ore and everything was still again, Welby heaved a sigh and lowered the shields. They were in complete darkness.

"*Circum inlustro,*" Raven whispered. A glowing white orb flared in her hand, and she flicked it to hover above them before she rolled onto her back and propped herself on both hands.

"Are you all right?" her companion asked.

"Yeah. You?" She sounded breathless but no one could blame her for that.

He drew a deep breath and sat slowly before he looked at her in the soft light. "I believe so, yes. *Circum inlustro.*"

A second orb darted from his finger to the ceiling, which was much closer than she had expected.

"Augeo." His small orb grew ten times larger and light spilled through the chamber.

Judging by the way the rubble had fallen and the blocked walls of yet another tunnel behind them, it seemed the cave-in that had dropped them there had taken the passage they'd traversed with them and simultaneously collapsed another one behind them.

Filling in one entrance by sealing off another. Whoever did this knew exactly what they were doing.

"Raven, I can't help but comment on—"

"I know what you're going to say." She brushed her dust-coated hair away from her face and sighed. "That I should have listened to you when you said to turn back. That it was reckless to try to save someone else before we knew we'd be able to save ourselves."

"That was—"

"I get it. But even if we'd turned back, we would still have ended up down here. That entire tunnel fell. We wouldn't have made it anyway."

Welby opened his mouth to protest but looked at the jagged and crumbled stone above them that had fallen on top of this hole into a lower tunnel and jammed themselves against the walls to create a new ceiling. "Yes, I see that's the case."

"Just so you know, I have a problem with leaving anyone to fend for themselves. Even if I end up in a cave-in because of it."

When he looked at her again, the corners of his lips twitched. "I'm not quite sure why you assumed I blame you for our current predicament."

Her eyes widened and she pushed herself fully upright

to sit up beside him. "Well, you tried to pull me back."

"Call it my survival instinct kicking in." He rasped a chuckle. "But we both chose to keep going after we felt the first tremors. I intended to say thank you."

"What?"

"For acting so quickly to cushion our fall." He shifted sideways and grimaced. "We're not dead but I imagine I'll be sore for quite some time after this."

She couldn't help but smirk at that. "Well...you're welcome. And the shields were a good call, so thank you for that."

Welby inclined his head and held her gaze as his closed-lipped smile grew. "Anytime." After a moment, he shook his head. "And when I say anytime, I want to make it clear I'm not referring to being caught in a collapsing tunnel while multiple unknown parties cast some of the most powerful magic I've ever seen."

Raven laughed. "You mean you don't wanna go again?"

"Ha! Not unless it's completely and utterly necessary. Although of course, if it were, I do hope you'd be there with me. To break another fall, at the very least."

The crooked grin he gave her in the half-light of their floating orbs made the new cavern in which they'd landed feel incredibly small and stuffy. A flare of heat raced through her cheeks, and she was acutely aware of how sitting there with Welby and surrounded by piles of rubble from a deadly collapse felt even more claustrophobic than when they'd ventured down the narrow tunnel above.

"Right. So...don't go into any other tunnels without me, then."

He nodded and chuckled softly again.

She pulled herself away from the surprising interaction between them, looked up, and scanned their new surroundings. "Speaking of other tunnels...I'd say we're lucky there are so many."

"They run for miles." The vet ran a hand over his dust-covered hair and a light cloud of dust and a few remaining pebbles flurried over his shoulders. "I imagine I might be the first man in history to thank the Swarm for what they've left behind."

Raven snorted. "You most certainly are. And thanks to the Swarm, I bet there are dozens of other entrances and exits. We'll merely have to find another way out."

"Agreed."

Raven! Leander's voice burst so forcefully into her mind that she sucked in a sharp breath and clenched her eyes shut.

I'm here. I'm okay.

"What's wrong?" Welby asked and leaned toward her in concern.

"Nothing's wrong. I guess a few hundred miles of mountain aren't enough to separate a mage and her famil-iar. At the least, they merely cause a delay."

What happened? The urgency in the red dragon's thoughts made her curse herself for not having tried to reach out to him sooner.

"A delay?" Her companion scooted closer. "I stopped sensing Gruene halfway through the first tunnel. Is there—"

"Give me a minute," she snapped and regretted her tone instantly. She looked at the man and nodded. "Please."

He stared at her but didn't say a word, so she closed her

eyes and drew a deep breath to concentrate on only one conversation at a time.

We're not alone down here, she thought to her familiar. *I think someone's collapsing the tunnels from the inside and they might be trying to keep anyone in Lomberdoon from following them. Welby and I were caught up in one of them but we're fine.*

Did you see the strange men?

No. I can't prove it yet but I think it was them. Their magic was...

It was too hard to explain, even through her connection with Leander and how easily he could usually discern her thoughts. That was more difficult than usual from who knew how far beneath the Brightsbane Mountains.

You have to get out of there, Raven.

That's the plan.

She opened her eyes and met Welby's gaze. "Did you see anything west of the mountains that might have been another tunnel opening?"

He shook his head. "We would most likely have heard of something like that. People are still wary of anything left by the Swarm. As far as I know, whatever tunnels did exist after the Great War were sealed beyond Lomberdoon's borders to reinforce the safety of the wall."

"Right. Except the one the people of Midway Outpost paved over with a cobblestone courtyard."

"Yes, that one seems to be the exception."

"So our best option is to keep moving until we find something that leads us to Lomberdoon."

The vet frowned. "All the tunnels we saw heading east had already been filled in."

"I know. But I seriously doubt the Swarm was worried

about crunching through the mountains on only one level so humans could pass through more easily thirty-five years later."

"Hmm. And you believe this…additional layer will lead us to Lomberdoon?"

"It feels like the best option right now. The only way we know of to get back to Midway Outpost was destroyed. And if whoever's down here operates on a strategy to collapse tunnels like this to keep what they're doing beyond Lomberdoon a secret, I don't think they'll look for anyone who's trying to get out."

"Well, then." He stood and offered her a hand up, which she accepted. When she looked at her hand in his, he released her quickly and gestured toward the massive pile of rubble that had fallen with them and now lay twenty feet farther down the cavern. "Lead the way, Mage Alby."

"Oh, now I'm leading huh?"

"There does seem to be much more room down here. And I may have abandoned my concern for being stuck."

She laughed and turned away slowly, although it seemed impossible to shift her gaze from him until her body forced her away.

Leander, tell Gruene we will continue through the mountains. There are way more tunnels down here than we thought and at least one of them has to lead into Lomberdoon. We can't get out the way we came in.

That will take you days.

Which is why we need to get moving immediately. We'll meet you on the other side.

Be careful, Raven.

You too.

With a nod, she skirted the giant pile of rubble and gestured for the man to follow. "Come on. We have a lot of walking to do."

After dusting his trousers off, Welby looked up and reached for his massive glowing orb where it bobbed beneath the collapsed and jammed ceiling. It shrank to its normal size again and darted toward them to illuminate a softly glowing circle around him from above his head. "And hopefully less falling."

"Yeah. That would be ideal." She waited for him to catch up and together, they progressed toward the other side of the chamber where another tunnel branched off to hopefully lead them east and into their kingdom. "Our dragons should be there waiting for us when we get out."

"Yes, Gruene and I have planned for something like this."

"Like what?"

"Being separated." He shrugged. "I understand some mages can sense their familiars over great distances, but that doesn't do much to form an accurate plan. She'll return to Havendom to inform Primus Kauler of what happened."

"Not without us, she won't."

"Raven, there's nothing more we can do—"

"Leander and Gruene will wait on the other side of the mountains until we get out." She stopped, which made him focus on her as she stared firmly at him. "No one will go to Kauler until we're all together again."

He frowned and turned his head slightly away but flashed her a sideways glance of frustration. "This entire scenario was impossible to predict. You couldn't have laid out a contingency plan for all of it."

"I didn't have to." Raven fixed him with a knowing smile before she walked toward the tunnel again. "You're right about mages sensing their familiars over great distances. Some mages even have more than one and can—"

"More than one what?"

"Familiars."

Welby's mouth dropped open and he walked stiffly beside her with his head facing straight in front of him. His wary sidelong glances continued. "Are you telling me you're one of those mages?"

"No. I merely trained with one."

He's looking at me like I told him dragons grow on trees instead of hatching from eggs. I'll keep Professor Worley and his four familiars to myself from now on.

The vet cleared his throat. "I still don't see how you can be so confident that Leander and Gruene will be where you say they'll be."

Raven shrugged. "Because I told him where we're going."

"You—"

It was incredibly difficult to hold back a proud grin at his audible bafflement but she managed it.

"Forgive my ignorance," he muttered as they stepped through the opening into the next tunnel and their light orbs darted ahead of them. "But it sounds like you're referring to long-range telepathic communication with your familiar."

She couldn't help a glance at the broad-shouldered

mage vet beside her, and her smile finally broke free. "Trust me, Dr. Welby. You're one of the least ignorant people I know."

His frown deepened but it was softened by what looked like a new impulse to laugh. Instead, he cleared his throat and shook his head. "And you, Mage Alby, are full of surprises."

CHAPTER NINETEEN

Leander snorted at the outer wall surrounding Midway Outpost, which he'd stared at for some time while he'd tried to locate Raven and learn what had happened to her in the tunnels. He'd spent hours pacing across the drying grass beyond the settlement since his mage and Welby had descended into the hole in the ground.

Gruene, however, had curled into a tight ball of black scales and claws yards away to watch the sunrise and hadn't said a word since they'd chosen their new location in which to sit and wait.

Now that he'd heard from his mage that their loose plan had changed, he was ready for action.

He turned and spread his wings halfway before he moved slowly toward the black female. "It's time to leave."

"We were told to wait," she muttered calmly. "That was the plan."

"The plan has changed," he snapped, lowered his head, and growled at her.

She raised her head slowly in the morning sunlight, her

black scales glistening, and swung her long neck to fix him with a glittering emerald eye. "We may be free, Leander, but our mages come first."

"Our mages are moving through the mountains and need us to be there for them on the other side."

Her eyes narrowed. "According to whom?"

He snorted and pawed the ground. "According to my mage. We need to leave."

Gruene paused before she rose languidly to her feet. A rippling tremor raced along the scales of her neck, down her flanks, across her back, and finally ended when she flicked her tail toward the sky.

I've told her what our mages need, and she's preening in the sun like a feline.

"Two days," she said. "That is my agreement with Chui. If we're separated, I wait two days before I return to Havendom to call for help. Not three hours."

The red dragon stretched his neck and screeched angrily at her. It would have been far more satisfying if he'd been closer and had done it in her face, but her wings twitched outward all the same and she shuffled two steps sideways and stared warily at him.

"There are humans in the tunnels, Gruene!" he snarled. "They destroyed the tunnel leading to that cursed hole in the ground. Raven and your healer can no longer return to us here and they expect us to be waiting for them on the other side of the mountains by the time they pass through."

She snorted and turned her head slightly away from him, although the intensity of her gaze betrayed her surprise and concern. "Pass through what?"

"The mountains." Leander extended his wings to their

fullest span and growled again. "You do what you must but I will not carry your mage simply because his familiar was too proud to hear the truth."

Gruene snarled and thumped her tail against the dirt. Her denial and anger were short-lived, however, because the realization of who she was talking to—the red male with blue fire she'd heard so many dragons talk about over the years—sank in. She lowered her head, took four ambling steps toward Leander, and paused. "How do you know this?"

"Raven told me. Yes, we hear each other's call more clearly than you and I hear our kin. I realize it isn't the natural way between any human and dragon or mage and familiar but I am sure. We take to the sky. Now. Unless you wish to explain to your mage why you turned against the information you needed and abandoned him to—"

She cut him off with a ferocious screech and spread her wings. Plumes of dragon frost erupted from her nostrils. "Do not accuse me of abandoning my mage."

"Then fly with me." With a snarl, he launched himself into the sky and wheeled southeast along the mountain ridges. He didn't need to look back to know the black female had grudgingly accepted his news as the truth —for now.

She doesn't trust me. The feeling is mutual. But if she trusts a mage's familiar who can tell her exactly what happened, that has to suffice.

The black dragon said nothing as she surged through the air to catch up with him. When she settled beside him and caught the air current, her wings stretched wide and the fluttering tips of their black membranes almost touched the red of his own. She curved her neck slightly toward him and caught his gaze. "Is he hurt?"

"No."

"Are they in danger?"

"They were. Your healer is fortunate to have Raven at his side."

She snorted. "Chui is a skilled mage. Not useless."

Compared to Raven, everyone is useless.

The red dragon pushed himself harder and faster across the sky as the first foothills of the Brightsbane Mountains rose steadily beneath him and his disgruntled flying companion. She didn't miss a beat and kept pace with him perfectly. That only irritated him even more.

"Where will they emerge?" she asked.

"Most likely from the mines."

"Then we'll wait for them there. But after two days—"

"It will take them at least that long to move through the mountains on foot. I will hear from Raven before then. Only if she tells us to return to the capital without them will we leave those mines."

Gruene snarled but didn't argue.

Leander had expected some resistance from her at least. It was hard to argue with another dragon who could speak to his mage across such a distance and through miles of mountain stone. But what he didn't expect was to hear the black female's rumbling laughter emanate from her throat and whip behind her with the wind.

"You find this amusing?" he growled.

"Two days at least. On foot. Humans are pitiful without our wings."

With a grunt, he narrowed his eyes and cast her a sidelong glance. She was already looking askance at him and her rumble of amusement only continued.

The red male had no intention of laughing with her. That was the last thing he wanted because her antics irritated him exceedingly and made it impossible for him to focus on anything but his irresistible urge to move away from her.

Still, he couldn't help but comment on her apt assessment.

"Yes. They are."

A glittering plume of dragon frost curled around Gruene's nostrils and trailed behind her.

Leander looked away quickly and focused on the direction of their flight. "At least concerning their ability to travel."

"You give humans too much credit, Leander."

"I believe in my mage. Beyond that, I have no opinion of the others."

"What about Chui?"

He looked at the black female, who narrowed her eyes and continued to rumble at him in the dragon equivalent of a chuckle. "Your mage is doing his job, exactly like mine."

"That doesn't answer my question, Leander."

His wings twitched at hearing her say his name but he recovered quickly. "It's the only answer you'll get."

"I think you—"

A piercing screech cut through the air behind them, much farther north than either Lomberdoon dragon intended to fly. Their conversation was entirely forgotten as they shared a wide-eyed glance. With an intrinsic knowing, they banked sharply in opposite directions to wheel and head back along the base of the Brightsbanes.

That was rage.

More dragon voices cut through the sky with the same ferocious urgency and echoed along the rocky peaks that stretched far to the east. If it had only been the sound of them, he wouldn't have been able to pinpoint where the dragons were with so much noise bouncing from different points.

But he could feel them—their surprise, their rage, and their indignation at facing humans in a world where dragons had been freed. Sensing the other dragons' emotions and their unwitting call for aid spurred both him and Gruene forward to do what they could—if they could do anything at all.

It's happening again.

The two dragons soared over Midway Outpost and raced north, urging each other wordlessly to move faster, push harder, and get there on time. They passed two more settlements much smaller than Midway Outpost and without any of the well-constructed outer walls or stone buildings the last free outpost in the unclaimed lands between kingdoms had boasted. After that, nothing but an open valley stretched west away from the Brightsbane Mountains.

The range began to curve even farther west instead of due north. Eventually, it would curve north again and stop hundreds of miles from the sea. He'd been over those highest peaks before and beyond them.

Leander couldn't see the location from here, but he could feel it—the place where he and Raven had flown with Connor and Calista to breach the thickest mass of those peaks in an attempt to reach the Valley of the Keepers. No storm cloud would swirl above to stop them now. Not since magic had fully returned. But the thought of drawing closer to that timeless place again—despite how much he'd enjoyed the Keepers' warm welcome of him and any other dragon—almost made him turn away.

"There." Gruene screeched and tucked her wings to dive toward the foothills.

They'd flown so high that it would have been impossible to miss the skirmish at the base of the mountains. He, however, had been too preoccupied with his memories from two years earlier to pay the close attention he'd needed to.

The black dragon had seen what he hadn't.

He dove after her and uttered a screech as he abandoned his private thoughts now that they'd found the source of the cries.

Seven wild dragons wheeled through the sky while some of them darted among a contingent of two dozen dark-haired, strangely clad humans who'd created an odd formation to face the clan. Fire breath and dragon frost blasted the valley floor where the humans stood their ground, occasionally joined by a bright burst of yellow or violet light.

Dragons with magic. At least some of them have rejoined their clans after learning what they can now do.

"Leave!" Gruene shouted over the constant angry screeches of the dragons trying to tear the strange humans apart. "East! Everyone must go east!"

None of the wild clan paid any attention to her. Why

would they, when they were being attacked by humans they'd never seen before?

Humans who smell like dragons and the sea. What are they?

Thick, heavy clicks sounded from the ground like a rusty door opening with agonizing slowness but much louder and more foreboding.

Leander scanned the human force and immediately found the source.

These strange men had erected multiple contraptions of wood, metal, and rope on the valley floor. Beside each sat a massive woven basket larger than his saddle, all of them filled to the brim with black-caked rocks glistening in the sunlight. Two humans at each contraption placed the ore in a bucket attached to a long wooden lever, and without knowing what such devices were called, he knew instantly what they were meant to do.

The closest machine clicked again as another human spun it on its swiveling base so the bucket faced the dragons who hurtled toward his party.

Another sharp click, thump, and creak of wood carried despite the cacophony of the irate dragons.

"Don't engage!" Gruene snarled and still attempted to gain the attention of the wild dragons too intent on exacting their revenge. "Go east! You must—"

The red dragon dropped like a stone toward the black female and pummeled into her from above as the black orbs were launched from the human device.

She screeched in fury and twisted her body as they both dropped several feet from the impact. "Are you mad?" She clawed at him and snapped ferociously before he finally managed to get the wind under his wings again and break away from her.

"The machines!" he retorted.

He thought she'd completely ignored him when she broke sharply away and beat her massive black wings in a fury to climb away from him.

This female thinks she knows everything.

Irritated, he banked again to fly toward the enraged wild dragons who ravaged the ground with fire breath, dragon frost, and magical bursts. He looked up to where Gruene wheeled over the entire battle and realized that she now saw what he'd seen not a moment too soon.

The men's contraptions on the ground flung glistening black rock one after the other into the sky, aimed at Leander's kin.

The black dragon bellowed furiously and swooped over the wild clan. "Retreat! All of you! Avoid the black weapons!"

Two dragons darted in front of her, snarled, and cast her livid glances before they continued their desperate counterattack.

These humans, however, posed a greater threat than any others the clan might have encountered. Worse, their scent enraged all of them, even Leander.

Their smell isn't the problem here. They're firing fungus at wild dragons. They know exactly what they're doing.

"Get out!" he roared at the clan. "You cannot fight this!"

A yellow female screeched and darted in front of him. "You see this with your own eyes. Humans turn their weapons on our kind."

"Leave them!" With a thick thump and creak, another

contraption fired its seemingly innocuous but very deadly projectile below him. The red dragon snarled, darted after the yellow female, and thrust her out of the way exactly like he'd prevented Gruene from being struck. She snarled and clawed at him, but at least the black fungus projectile hadn't found its target. "Do you know me?"

"Not as a traitor," she snapped.

"There is no betrayal. Get your clan east. If any of you are hit, you will not see more than five days."

It was either the way he'd said it or maybe word of the fungus-infected dragons had already traveled this far northeast, but the yellow female took another look at the large weapons that fired black fungus and screeched. "East!"

The others faltered in their attack as their clan leader issued the same cry of retreat that had come from the two saddled but riderless dragons who'd come out of nowhere.

That gave the humans on the ground enough time to reload and aim again, this time at slower-moving targets.

With a furious bellow, Leander dove. This time, it wasn't toward any other dragons to force them to safety but toward the contingent of men who shouted incomprehensible commands at each other and tried to ready their devices.

His fire breath burned deeply in his belly as he raced toward the foreign attackers.

More than fire. I will bring them death.

When the column of flame erupted from his open mouth, it seared the ground with a spray of smoke, cinders, and dirt. He didn't need Raven in that moment to help direct his attack and hadn't for years. At the same time, he also didn't need her to tell him that mere fire breath from any other dragon wouldn't do the job.

The men below him screamed and flung themselves out of his line of fire. Some of them cast weak and ineffective spells at the red dragon who scourged their formation. Those that struck Leander's flanks and legs did little more than sting when they glanced off his scales.

When he reached the end of the formation, he streaked straight up into the sky, flipped, and rolled to right himself before he swooped onto the humans again. His fire breath never faltered and arced in the sky with him to deliver a spray of deadly flame over the valley.

By the time he raced toward the men and their cursed machines again from the opposite direction, his fire breath had morphed from its raging orange-yellow to the bright, blinding blue of his deepest flame.

Although he couldn't be sure, he'd always suspected that the Blue Flame spell Raven and Welby had used was a mage's spellcast manifestation of what he could produce on his own.

The blue fire swept into the men's machines and fragments of wood and metal scattered in all directions. Some of the humans were caught in the blast, but their agonized screams cut off quickly when their bodies fell amid the blaze. Most importantly, the baskets of black fungus-caked ore used against the wild dragons of Threndor burst into blue flame and were quickly devoured by it.

A single pass was all he needed to consume the entire cache. The humans who hadn't been trapped by his blue dragon fire swarmed toward their fallen comrades and shouted angrily in words he couldn't understand. It didn't matter. They'd given their message to the wild dragons and had received one from the large red male in return.

Whatever they were doing, it would not be tolerated. No aggression directed against any free dragon of Threndor, wild or trained, would be without repercussions.

Gruene wheeled away from the massive plumes of smoke that billowed from the humans' destroyed formation. She uttered an almighty screech that meant only one thing—they were finished there.

Now, she fully expected the wild clan to follow her, at least for a brief conversation about what they'd seen.

The black female's call was so powerful that Leander momentarily forgot himself and the fact that they had stumbled upon this skirmish together—that their mages were together beneath the mountains as well as they tried to push through to the other side and the borders of Lomberdoon.

If I didn't know her, I would have followed her anyway. She thinks rallying wild dragons is as simple as sounding like she's in control. Ha. She has no idea what Raven and I have done.

When the dragons had all converged again behind their rescuers, Gruene darted to the closest mountain ridge and settled on a bowl-shaped plateau below the first range of mountains that climbed steadily higher toward the sky in either direction.

He landed beside her with a snort. "Calling a private audience, are we?"

"We have to let them know what's happening. That Chui and Raven are already looking into who those strange men are and what they're doing here—why they're attacking dragons up and down the Brightsbanes."

The red dragon couldn't disagree with her on that so he pawed the ground and waited as the wild clan of seven landed one after another on the plateau.

Once they had all settled, the yellow female leading the clan tossed her head and turned it from side to side, although she kept her gaze on Leander the whole time. "Some of us had begun to think the first free dragon who still claimed a mage had forgotten who he was."

"Some of you would have been wrong," he muttered.

"It appears, however, that he hasn't forgotten why we followed him this far south in the first place."

If she thinks this first free dragon with a mage can so easily forget blue dragon's fire, she must not have been there to see me use it around the others.

Leander stretched his neck as high as he could to view the entire clan. "You did not follow me. You followed your own council toward freedom and safety."

"Both of which the world of humans no longer affords us," a beige male added. "You saw what they did."

"Those humans are not of our world here, and you know it." He swept his gaze slowly across the small clan and met each of the other dragons' wide eyes in turn. "They do not belong here."

"They are here all the same," the yellow female said. "And they attacked us."

"It's not the first time," Gruene said. "We both have mages, and they're doing what has to be done to ensure that these attacks stop. But there is a greater danger here for dragons, and it is not the humans."

The clan shifted uneasily and all of them turned their

heads toward their leader. She lowered her head. "The sickness."

"Yes." The black dragon studied them, searching for the telltale signs of infection. "Did their flying weapons touch any of you?"

"It was moss," a ruddy-orange male snarled. "How is that—"

"It was the fungus that is decimating our kin with infection and plague," Leander interrupted. "It does not kill as swiftly as teeth or claws, but it does kill. After we lose our minds."

"No," the clan leader said. "None of us were touched. But if we were?"

"If you were, our mages have the cure," Gruene said.

"We have the cure." Leander met her gaze and curved his neck to look at the saddlebags strapped tightly to his riderless saddle.

The black female uttered a low growl and muttered, "And no one to distribute them. Unless you can grow opposable thumbs as well as speak to your mage when you're apart from her."

He snorted. "Don't be—"

A soft purple light glowed around the straps of one saddlebag and it unfastened itself. The top flap flipped open and one of the potion vials elevated to float in the air in front of Leander's face.

"This is the cure?" A small, almost runtish wild female with a massive scar that slashed down her violet right wing tilted her head almost ninety degrees. "It is so…small."

Gruene's emerald eyes widened, but nothing more of her surprise showed.

Hearing of dragons with magic is one thing but seeing it? She's spent too much time with military dragons and not enough with those who had far more to do with magic from the start.

The red dragon swung his head to face the clan. "It will protect you. The plague spreads quickly from dragon to dragon. Take these now and go to the eastern mountains on the far side of Lomberdoon. As long as you stay away from these mountains here, there is no threat even from strange humans."

"And tell any others you see to not engage those humans," Gruene added. "Without the cure, they will fall to the dragon plague."

The yellow clan leader's wings twitched outward and she snorted.

Her magic-wielding clanmate acted instantly and six more vials rose from the saddlebag before they drifted across the plateau toward every wild dragon's head.

Leander looked only at the yellow female. "It is safe."

Seven wild jaws opened and seven glass vials of the potion disappeared between bone-crushing jaws to spill Welby's invaluable concoction down seven dragon throats. A few of them sputtered and shook their heads. The yellow female stamped a forepaw into the dirt and snorted again. "Where will you go?"

"To bring war. Once every dragon here is assured of their safety from such a plague."

The clan leader raised her head and glanced quickly at two of her clanmates who stood closest to her. "We came here for peace, Leander. Perhaps we did not follow you from the endless valley by the sea, but we will follow you to war with any human who does not understand the way our world has changed."

He didn't move a muscle.

The yellow female had given him her allegiance on behalf of her entire clan and perhaps even others if she knew them well enough. All he had to do was give the word.

Not until Raven is ready to give the word with me.

The gathering between the clan and their new allies ended. The leader screeched and darted into the sky before she banked away to head due east. Her clan followed and uttered consenting cries as they departed. Leander turned his head to watch them vanish over the next peak, then caught the last glimpse of purple light around his saddlebag as the magical dragon's final show of gratitude slid the strap through the buckle and pulled it taut.

Gruene regarded the fading light for a moment before she fixed him with one emerald eye. "You have already brought war to those strangers on this continent."

The red dragon stared at her, unmoved. "I prefer to call it a daring rescue."

He had no idea why he'd felt the need to reframe it like that and was as furious about foreign humans attacking any dragon with the black fungus as he had the right to be. Perhaps even more so because those men knew what they were doing. They'd fully intended to infect as many wild dragons out in the open lands as possible.

But it had been a rescue.

His companion lowered her head and tilted her muzzle downward until all he could see of her face were the luminous green eyes that blazed from within the onyx-black ridges that encircled them. "I thought you were trying to wound me."

Leander stepped away from her. "If you're wounded by words, it's no fault of mine."

"When you struck me from the sky."

He turned his head and wished he could escape her gaze like he'd done since he and Raven had landed at the Legion base in Havendom.

What does she think she's doing?

"I would call that a daring rescue as well, Leander." Her wings rippled outward in an oddly alluring unfolding and another plume of dragon frost curled from between her scaley lips to coil toward his snout.

Startled, he stepped sideways to avoid whatever she was attempting to do with that and turned to face southeast again. "I made it clear that I do not intend to carry your mage for you. That's all it was."

"Of course."

Gruene's coy acceptance of his refusal to be caught in her games made him want to turn and unleash another column of flame to burn away the annoying dragon frost.

She won't get what she wants from me. *Whatever that is.*

With nothing else to say, he launched skyward and beat his wings to carry him toward the narrower, lower peaks of the southern Brightsbanes, where they would wait for their mages to return. She took flight almost as soon as he did, and she matched his pace with ease as they soared toward Lomberdoon's southwestern region, their wingtips inches apart.

Despite how much the black female agitated him with her ridiculous displays, a certain pride to have her at his side filled Leander. At least they wanted the same thing as far as the safety of dragons was concerned. Certainly the safety of their mages and the humans who had gone through too much in the last few years to not believe the freedom of dragons—and fighting for their rights to maintain that freedom—was important.

Raven, he thought to his mage and searched for her presence despite knowing that she and Welby were somewhere far beneath the mountains. *There is far more at stake here than we thought.*

CHAPTER TWENTY

Raven received the message from Leander with perfect clarity, even deep underground. It was an unexpected warning, of course, but what took her completely by surprise were the images thrust into her head one after the other.

Her familiar had sent her a visual of everything he and Gruene had been through with the wild dragons and the foreign humans who had attacked them.

She gasped, staggered sideways, and braced herself with a hand against the tunnel wall.

"What is it?" Welby hurried toward her, his brow creased deeply in concern.

The young mage shook her head, drew a deep breath, and regained her balance. "Leander."

"Is he okay?"

"He's fine. Gruene too. They—" It took her a moment to put all of Leander's images into words. Since she and her familiar had discovered they could hear each other's voices in their minds—and that he could read her thoughts whenever he wanted to—they hadn't communicated like this with actual memories and visions in a long time. Finally, she lowered her hand from the wall and met her companion's dark, intense gaze. "They found the strange men."

He tilted his head and studied her. "How do you—"

"I saw it. Leander showed me."

"I meant how do you know it was them? The men we've been looking for. There are many odd humans across Threndor, so unless we're completely certain—"

"They attacked with the fungus." Raven clenched her jaw and held her resolve against the flickers of horror and fury and an urge to take action that flitted across the vet's face. "With…catapults, I think, aimed at wild dragons. And they have a massive store of that fungus. Whoever they are, those men know exactly what they're doing. They know it causes Weeping Disease and they're deliberately trying to infect any dragon who flies overhead."

The vet responded with a low, frustrated growl. "Where are they?"

"To the north. Still west of the Brightsbanes, so they haven't entered Lomberdoon. That's the only good thing I can get out of— Wait."

He straightened and stared at her as a slow smile spread across her lips.

Leander's urgency when he'd reached out to her had rushed through with the threat that these foreign men posed at the surface, so it had been the first thing she'd focused on. But now, as she sifted through all the images, something else caught her attention.

Of course he'd send me an actual vision of what he did instead of simply saying they took care of it. Showoff.

"Raven?"

She laughed. "Sorry. Correction. They had a massive store of black fungus to launch into the sky."

Welby shook his head. "I don't understand."

It was a small victory in the grand scheme of things, especially if there were more men in this apparent war party than only the few dozen their dragons had encountered. But she couldn't help but grin as she sifted through the memory again before she focused on her mission partner. "He destroyed it."

"The army?"

"The fungus. All of it."

He was silent for a moment, then sucked in a sharp breath. "I understand he's a powerful dragon, but fire breath isn't enough to—"

"Blue fire."

"The Blue Flame is a mage's spell."

Raven raised an eyebrow. "Hmm. I wonder where they got the inspiration for something like that a hundred and fifty years ago. And before you try to remind me that Leander wasn't alive a hundred and fifty years ago, I know that. I also know he's not the first dragon to have ever mastered that ability with his fire breath. We've had way too many weird reactions from it for it to be a one-dragon ability."

The vet chuckled in wary disbelief, turned away from her, then turned back. "I assume you're not referring to humans running and screaming in terror."

"Only when the raiders arrived in Azerad. But I was mostly referring to non-humans."

They moved down the next tunnel in silence for a

moment and the veins of Smithheart ore around them glowed softly within the dark walls.

Welby sighed. "Honestly, despite being forced to traverse the width of the Brightsbane Mountains on foot and underground, I'm looking forward to seeing what you pull from your sleeve next."

She grinned at their bobbing white lights ahead. "You know what? Me too."

The farther they walked, the more the walls around them glowed with the bright silver light of the Smithheart ore. The mages passed through tunnel after tunnel and cavern after cavern and occasionally stopped to eat the strange cubes of a tasteless, gooey substance Welby pulled from his incredibly full satchel and called his "emergency rations."

They were far more filling than their tiny size indicated, and Raven didn't bother to ask what they were made of or how chewy cubes that felt like eating undercooked bread dough could keep them alive for the days it would take them to travel the entirety of the Swarm's underground tunnels into Lomberdoon.

Fortunately, he also knew a spell that pulled water from the soil around them and into a shallow metal cup he kept in his satchel. It was, of course, enchanted with the same cleansing spell she had once tried to use on the first infected dragon she and Leander had encountered and again used by Welby to discover the perfect combination for the Weeping Disease cure.

On that first day, they avoided the tunnels that looked

like they would branch off to the north or south and usually were presented with an additional option to cross entire caverns and eventually move east. The thick veins of glowing Smithheart ore kept their path relatively well-lit to the point that the glowing orbs were hardly necessary. When they both finally agreed it was time to call it a day—despite not knowing if it even was still day on the surface—the mages settled to eat more emergency-ration cubes, share a small cup of conjured water, and try to get comfortable enough that they could sleep for at least a few hours.

It wasn't the first time Raven had slept in the wilderness beyond Lomberdoon's border and on the dirt instead of in any bed at all. But it was the first time she'd slept in a cave without Leander since she'd been abducted by the mega-dragons who'd made Windroot Pass their home over the last few years, and that made this little trek through the mountain feel terribly familiar.

But this time I'm not alone. Welby's with me. And there aren't massive dragons from across the sea forcing themselves into a cave to either talk to me or eat me. Merely an army of foreigners who built actual machines to attack the dragons here and infect them with a deadly plague.

When they'd been walking, the glowing ore veins all around them had seemed like insufficient light to illuminate everything she wanted to see and investigate in the passages. Now, however, as she lay on her side with her back to the wall and nestled her head in the crook of one arm, she found the low light nothing but obnoxious.

A particularly thick vein of Smithheart ore protruded six inches from the wall above Welby. The man had chosen to lie on his back, his head resting on his satchel and his hands folded on his chest. The ore's light was brighter than anything else in this cavern, and she blamed it for keeping her awake longer than she wanted to be.

What she wouldn't quite admit was that despite her exhaustion and her frustration with sleeping under the ore's light, what kept her up was the fact that she couldn't stop looking at Chui Welby asleep on the opposite side of the cavern. He had chosen a place only a few feet away from where the walls converged into yet another tunnel that they'd take in the morning.

In sleep, he didn't look anywhere near as serious and down-to-business as he had the first time they'd met so she and Leander could escort him and Gruene south to "take care of the rabid dragon problem." He had no doubt tried to maintain his professional expression the entire time they'd worked together on this particular mission—which had turned into something neither of them could have fathomed almost two weeks earlier.

But maybe he's dropped a few of his walls, right? Or at least he's trying. And I don't think I've dropped any of mine at all.

Thinking of her reservations about getting close to people in general made her close her eyes immediately. She now thought of William Moss and the walls she'd put up between them too.

It's not my fault he can't make his mind up. Oh man, we went on a date. I didn't exactly tell him there wasn't anything between us and now, I'm sleeping under the mountains with a tall, handsome dragon vet I work with. One who feels comfortable enough to call me Raven instead of Mage Alby. Why am I even thinking about any of this right now?

She forced herself to relax, although sleep seemed impossible now that she'd settled down to attempt it.

I hardly think now's the time to worry about your feelings, mage.

Leander's unexpected voice in her mind—a little faint but still very much there—made her suck in a sharp breath.

Welby turned his head slightly toward her. "Is everything all right?"

Crap. He's been awake this whole time too? Does he know I've been staring at him?

"Yeah, I'm fine," Raven muttered. "Leander says good night."

"Ah. Then good night to you both, I suppose." He regarded her for a little longer, flashed her a small, weary smile, and adjusted his head on his satchel as he closed his eyes again.

She closed hers too and focused on reaching out for her bond with her familiar. *We stopped to rest. I don't even know what time it is but we're both too tired to keep going for now.*

The sun set two hours ago, he replied. *Have you found anything?*

Only more tunnels leading east. We're moving as quickly as we can. What about you and Gruene?

Her dragon was silent for so long that she wondered if the connection between them was as strong as she'd thought. Maybe the miles of mountain between them was enough to keep them truly apart.

We're waiting for you at the mines, he replied finally. *There is no sign of invaders inside the kingdom but if we do not act soon—*

I know, Leander. She drew a deep breath, exhaled slowly,

and tried to not make too much noise in the cavern where every sound was amplified with echoes across stone, hard-packed earth, and glowing ore. *We'll get out of here soon. Then we'll do what we have to do to stop this.*

Be careful.

You too.

That was all either of them had to say and it didn't surprise her at all that even a short conversation with her dragon—even across miles and weighed down by the urgency of their changed mission and the threat hanging over all their heads—gave her the comfort she needed to finally fall asleep.

She woke to a soft rustle as Welby strapped his satchel over his head and dusted his clothes off.

Raven sat, rubbed her eyes wearily, and looked around the unchanged cavern.

"I can't imagine that was more than a few hours," he muttered. "But I couldn't stay asleep."

"That's fine. I'm ready to keep going if you are." She pulled her hair out of her face and pushed slowly to her feet with a grimace.

Sleeping on rock and dirt isn't my favorite. My shoulder's gonna be sore all day.

"I'll be down here." He pointed at the tunnel beside them and cleared his throat. "If you need a minute to…"

"Thanks." She turned away from him quickly and hurried along the wall of the cavern to answer the call of nature in a cave that offered little privacy and even less in the way of personal morning hygiene. After everything she'd done and been through in the last two years at least— all the times she'd been stranded, abducted, camped out in the middle of nowhere with nothing to do but to keep pushing forward—squatting in an underground cavern with a dragon doctor waiting for her in the next tunnel didn't even make the list of her most uncomfortable situations.

Once she'd attended to her needs, they moved through the tunnels again with a little more stiffness in their muscles than the day before. The glowing ore illuminated the way for them.

Conversation was lacking, which was understandable. When Welby withdrew more tasteless rations from his satchel and offered her a gummy cube, she accepted and finally had to break the silence.

"Leander and Gruene reached the mines."

"Oh? Good. Did they see anything else?"

"Nothing in Lomberdoon so far. But if that changes, we'll know."

"I have no doubt." He popped a cube into his mouth and chewed without expression.

Raven tried to not wrinkle her nose at the strangeness of flavorless goo that made her feel instantly full the second she'd swallowed the last of it.

"You know, when I first heard about the infected dragons and that I'd be escorted south by one Mage Alby in the STAR division, I already knew you were a skilled rider at the very least." Welby cleared his throat. "But I find it surprising that no one bothered to mention the other assets on what seems to be your impressive…uh, resume."

She laughed, dusted her riding leathers off again, and shrugged. "I guess that's part of being in the Legion. Who I was and what I did before I joined STAR doesn't matter."

"It matters very much, Raven."

When she looked at him in surprise, he smiled at her, although it seemed more like regret and disappointment than anything else. "I appreciate that. Truly. But I'm happy where I am with the Legion right now. If it means I still have to work my way up, that's fine. Besides, I think most people have a tendency to forget the bad times and all the close calls when everything's...you know, peaceful. Going so well—or at least when they think it is."

"That's an accurate assessment of people in general." He nodded and his frown deepened. "I know you haven't asked for my opinion, but may I say something else?"

"Sure."

It's not like there's anything to stop him right now. We're alone under the mountains.

"I can't help but think the entire Legion is doing themselves a disservice by relegating you to the STAR division without utilizing everything you've gained from those bad times and close calls, as you put it. They're doing you a disservice. And when we return to Havendom, I don't have much confidence at all in the military's ability to handle the full scope of this situation if they don't put you at the forefront."

Raven rolled her eyes and laughed wryly. "Yeah. Tell that to Primus Kauler."

"I plan to."

She stopped and leaned away from him to search his

dark gaze for any hint that he was messing with her. "What?"

"With your permission, of course. Civilian hearsay and rumors don't carry much weight with the Legion, as well they shouldn't. But perhaps an eyewitness account and a strong recommendation from the contractor responsible for ensuring every Legion dragon is hale enough to perform their duty may be enough to plant a seed in the primus' mind."

For a moment, she didn't know what to say and she had to pull her gaze away from Welby's dark, glittering eyes to collect her thoughts. "Thank you. But I'm not sure he's open to consulting civilians on wartime strategy. Things have changed considerably in the last few years, but the military and the Consortium at the king's fortress are a little…harder to convince of anything. As far as I know, they always have been."

"Then perhaps it's time for even more change."

She cast him another glance and nodded.

I guess if a seventeen-year-old mage student can save everyone from the chaos of magic returning and convince the entire kingdom to free the dragons in every stable and on every ranch, a vet working for the military can make a few changes of his own.

They headed down the tunnel again, and her curiosity got the better of her like it always did. "You're not merely a contracted Legion vet. Are you?"

Welby started and the corner of his mouth twitched again, although he stared directly ahead at the tunnel illuminated by so much ore around them. "I am now."

"And before that?"

"Before that… Well, I suppose I was trying to find out what I truly wanted."

She chuckled. "You're not gonna tell me, are you?"

"You know, you haven't exactly divulged all the mysteries of your past either."

"Ha. Fair enough."

He glanced at her but lowered his head as if trying to hide his smile from her. It didn't work. "But when all this is over, I would very much enjoy the opportunity to sit and discuss it with you. Perhaps even to hear a little more of Mage Alby's past exploits before she became a STAR mage and received her orders to accompany a contracted Legion vet on one incredibly complicated assignment. If you'd like."

Raven swallowed thickly and nodded. "Yeah. Maybe."

Is he that curious about all the stuff I've done that no one wants to talk about? Or did the dragon vet ask me on a date?

The fact she was even questioning that possibility seemed absurd in their current circumstances, but she couldn't help but smile a little at the thought.

Sharing past mysteries. I guess that gives us both something to look forward to when all this is over. I seriously hope it doesn't take as long to convince Kauler of this massive threat as it took to convince the Consortium to free dragons.

CHAPTER TWENTY-ONE

After hours of walking through more tunnels and caverns
—occasionally stopping to deliberate which branch was
most likely to take them east instead of throwing them off
their course—the two mages made an unexpected and
highly disheartening discovery.

They'd finished sharing another cup of water collected
by Welby's spell, and when Raven returned the empty cup
so he could tuck it into his satchel again, she pointed at the
ceiling and muttered, "*Circum inlustro.*"

Another white orb rose from her fingertip to bob along
the tunnel in front of them and she nodded. "We have to be
halfway through these mountains by now, at the very
least—"

"Raven." Welby touched her shoulder gently, most likely
to catch her attention.

Despite the warmth that flared in her cheeks with his
gesture and an acute awareness of how close they now
stood, she couldn't ignore the urgency in his voice. "What?"

"You summoned a light."

She frowned. "Yeah. It's a little dark in here. I suppose it's not all that surprising when we're under—"

Reality pushed through. That was the problem, and it was surprising because they were still surrounded by ore veins giving off their usual glowing silver light. Despite this, it was a little dark.

Oh no.

With a flick of her fingers, she pulled her white orb closer and directed it toward the tunnel wall and the closest ore deposit. The Smithheart still glowed, yes, but was now coated with a dark film that glistened under her magical light. "Fungus."

"Unfortunately, yes." He summoned a light as well and directed it along the tunnel walls and ceiling around them. "It's still here."

"I…well… We don't know it's the same black fungus. It could be anything. We should test it, right? Take another sample."

"I've spent more hours than I care to admit handling the previous samples under intense scrutiny, Raven. I have no doubt that this is the same fungus."

Her heart sank and the tunnel walls that hadn't bothered her at all over the last two days suddenly felt like they were closing in around her. "We didn't destroy it all."

"We didn't know there was more." Despite his certainty that this was the same fungus that they'd eradicated with the Blue Flame months earlier, the vet withdrew another vial and tweezers from his satchel and scraped another sample off the closest ore deposit as she had suggested. "But it never hurts to be sure."

It won't help us at all to be sure that this is the same fungus if it's already grown this far through the mountains. It will take forever to destroy.

She watched him work quickly and tried to keep her concern under control. They didn't have to talk about what this would mean for their mission or whatever strategic response Primus Kauler might order once they returned to the capital and told him of what they'd seen. It might have been too dire to voice aloud anyway.

They were back where they started, with live black fungus still growing within the tunnels beneath the Brightsbane Mountains that connected somehow to the mines along Lomberdoon's border. Those same mines opened into the kingdom and had brought the fungus to wild dragons.

Worse, they now also faced a threat from an unknown force beyond the kingdom walls—an army of strange men who'd built contraptions for the specific purpose of infecting any dragon they found.

"We need to keep moving," Welby muttered as he fastened the straps of his satchel. "Quickly."

"Yeah."

Fueled with new urgency, the mages navigated the twisting passages beneath the mountain at a much faster pace than they'd taken before. If they'd gone any faster, they would have jogged through the tunnels, and she fought hard to not break into a run.

The next two caverns they encountered held the same discouraging evidence—thick layers of black fungus coated the Smithheart veins and dimmed the light. The fungus' dense, glistening presence made her stomach turn.

There's enough here to infect every single dragon on the continent. And someone's been mining it to do exactly that.

Welby's lips were pressed together in a tight line as they hurried down tunnel after tunnel. His frown darkened until he wore a perpetual scowl without once breaking out of it.

Soon after that, they stumbled into yet another cavern that had been used by the men who had mined these tunnels clandestinely as another temporary camp.

Raven stared with wide eyes at the similar piles of discarded refuse, tattered blankets, a few broken mining tools, and the remnants of odd runes that had been carved into the cavern floor. It was almost exactly like the camp remains they'd found in the cavern with her STAR unit. "They've moved between different sections of the mountains."

"It would seem so, yes." He glared at the chunks of wall that had been broken away by the men who'd made this camp and who knew how many others. "I don't understand why they've moved like this and left behind so much evidence of their presence."

"They're mining rare ore in a place that's filled with it and taking the fungus to use as a silent weapon against dragons," she muttered. "I don't think cleaning up after themselves is all that high on their priority list."

"But ensuring that no one discovered their presence might be."

"No one on Threndor wants to snoop around in the tunnels left by the Swarm." She kicked a woven basket that had been ripped in two at some point. It toppled across the cavern floor. "The authorized miners are only doing it for the ore and the opportunity of steady work. We wouldn't even know about any of this without the Orion mine."

"Which means that whoever these men are, they still don't know that anyone has discovered their presence here."

"Well, they've covered their tracks well, haven't they, by collapsing all those tunnels we found along the western edge of the mountains? They've probably done that all across the range, and the miners won't even go far enough into the mountains to notice anything at all."

The mages shared a wide-eyed, highly concerned glance, but Welby looked away quickly and stalked forward. "The only thing we can do at this point is keep going. The sooner we reach our dragons, the sooner we can cut this off at the head."

That was the first even remotely violent thing she had heard him say but it felt entirely appropriate.

Like a snake. First, we had the Swarm tunneling through our mountains and destroying our kingdom. Now, we have a snake from some strange place that smells like the sea and is taking advantage of everything the Great War left behind.

They discovered various tunnels that had collapsed and prevented them from moving in the direction they wanted. This only proved Raven's theory that these unknown men had strategically filled in certain passages around them to ensure that no one discovered their presence. But there was always another way out of the tunnels, and she and Welby were forced to navigate those that took them either farther north or farther south than they preferred. Unfortunately, they had to get out so had no choice.

By the time they'd crossed through a sixth abandoned camp, she had begun to feel like they might never escape. It didn't come anywhere close to making her accept defeat and resign herself to spending the rest of an incredibly shortened life trapped underground. If she were anyone else, it might have.

Raven Alby, though, only found herself fueled by a renewed determination to do whatever it took to get them both out to the safety of the surface and to reunite with their dragons.

We have a kingdom to save. Probably all of Threndor. Again.

When Welby said he wanted to stop to eat another cube of emergency rations and pull more water from the walls, she let him focus on that while she scoured the walls of the next chamber they'd entered.

It was the first one they'd reached that didn't seem to have any other tunnel entrances than the one from which they'd already emerged.

"Raven, we have to eat. Then we'll turn back and find another—"

"We're not turning back." She walked slowly along the edge of the chamber wall and wanted to push against the stone in her frustration but was repulsed by the coat of black fungus that covered every deposit of faintly glowing ore. "We can't."

"We were fortunate enough to have come this far already without reaching a dead end. It's a minor setback. I've left a trail of where we've already been."

"The last cavern with other tunnels is at least an hour

behind us. And we're not down here to explore what leads where. We have to get out!"

She kicked angrily at a pile of loose rocks and they lurched against the cavern wall. Instead of the sharp crack of stone on stone that would have at least been a little satisfying, they met the thick coating of black fungus with muffled thumps before they toppled uselessly to the dirt.

"May I make a suggestion?" the vet muttered.

"I'm not panicking."

"I never said you were. I do, however, think a little nourishment and a short rest will go a long way to clear both our heads right now."

Raven spun away from the wall and glared at the man. But the second she saw his face illuminated beneath his orb of light above his head, her anger softened.

He's as frustrated as I am and feels as useless. Jeez, if I look anything like he does right now, anyone who saw us would think we've spent months down here instead of only a few days.

"Please." The vet extended his hand with another taste-less cube of rations settled in his palm. "Eat. We can devise a new plan."

"We don't need a new plan," she muttered as she walked toward him. "We only need to finish this one."

"We will."

She took the cube from him and popped it into her mouth. He watched her for a moment, then gestured at the dirt before he sat first. While she chewed slowly and tasted absolutely nothing, she joined him and crossed her legs beneath her. "We don't even know how close we are to the mines."

"Closer than we were yesterday." He popped another

emergency ration into his mouth and chewed thoughtfully as he gazed around the cavern. "I don't think the Swarm cared much for directional accuracy."

She snorted. "No, probably not."

"But we will get out."

They sat in silence, both mages somewhat grateful for the chance to sit and rest again even though it had been forced upon them by their first dead-end cavern.

It must have taken serious magical power to destroy these tunnels in the first place. I felt it when the first one collapsed on us. I have no idea what spell they used, but maybe it isn't about the spell itself.

"Do you know any battle magic?"

Startled by her question that came seemingly out of nowhere, Welby choked and cleared his throat hastily before he met her gaze. "Are you expecting an imminent battle before we leave these mountains?"

Raven sighed. "No. Hopefully not. But do you?"

He held her gaze and frowned. "A little. Of course, I can't say I had War Mage Barnasis as my trainer, but I've picked up a few spells here and there."

"What about destruction?"

"No. Nothing as advanced as that."

Ignoring her frustration—and the gnawing feeling that if they didn't get out of there soon, the threat from the hidden army on the other side of these mountains would only be that much worse—she forced a smile and pushed to her feet. "Well, then, Dr. Welby. Today's your lucky day."

"I'm sorry?"

"Come on. Stand up."

The vet chuckled lightly but it sounded like he thought

she was insane. "I don't see how this is an appropriate time for a private lesson in battle magic."

"It's the perfect time." She extended an open hand toward him and nodded. "And I assume it will be much easier to train a mage who's already received his robes than a few mage students who hadn't yet learned how to get along."

"What?"

"Nothing. It doesn't matter." She wiggled her hand at him. "Get up."

Bella would have laughed at that. We were at each other's throats until we realized we could do serious damage when we needed to.

After removing his satchel from his lap to place it on the ground, he took her hand and let her pull him to his feet. "And you're going to teach me destructive battle magic. Is that it?"

Raven released his hand and grinned. "I'm no War Mage Barnasis but I have trained an entire Legion division how to fly like Leander and me—or as close to that as anyone else is likely to get. Are you ready?"

A weak chuckle escaped him. "Not even remotely."

"Here we go."

She drew from all the hours she'd spent with Bella Chase under Alessandra Barnasis' gruff and arguably deadly tutelage to explain the basics of the spell to the mage vet. Welby was a quick study, which made sense. He'd already had experience with spellwork and perfecting control over his magic. It was, however, the first time he'd been instructed by a military mage who'd had her mage's robes for only a few months. His surprise and amusement traced through her entire impromptu lesson, but he listened intently and did everything she instructed.

When they'd finished, he smirked at her. "You might have a future in training with battle magic as well."

"I'm the only mage in the Legion." She cocked her head. "But magic is for everyone these days, right?"

"I'd recommend starting with something less destructive. If you were to ever head down that particular career path."

"Not in the military. Destructive is exactly what they're looking for. Okay, let's give it a try."

With his smile twitching in and out of existence as he tried to concentrate on the task at hand, he turned away from her and faced the far wall of the chamber. "Before I start attacking the only thing keeping miles of mountain stone from rumbling down all around us…"

"You felt the kind of magic that collapsed that first tunnel we entered." She raised an eyebrow. "It took a huge amount. They were chanting down there too. I wouldn't worry about the walls coming down." She pointed across the cavern without looking away from him and muttered, "*Verecundia.*"

A streak of blinding opalescent light streaked from her hand and into the wall.

Welby grimaced, but the only effect her battle magic had on the cavern was a crack of stone, a puff of black fungus that dispersed into the air, and small pebbles that bounced onto the floor.

No rumbling tremor followed, nor any shift of the walls that protected them from being crushed by the mountains.

"See?"

"That was…daring."

"That was a demonstration." She stepped toward him and turned to face the opposite wall before she clapped him on the shoulder. "Now, it's your turn."

In her excitement to teach him the spell and take their minds off their predicament, she hadn't even thought about what she was doing touching him like that in such a friendly manner. Honestly, it had felt like clapping Henry on the back whenever she wanted to reassure him.

Except joking with her best friend didn't make her cheeks grow warm or her arm immediately withdraw to hang awkwardly at her side.

We're trapped under the mountains and I'm worrying about a friendly nudge. Quit thinking like this, Raven. We have work to do and even if Welby thinks we're training for fun during a break, we're gonna use this to get the hell out of here.

He studied her warily for a moment, then took a deep breath and focused on the opposite side of the cavern. "*Verecundia.*"

The battle spell launched perfectly from his outstretched hand and streaked across the chamber. It struck the wall with what she only assumed was perfect precision since she didn't know exactly where he had aimed. If his magic was anywhere near as accurate as his use of a longbow, it was probably perfect.

Another puff of black fungus disintegrated beneath the blast, and more stones cracked away from the wall to crumble onto the dirt.

Welby chuckled. "That's an excellent spell to keep in any mage's arsenal."

"And you didn't even look like you were trying."

"Training with a war mage or not, Raven, I did graduate from mage school."

"Which one?"

"Mandrose Academy—"

A rumbling growl issued from the cavern wall where he'd struck it with the incredibly powerful spell. More large rocks broke away and slid down each other to spill into the cavern.

He snatched her hand in his and hauled her with him. Both mages raced across the huge space toward the tunnel they'd used to get there, momentarily deafened by the roar and crack of the wall they'd assumed was solid but now gave way beneath a single unwitting battle magic attack.

By the time they darted into the far tunnel, though, the sound had softened into a low patter of rocks cascading over each other. It was nothing like the chaos of being in the middle of the last cave-in, and when they pressed their backs against the wall of the tunnel to catch their breath, the noise stopped.

"That…" Raven swallowed. "That wasn't supposed to happen."

"And you said it was my lucky day." His voice was completely flat, his statement most likely intended to carry much more sarcasm or at least a little judgment over her mistake. Instead, it made them both laugh.

When she realized his hand still clamped hers tightly, her laughter died. He noticed it as well a second later and released her gently before he cleared his throat. "Honestly, though, I'd expected more dust and rubble." He leaned forward to peer through the end of the tunnel and into the cavern. "And for that cavern to be gone now."

"What?" She pushed away from the wall and walked cautiously toward the opening.

The cavern was still intact. A small cloud of dust drifted to settle slowly around what they'd both expected to be a massive accidental collapse, but that was it.

"Then what did we hit?"

"Raven, I honestly wouldn't—"

"Investigate?" She looked at him over her shoulder. "That's why we're here, isn't it?"

Without waiting for a response or to catch whatever expression moved across his face, she stepped into the chamber and immediately found the source of what she'd thought for a moment would be the end for both of them.

Did we...open another tunnel?

"You need to see this," she called to him as she moved forward.

"More surprises beneath the mountain," Welby muttered. "Exactly what I was hoping for."

She fought back a laugh.

So he can be sarcastic. We merely have to think we're almost dead first.

When she reached the pile of loose rock and rubble that stretched six feet from the cavern wall, her heart leapt into her throat. "I can't believe it."

"I struck the wall with battle magic. Expecting at least a little damage after that is hardly—" Her companion stopped beside her and drew a deep breath. "Oh."

Raven turned her head to look at him and grinned. "I believe you've reopened another collapsed tunnel with that battle magic, Dr. Welby."

He glanced at her and immediately looked at the

opening in the wall again. "I had a fairly proficient instructor."

"Ha! Lucky day for both of us, I guess." She stepped over the thinnest layer of loose rocks that had spread over the cavern floor and bent forward to peer up the incline of the landslide they'd produced. With a flick of her fingers, she called her white orb that had rested in the center of the cavern and sent it hurtling through the small space between the broken cavern wall and the mountain of debris. The light flickered over the stone, traveled swiftly upward, then vanished and faded into a soft glow.

It was enough to see what looked like another chamber above them.

"It goes up."

Welby joined her on the teetering layer of broken rock and bent to examine the new makeshift tunnel they'd made. "Into another chamber."

"It looks like it."

"The fungus growing on these walls certainly succeeded in masking another cave-in. And that's quite a narrow opening."

"Well, if you get stuck, you now know how to blast out again."

His head whipped toward her in surprise before he responded with the first real burst of laughter she'd heard from him since they'd met. She couldn't help but laugh with him.

"Has your optimism always been this infectious?"

She met his gaze and shrugged with only one shoulder. "I guess it depends on who's with me to catch it. Are you feeling optimistic?"

"And curious." He turned to retrieve his satchel from the ground where he'd left it, and she peered up the landslide into the next chamber above them.

This might have saved our lives—or at least extra hours wasted trying to find another tunnel leading east that hasn't been destroyed. And he didn't think it was a good time to practice new spells.

Welby returned and gestured up the pile of loose rock. "After you, Mage Alby."

"Thank you, Doctor." They both chuckled again and the STAR mage stepped cautiously up the incline until she had to use her hands to crawl up the slope they'd created.

It's not only chivalry on his part. If he fell and took me with him in another landslide, we'd have additional problems to deal with.

Her stomach lurched when an unbidden image of them tumbling down the rubble to land on top of each other in a heap entered her mind.

Yeah, super romantic. Quit being so ridiculous and climb, Raven.

CHAPTER TWENTY-TWO

The upward-sloping tunnel had looked much shorter when Raven sent her orb of light there to investigate but it took her and Welby at least ten minutes to carefully navigate the lower half of the rockslide and all the crumbling shale and chunks of stone beneath them. A surprising amount of Smithheart ore was visible inside the actual landslide and all of it glowed beneath their hands as they hauled themselves up toward the narrow space.

The vet chuckled occasionally between his grunts of efforts until she finally had to ask him what was so funny.

"I've done many surprising things over the course of my career," he replied. "But crawling up a pile of loose rock after accidentally blasting what I hope is our final escape route out of the mountains may be at the top of the list."

"Well…" She tested the next handhold above her, thankful that the instability of the loose rubble wasn't as bad now that they had climbed higher. "You're about to add far more surprises to that list once we get out of here."

"Oh? Such as?"

"For one thing, trying to convince the primus of Lomberdoon's Royal Legion that he needs to put a freshly robed mage at the front lines against a foreign invasion from…uh, somewhere we don't even know yet."

"It sounds as if you doubt my powers of persuasion, Mage Alby."

"Not even a little, Dr. Welby." She smirked at the ridiculousness of their banter like this as they clambered up a landslide that still might give way beneath them at any minute. "But I do doubt Kauler's ability to be persuaded."

"So I take it that means you're open to letting me try."

"The chain of command doesn't apply to you, right? Go for it. I merely hope he doesn't get too offended by it and decides to send the Legion vet off base for getting too involved in military matters."

"And why's that?"

The amusement in his voice instantly made her realize what she'd said and how it probably came across.

Crap. I basically told him I want him to stay on base. Or that's the way he took it. That's not even how I meant it. I think.

It took her a moment to think of an answer that wouldn't sound like she was trying to unsay it, and she paused to make a show of reaching for the next handhold and tugged experimentally at it to be sure it was safe. "The Legion would lose an excellent dragon doctor. And until we know this fungus is completely contained—not to mention the unknown army that has to be taken care of first—Kauler getting rid of you would dig us all into an even deeper hole."

"Ah. I see your point."

Now, the man sounded disappointed, which also wasn't

at all what she'd intended. Raven rolled her eyes and cursed her inability to find the right thing to say without making it sound like something completely different.

"And I'm very sure Leander would be disappointed to not have Gruene chasing him around all day."

Welby snorted. "Yes, what a pity that would be. And a damper on my familiar's spirits too, no doubt."

Okay, maybe that leveled things out a little. We can joke about our dragons missing each other instead of thinking about how weird it would be to not be working together. Or getting trapped in tunnels.

Finally, she reached the top of the slope and grinned as she crawled on her hands and knees through the final narrow opening they'd created in the side of two caverns. "This is it."

When she pushed to her feet, she turned immediately and peered down the slope at him. "You're almost here."

"I appreciate the encouragement." He grunted, pulled himself up again, and scraped his massive shoulders against the walls of what probably wasn't supposed to be a tunnel at all. "I swear on my mage's robes, if I get stuck now, I'll—"

"Here." She leaned into the opening, grasped the wall above her head with one hand, and extended the other toward him. "You got it."

He slapped his hand into hers and held it tightly as he grimaced and struggled to push through the opening. She stepped back to brace herself, grasped him with both hands, and pulled with all her might.

Oh, jeez. Either he's stuck or he's way heavier than I thought.

The clack and echo of rocks sliding into the other

cavern below them made her increase her effort. The vet growled and hunched forward before he kicked off with a mighty shove. At the last second, the top of the mountain they'd climbed gave way and slid from beneath him.

Raven cried out with the effort and leaned back as far as she dared to put all her weight behind hauling him over the edge. For a moment, she didn't think it would be enough, but he squeezed through the opening and stumbled forward. She staggered and would have fallen if he hadn't yanked her toward him and wrapped his other arm around her.

The rest of the hill they'd climbed avalanched with a roar as stones and ore deposits tumbling noisily. She clenched her eyes shut against the deafening collapse and tried to catch her breath.

When the echoes faded, her fear of losing her mission partner to another cave-in was instantly replaced by the agonizing awareness of how closely she was pressed against him and how tightly his arm around her waist held her there. She opened her eyes and discovered that she only came up to the center of his broad chest.

Okay, this is not exactly falling on top of each other at the bottom of our escape route but it's still too close for comfort.

Welby released her gently and stepped back to peer down the steep drop behind them. "Are you all right?"

"Yeah." She brushed the hair out of her face and cleared her throat. "Yep. You?"

"Well, I haven't been buried alive." He turned toward her with a crooked smile. "And I've been rescued by a mage in a red leather uniform. So I'd say—"

His smile disappeared when he looked over her shoulder.

That doesn't look good.

"What?" Raven turned stiffly and saw exactly what had cut him off.

They'd climbed into another cavern that had been used as a makeshift camp by the army mining clandestinely beneath the mountains. The remnants of that camp, however, were nothing more than brittle black shapes burned all the way through. Streaks of char and ash were scattered across the cavern floor, and now that she saw it with her own eyes, she smelled the lingering odor of fire and of everything it had consumed.

Although it hadn't consumed everything, she realized after a moment's scrutiny.

"No." Raven staggered forward and scanned the high walls of the massive space.

This was the tunnel entrance she'd emerged from with Dr. Welby and her team of STAR legionaries almost a month earlier. She recognized the small lip that had served as stairs into the chamber. Without a doubt, she knew that if she hurried through that tunnel, she'd find the remains of the hasty, desperate barricade the Lomberdoon miners had erected toward the end of the Orion tunnel.

Of course, she should have been ecstatic that they'd stumbled across a cavern and a tunnel they knew. It would lead them out into the mines in Lomberdoon's southwestern region where Leander and Gruene were waiting for them. But her heart sank instead.

"You said the Blue Flame was the only thing that could

destroy the fungus." She spun to meet Welby's gaze. "You said it would work."

"It did work." His hands were clenched into fists at his sides and he gazed around the cavern in disbelief. "I tested the spell myself on a smaller sample before we left Havendom to burn it all away."

"So why is it back?"

She couldn't wrap her head around how a spell they knew would work had failed to eradicate the black fungus in a cavern that hadn't previously had any other exits or entrances. Nothing could have entered there until they had accidentally uncovered the hidden tunnel that had already collapsed long before their first venture down there.

Welby shook his head slowly. "I don't know."

"That doesn't help us." Raven marched across the cavern toward the wall and almost reached out to claw angrily at the fungus with her bare hand. She stopped, picked an ash-covered rock up, and thunked it against the wall instead.

The fungus scraped away beneath the stone and drifted to the floor like a thick black leaf. She scraped the stone repeatedly to peeled away dense layers of the growth that should have been completely eradicated—the fungus they thought they'd already destroyed to keep Lomberdoon's dragons safe.

"How is this even possible?" She snarled her fury and frustration. "We burned it out!" She threw the makeshift tool aside and stepped back to glare at the wall. "If we can't get rid of it, how are we supposed to keep them safe?"

"Raven, I'll take another look at the samples," he offered, his voice laced with boiling anger and resentment that matched hers. "But right now, we need to get out of these tunnels and back to our dragons."

She extended her hand toward the wall, her chest heaving, and recited the words of the Blue Flame she'd studied a month before to make sure she had it right. Blue fire burst from her palm and struck the wall four feet in front of her.

"Don't!" Welby darted toward her but the fungus had already caught flame. The powerful magical fire bloomed across the wall, ate away the deadly growth, and spewed blue sparks with the nauseating fumes of the putrid, oozing plant that had already caused them so many problems.

She was ready to try to blast every trace of glistening black growth off these walls again if she had to, but he caught her hand and held her back.

"Let me go." She struggled against him but it was hopelessly ineffectual when the man was almost twice her size and so much stronger. "I'm serious!"

"We know from the last time we cast that spell, we can't stand in this chamber when it goes up in flames. We almost didn't make it out the first time—"

A loud pop and a series of sizzling crackles erupted from the wall as even more of the fungus caught fire. The blue flames flared with incredible strength and streaked away from the wall toward them.

"*Eatenus exstinxisti!*" Raven shouted. A gust of wind burst from her hand and swirled in a vortex aimed at the blue blaze.

It was enough to make the flames surge even closer to them with a roar. Welby jerked her against him, wrapped his arms around her, and spun them before he stumbled forward with his back to the blaze.

The heat he'd expected in his daring and probably useless attempt to protect her never came. Instead, a massive splash against the wall was followed by a violent hiss of flames being quenched and more wet splatters on the dirt behind him.

A moment later, the cavern fell completely silent except for the steady patter of water dripping onto the ground.

Raven stiffened in his arms, bent uncomfortably back as he leaned over her and pressed her tightly against his chest. "Chui, unless you're fireproof, I don't think this would have done much to save either of us."

She hadn't meant to call him by his first name, but the tension of this entire situation already ran so high that she'd blurted it without thought.

He looked at her with wide eyes, searched her gaze, then straightened and pulled her upright with him. Slowly, he released her from his arms and shook his head. "Well, I…" He cleared his throat and studied her carefully. "I'd intended to cast another shield but it seems that was completely unnecessary."

"Yep." She looked behind him at the wall where she'd doused her blue flames.

The vet turned to study what she'd done and stroked his chin. "I assume you already planned to use that spell after attacking the fungus."

"Not really." She grimaced. "But you used it to put fire breath out in the valley the other day, and I thought it was worth a try. I'm sorry. I should have said something—"

"There's no need." His voice was flat again and

completely distracted as he stepped slowly away from her and approached the wall.

The water she'd conjured to douse the blue fire still dripped from the wall and trickled in small rivulets to form puddles on the floor. Where her spell had set fire to the black fungus, the stone was entirely clear. Huge deposits of Smithheart ore glowed brightly now that they'd been released from the dark film that had covered them.

He peered closer, sucked in a sharp breath, and waved her forward. "Come look at this."

Raven complied reluctantly but wondered what in the world would be so important after she'd almost burned them to a crisp so close to leaving the mountains. When she stopped beside him, he pointed at the wall where the charred edges of the black fungus stopped and the cleared stone began.

"Look at that."

She squinted and peered closer but couldn't immediately see what he did. Then, the fungus moved.

It slithered at a snail's pace across the wall and extended hair-thin tendrils of black that snaked to the closest deposit of brightly glowing ore. The second it touched the gleaming natural metal, the speed of its movement and growth intensified tenfold. Within seconds, a few slivers of fungus bloomed into another patch of dark, glistening growth that covered the ore completely like a well-adapted parasite and dampened the silver light. It was as thick and disastrously healthy as the rest of the fungus she hadn't managed to burn from the cavern a second time.

"The ore," she whispered.

"Right." Welby nodded. "If the miners keep coming down here for more—"

"No, that's not what I mean." She pointed at the wall where the rapidly growing fungus had finally stopped its alarming regeneration and had settled again after a few seconds of wobbling on top of the ore like a bowl of pudding. "The ore is the problem."

He frowned at her. "I believe that's exactly what I said."

"Not mining it, Chui. Being fed by it." She had called him by his first name again like they'd known each other for years instead of only a few months. Still, she was too excited by her newest revelation to let herself be bothered by a few irrelevant details. "The Blue Flame works. I burned this fungus off in seconds, exactly like we did the first time we were here. And all your tests told us we'd get rid of it for good with that spell, so we thought we had. But your tests didn't include the ore."

"I'm not sure I follow. Why would I test ore if it has nothing to do with—"

"Believe me, it has everything to do with the fungus. You saw the way it was regrowing, right? It was slow and almost desperate until it reached the ore. Then, it practically exploded. There's something about this Smithheart ore in these mountains that makes it grow so quickly— even if it's been burned out by the only magic that can stop it."

"But the Blue Flame consumed this entire chamber the last time we were here." He peered at the glistening plant again and shook his head. "A chain reaction in highly flammable fungus that caught fire to everything in seconds. There would have been nothing left to reach the ore for this kind of regeneration to occur. I'm sorry. It's an excellent theory but the holes are too big to fully support it."

Raven stepped away from the wall, folded her arms, and regarded him with a challenging expression.

"What?" He turned to face her and his eyes widened in incomprehension.

I'm gonna have to spell this whole thing out for him, aren't I? I can't blame a vet for not putting all the pieces together when this has nothing to do with animals or his profession.

"I know it doesn't make sense the way you're thinking about it," she told him and fought a smile. "But the only hole we missed is the one that will prove my theory."

"Raven, nothing could have withstood the Blue Flame—"

"It didn't." She turned partially away from him and glanced across the cavern.

He followed her gaze. "At this point, I'm more interested in knowing what makes you so confident, so if you could please..."

He paused, straightened, and tilted his head. "That hole."

"Yeah."

"I see." A frown flicked across his brow before he sucked a sharp breath in and pointed at the destroyed wall of the cavern through which they'd climbed from the level of Swarm tunnels below. "We didn't miss anything the first time. The fungus was destroyed."

"Yes." She grinned.

"But the cave-in from some other tunnel, maybe even one beside this cavern or higher above us..." He glanced at the ceiling. "That would have happened after we burned the fungus in here."

"And once the walls came down, that gave the fungus in every other tunnel in these mountains an opening to slip through and grow again. Because of the ore."

"Raven! You're brilliant!" Without any warning, he swept her into his arms and pulled her in for an embrace she hadn't been remotely prepared for.

For a moment, she let herself hug him, glad that someone else had followed her train of thought and agreed with her. That combination had been rather lacking in her experience over the last four years.

But then she noticed how different it felt to relax into the embrace of this tall, broad-shouldered, muscular dragon doctor. It was too unfamiliar and too unlike the embraces she'd shared with William. Thinking of the young dragon trainer made her instantly feel guilty for enjoying this as much as she did.

She pulled away gently, swallowed, and looked around the chamber again, her cheeks flushed.

I'm always gonna be red in the face around him, aren't I? Thank the Source he's too polite to say anything about it. There's no way he doesn't notice.

"What's wrong?" he muttered.

"I'm…uh, trying to think about how we can fix this now that we know the fungus is practically unstoppable as long as it's in these tunnels." It was a legitimate concern, although the twist of the truth to avoid what was on her mind still felt like a massive lie. She couldn't stop there. "Do you think there's any way we can discover how this ore is…I don't know. Boosting growth properties? If we can do that…"

"We may find a way to reverse the effects and possibly eradicate them. At least long enough to burn the fungus from every location in these mountains. Hopefully."

"That would take casting the Blue Flame innumerable times in a short space of time." Raven ran a hand through her dust-encrusted hair, snagged her fingers on the ends, and gave up. "But it's a start."

"There are more than enough mages in Lomberdoon to accomplish that task with a combined attempt. Yes." His eyes glinted with excitement and renewed hope as he caught her shoulders and bent to meet her gaze. "Like I said. Utterly brilliant."

Her automatic smile was a combination of guilt, discomfort at how close he leaned toward her, and over-whelming pride in what they'd discovered. "Thanks. But it wasn't only me—"

"I would never have seen it on my own. This changes everything."

She had no idea what to say to that, so she kept her mouth shut and stared at the eagerly hopeful dragon doctor. He seemed to be considering new tests and strategies for how to bring this brand-new plan of theirs to life, and she finally had to pull him out of his thoughts by moving away from his hands on her shoulders. "We're still not out of the proverbial fire yet, though."

"Hmm?" Welby blinked quickly, met her gaze again, and released her. "No, of course not."

"And we still have a long walk ahead so we should get going."

"Right. The final stretch." He chuckled. "I can't tell you how glad I am that we won't have to walk back to Havendom."

"Ha. No, we won't. I'm ready to get back into the sky." She moved toward the entrance of the tunnel the Lomberdoon miners had named Orion and broke into a jog. "I assume vet training probably didn't include running through mines, right?"

He wrinkled his nose. "It most certainly didn't."

"Do you think you can keep up anyway?"

Chui laughed. "Trust me, Raven, I've done my fair share of running. As long as nothing gives way beneath my feet again, I'll be right behind you."

"Good." She flashed him a wide grin over her shoulder and continued toward the tunnel entrance. In seconds, she'd jumped onto the ledge and had disappeared down the Orion tunnel toward the mining site constructed within Lomberdoon's southwestern border.

"Just because I can run doesn't mean I enjoy it." The vet gritted his teeth and quickened his pace across the cavern to catch up with the redheaded mage.

Leander. Raven searched for her familiar's presence and reached out in an almost desperate attempt to find him until his voice entered her mind without warning.

We're still here. Are you close?

We found the Orion tunnel and we're heading out that way now.

He didn't have to think anything for her to feel the rush of pride and joyful excitement from her dragon beneath the urgency of everything they still had to do. Still, she couldn't let him get his hopes up yet.

There's another problem, though. The fungus isn't gone. We didn't destroy it.

The healer's spell was flawed?

No, it has nothing to do with the Blue Flame. That was perfect. It's the ore. I need to focus on running in case there's another collapse or something else we didn't expect. I'll explain as soon as we're there.

Hurry.

She pushed herself even harder and heard Chui's heavy footsteps and steady although slightly faster breathing behind her.

They'd have at least six hours on their ride to Havendom to tell Leander and Gruene what they'd discovered during their trek through the Brightsbane Mountains. Once there, they would probably have to relate the tale all over again with a few added explanations to get the severity of it all across to Primus Kauler. Hopefully, the military would listen to a young mage when it counted. This time, she wasn't merely a student trying to break all the rules and make her own traditions.

Raven knew what she was doing.

As the floor of the Orion tunnel started to angle upward toward the surface and the glow of the Smithheart ore faded beneath the bright light that spilled in through the entrance, she realized they had one more serious problem to deal with on top of everything else.

The tunnel we crawled through to the last cavern collapsed after we'd already cleared the fungus the first time. If it was done deliberately, it means the foreign army has already been through the mountains—this close to Lomberdoon and within the last month at least.

CHAPTER TWENTY-THREE

The reunion between both mages and their dragon familiars was intense and by necessity, short-lived. Raven and Chui mounted quickly, and they took to the skies to fly as fast as they could to the capital.

On the way, they had enough time to share the stories of what they'd seen over the last few days—and to grow a little anxious over how long it would take them to get to their destination. They needed to alert the Legion Primus to a slew of new threats and obstacles in their way with real urgency.

The vet voiced his plan to cast a Full Appearance to his Advisory Mage friend in the king's fortress and at least get word to Kauler that they were on their way and that he needed an urgent meeting with the primus to discuss what they'd found. She agreed it was the best way to handle this, then stopped him.

"Don't give your friend all the information. Only that you need to speak to Primus Kauler."

"Raven, this concerns everyone in the king's fortress as

much as it concerns the military. Including King Vaughn. If my friend knows what needs to be discussed beforehand and speaks to the king, we'll save ourselves valuable time and not have to deliver the same report ad nauseum."

"I know. I agree with you a hundred percent on that part, but I—" She shrugged and tightened her grasp on the pommel of the saddle she didn't need to use. "How well do you know this friend of yours?"

Chui frowned. "Well enough to think this is a good idea. But now I'm starting to reconsider. If you have another suspicion, I'm the last person to tell you to keep it to yourself. Especially now."

"You mean about the foreign invaders living under the mountains?"

"Or any other facet of this entire situation, yes."

She swallowed and drew a deep breath. "No. I don't have any suspicions. At least none I can prove right now. But the last time I asked for help from mages in Haven-dom, their response was…beyond frustrating."

"They didn't believe you."

"Yeah, that's part of it."

The other part was that they didn't want to believe me because it meant their whole world was changing and they had to adapt. I seriously hope the Consortium has assigned new mages and managed to change with the times during the last two years.

"You know what? That's my personal issue and it has nothing to do with this." Raven waved her hand toward him in a conciliatory gesture. "Tell the Advisory Mage whatever you want. At this point, it might not even matter."

He inclined his head, although he couldn't lower his

voice as much as he would have if they'd walked side by side again instead of flying on dragonback. "I hope you know by now that I hold your opinion in high regard."

"Thank you. But I can admit when I don't know everything and I can't see the future."

Not like that old wizard Pete everyone thought had lost his mind. He knew what was coming and no one wanted to listen to him either.

With a nod, Welby returned his focus to casting the Full Appearance in the saddle while Gruene and Leander soared over the towns and villages of southern Lomberdoon and headed northeast.

The red dragon's rumbled amusement vibrated through the saddle, and Raven leaned forward to stroke the base of his long neck. "What?"

"You seem to have released a few old grudges in recent months."

She rolled her eyes. "I don't hold grudges."

Her familiar swiveled his head to fix her with his glowing yellow eyes. "Not anymore."

And something happened between you and the healer under so many tons of rock, he added in her mind. *I can tell.*

We can talk about that later. And then we can talk about how you and Gruene seem to have no problem flying next to each other.

He whipped his head forward again and snorted. *Or we could not talk about it at all.*

Hey, yeah. I like that idea too.

Raven smirked and glanced at the vet as he spoke to his friend she still couldn't see through the window of the Full Appearance spell. It was impossible to not notice that he didn't say a word about what they'd found or why it was so important to speak to Primus Kauler, only that it was an urgent military matter that couldn't wait.

Wow. He took my suggestion.

That made her smile grow a little more and helped with the feeling of impending chaos she knew they'd walk into, hopefully sooner rather than later. If they waited too long, it would only get worse.

When he regained consciousness, Connor Alby didn't immediately remember where he was or how he'd gotten there. The only thing he could think of for the first few seconds was that it was so incredibly dark, he couldn't move, and his ankle flared with pain. That was probably what had woken him.

He grunted as he tried to reposition himself and heard a few small stones clacking across other stones somewhere very close by.

The sound seemed to trigger his awareness and it all came rushing back to him.

So I'm still not dead. Funny. They say cats have nine lives but no one ever talks about how many a mage gets. I must have had at least two dozen by now.

His throat was dry and he had to clear it several times before he managed to croak the words of his first spell as a not-dead mage. "*Erigo.*"

The top few rocks that had buried him in a massive pile illuminated with yellow light, then elevated from where they'd settled and moved from the pile to drop on the dirt.

At least his fingers hadn't been pinned by the debris as well or he'd be stuck there far longer than he wanted.

I've already been here too long. There's no way to tell how long exactly, but it's precious time I won't get back.

Little by little, he worked at the rubble pile by spell-casting alone until he could finally free his arms enough to try to dig himself out. That quickly proved futile, so he unburied himself completely with repeated levitation spells until his body collapsed onto what was left beneath him.

With a groan, he rolled onto his side and tried to push to his feet. The amount of effort such a simple act took was tremendous.

Come on, old man. If the mountain can't kill you, a little weakness won't finish the job. You're better than that.

On shaky legs, he finally managed to stand and wobbled a little before he took a moment to look around. The ore veins that streaked through the small cavern all around him glowed with an unfamiliar brilliance, which he recognized as the Smithheart's natural potential when the raw metal wasn't covered in the gunge of black fungus he'd seen so many times before. It provided enough light to see that he'd fallen far below the tunnel he'd almost escaped. Unfortunately, it also revealed that while this small chamber had once had two additional tunnel exits he might have taken, it now contained only one.

That's fine. I'll keep going until I'm out of these mountains or drop dead. Assuming the Malendesh don't somehow discover me first.

Casting another illusion on himself with the Fade was out of the question now. He simply didn't have the strength. Instead, he pushed himself toward the only open tunnel and staggered on weak legs that made him feel his age.

By the time he reached it, he was out of breath and had to stop again.

You'll never get out of here like this. It'll take you months.

A wave of debilitating hopelessness washed over him and strengthened as his last reserves of energy faded quickly. Without food or water to rejuvenate him, he couldn't recover his strength. Worse, his ankle sent a lance of searing pain up his leg and into his hip whenever he stepped on that foot.

"Rest, then," he whispered. "Only a little while. See how long it takes without focusing on invisibility."

A weak chuckle escaped him as he stumbled sideways and practically sagged against the tunnel wall. He most likely would have fallen into it—maybe even battered his head against the stone or the ore and knocked himself unconscious again—if he hadn't reached out to support himself with a hand on a particularly bright deposit of Smithheart ore.

The second his hand touched the glowing raw metal, his heart raced at three times its previous speed and the energy that tingled up his hand and into his arm made him gasp. Anyone else might have thought he had finally reached the end of his days and his body was merely giving out as he sagged against the wall and the glowing ore.

He'd only faltered momentarily because he couldn't believe what was happening.

Magic.

Strength surged into him, traveled up his arm, and

spread through his entire body. The weakness vanished and the agony in his ankle faded quickly until it was nothing more than a bad memory. The source of his magic he'd all but spent in an effort to remain undiscovered by the Malendesh and to warn away the strangers who'd approached the cave-in at the last second returned immediately.

Connor drew in a massive, searing breath like he'd held it for the last few weeks. When the strange and entirely unexpected transformation finished, he removed his hand from the ore deposit. The tingle in his arm faded and the ore pulsed with a slightly stronger light before it returned to its normal glow.

The ore.

He leaned closer to peer at the raw metal and laughed in disbelief.

This isn't even Smithheart at all, is it? By the Source, we've all been duped by nature at its finest and the return of magic. And now we're being undermined by Malendesh forces because Lomberdoon was too blind to see what we had under our noses.

Now everything he'd overheard the foreign contingent saying made complete sense. Even without understanding every single word of Spirgul, he fully understood the complete context.

Malenspire had sent their men south from their island nation to explore the shores of Threndor. How they'd known about the ore and its magic-bolstering properties, he couldn't say, but they were there now.

They had discovered this ore's ability to magnify their new magic, which made it indescribably powerful when an entire force combined their magic and used the ore to fuel it. Their purpose was to collect enough to strengthen an entire army—maybe even an entire population—and use their discovery to make them more powerful than they'd been in centuries.

Unless they were thwarted, they would be strong enough to have a real chance in a fight against any other military force on Threndor—maybe even to invade.

Lomberdoon was the closest sovereign kingdom to the Brightsbane Mountains. It was closest to the mines and the nexus of power the Malendesh were stealing under their noses, and no one even knew they were here.

Without having announced their presence on Threndor, the Malendesh were most certainly operating with the intention to preserve their element of surprise for the right moment. That certainly made this an act of war.

Connor staggered forward, realized how unnecessary it was to move slowly now that his full strength had returned, and straightened.

I have to let someone know. More importantly, I need to get the hell out of these damn tunnels.

He raised both hands in front of him. "*Loquimi magus Kyrie Athena.*"

The window of light that shimmered in the air in front of him was blinding, the casting window more powerful and instantaneous than he remembered in a Full Appearance spell. War Mage Athena's angular face and short silver-blonde hair filled the circle. Her eyes widened.

"Connor."

"I'll make this brief." He cleared his throat and gave her a laughably terse summary of what he'd discovered. The entire time he spoke, she didn't so much as blink. He hadn't expected much of a visible reaction at all from his old friend who'd helped him and Raven more than he could have hoped for two years earlier. Now, he was calling on her again.

"I need a friend with resources to help me handle this before it gets any worse," he finished.

She glanced at something beyond the window of the Full Appearance spell that made it look like she was peering over his shoulder, then tilted her head. "You no longer have only one friend with resources in the capital, Connor. Unless, of course, my intel network has finally failed me and your granddaughter hasn't joined the Airborne."

He frowned and still deeply regretted his inability to see his granddaughter off to her new stage in life. But if he'd been there with her, he would never have made this discovery. "They aren't mistaken. Raven is with the Legion."

"And yet you're contacting me for this issue." Athena pressed her lips together. "Neither one of us can pretend Raven is too ill-equipped to deal with this."

"No. But we don't have time to skirt diplomacy with the king and his military leaders. And Raven has her orders, whatever they are. She can't abandon her work to join me. I need you, Kyrie."

"To do what, exactly?"

"To gather the last of the proof we need before the Malendesh take their ships laden with our ore across the sea to Malenspire." Connor smirked. "And to add your strength to mine. I look forward to blasting out of the belly of the mountains."

CHAPTER TWENTY-FOUR

When Raven and Chui were all but escorted to Primus Kauler's office on the Legion base, she'd started to let herself hope that making their report and getting immediate orders to take action would be easier than she'd expected. She shouldn't have.

The commanding officer let her make her report up to the point where they'd followed the wild dragon who'd dropped out of the sky to her clan to give each of the others the Weeping Disease cure and he interrupted with a sharp clearing of his throat. "Were all the wild dragons cured?"

"Yes, sir. But—"

"That was your mission, Mage Alby. Your orders were to not return until the situation was handled with complete success."

"Primus, there may still be—"

"Did you return without assessing the state of other dragons out there infected by this disease?"

Raven gritted her teeth. "There's no way to know that we found them all because the fungus—"

"You've spent long enough separated from your division, Legionary." Kauler raised his chin from where he sat behind his desk and glanced pointedly at the door. "Get back out there and finish the day's training with them. You're dismissed."

For a moment, she couldn't believe what she had heard. He had dismissed her before she'd even had a chance to mention the foreign men who'd built catapults to infect every dragon on Threndor unfortunate enough to get in the way.

She stared at her commanding officer and the primus tilted his head. "Orders, Mage Alby."

"Sir." With a glance at Welby, she clenched her jaw and started to turn toward the door.

"Primus Kauler," the vet said and stepped forward. "With all due respect, sir, I'd like to request Mage Alby's presence while I deliver the rest of our report."

The primus frowned and she froze halfway between her mission partner and the office door, completely without a clue as to whether she should leave or take her chances and stay.

"The discoveries we made would not have been possible without Mage Alby's expertise," Welby continued. "And I firmly believe continuing to consult her on what we face will be far more beneficial than dismissing her now to train with her division. Beneficial not only to Lomberdoon but most likely the entire continent at this point. Sir."

With a heavy sigh, the officer darted a glance at Raven,

fixed Chui with an irritated expression, then raised an eyebrow and nodded. "Make it quick, Dr. Welby."

"As quick as I can given the gravity, Primus."

Kauler's eyes widened briefly and he leaned back in his chair and waited for the vet to continue with the more threatening details of their mission report.

Raven turned to face her commanding officer and took his nod as approval for her to stay in his office.

So there's no chain of command for the civilian contractor. Mostly. Since when is a military leader so quick to listen to a civilian anyway? Henry was right. No way is Chui merely a vet.

Despite the new level of mystery revealed about her mission partner—and maybe he was even turning into something more if she ever let herself entertain the surprising idea—she stood perfectly still and at attention while he recounted everything that happened after they'd healed the wild clan beyond the mountains.

Her commanding officer listened with narrowed eyes and didn't interrupt once, which only aggravated her that much more. Maybe after this was all over, he might be a little more open to letting his STAR mage complete more than one sentence a day.

When Chui finished his account of events, the primus looked from one to the other and pressed his lips together. "I knew I'd hear about this eventually. Although I didn't expect it to happen all at once, inconvenience doesn't change a damn thing. It's our job to take care of it."

Raven leaned toward him. "Sir?"

Kauler sighed. "The last few weeks since the two of you went south, I've received five more reports of serious problems out that way. Nightly disturbances, a few destroyed barns, and two accounts of even more dragons who got themselves sick and lost their minds because of it."

She shook her head. "Primus, they didn't get themselves sick."

"Yes, Dr. Welby explained what's happening down there. And while I imagine the two of you are ready and eager to mount up and get back out there to handle the situation beyond the mountains, we have an internal operation that needs our immediate attention. We'll hit two dragons with one cure, as it were."

Kauler smirked at his poorly timed play on words, but when the two mages who stood stiffly in his office didn't react at all, he glanced at the ceiling and adopted his straight-faced seriousness again. "Harpertown's had an especially hard time with an influx of these infected wild dragons. The surrounding towns and villages have sent complaints, but Harpertown's the biggest so we'll go there. If anyone wants to sit in on the meeting, they can get themselves from Brighton or Heatherwood or wherever they are and join us then."

"A meeting?" she asked.

The primus ignored her and nodded at Chui. "Dr. Welby, I want you and your...assistants to focus on making as many of those cures as you can in the next two days. You'll have help to take them to Harpertown and a unit dedicated to helping you distribute them. And you'll have to explain to the citizens losing their dragons or their livelihoods to this fungus disease exactly what's happening and why this cure will solve their problems."

"You want me to head a crisis meeting," the vet muttered. "Primus, I'm not a public speaker."

"Which is why I'm sending one of the Arbitrator Mages from Havendom with you to stand in as support. As well as STAR."

Raven balked at the suggestion. "Primus, STAR should be beyond the mountains. Tracking down the invaders—"

"And you will be, Mage Alby. As soon as Dr. Welby and Mage Ectorio conclude their business with this meeting. We can't stop a war before it truly begins if our kingdom is tearing itself apart from the inside. And we all know what happens when no one gets the answers they deserve because those in Havendom don't think it's important to provide the necessary information."

She pressed her lips together and nodded.

At least he's not trying to keep this a secret to prevent an uprising. I guess he learned that lesson with curing the Legion dragons.

"So." Kauler inclined his head toward Chui again. "As many doses as you can manage in the next two days. You'll have the townspeople to thank for mass distribution once you show them how it's done. The dragons who aren't already infected will be inoculated like the Legion. The rest? Well, I'll leave that in your capable hands. And Mage Alby, make sure your division is ready to move out the day after tomorrow—fully prepared for combat. I expect that's exactly what we'll find on the other side of those mountains, assuming it doesn't find us within our kingdom borders beforehand."

"Yes, sir."

Both mages turned to leave the office. Once the door closed behind them, she couldn't hold back a small smile. "I completely underestimated the way he listens to you."

Chui leaned toward her and muttered, "The primus and I answer directly to the same king. I'm the only one of us who doesn't have to go through the military first to get an audience."

"Wait, what?" Raven stepped away in surprise and frowned teasingly at him. "I thought the military contracted you."

"They did. At King Vaughn's recommendation. Like I've said before, Raven, I would love to sit with you and discuss all the unanswered questions we both have—about each other specifically." He paused and his smile widened enough to make his gaze more than merely friendly. "But right now, we both have important things to prepare for."

"Right." She nodded. "I guess I won't see you for two days if you're busy making more potions."

"Unfortunately, no. But I do have the best mage in the Legion to escort me south for this meeting with the townspeople."

She glanced at the ceiling and shook her head. "I'm the only mage in the Legion."

"You know, I imagine there's a reason for that."

After leaving her meeting in the Legion tower, Raven stalked across the training grounds and met up with her division. They were finishing their formation drills and flight maneuvers and Maximilian grinned when he saw her. "Mage Alby's back!"

The legionaries stopped what they were doing and dragons swooped out of the sky with their riders to gather around the mage who'd led their training until her latest orders had sent her away. Now, they were all about to leave Havendom with her in two days.

She couldn't field every question about where she'd been and what she had done. As the other cohorts who hadn't been posted for patrol duty around the kingdom left the field to head toward the outdoor mess hall, she gathered her division and told them everything they needed to know. This included the wild dragons, the foreign force that had secretly traveled to Threndor and found the tunnels under the mountains, the magic-boosting ore, and the catapults. Finally, she shared the orders about the meeting they would attend in Harpertown to both reassure and enlist the help of the townspeople to prepare the kingdom and especially Lomberdoon's dragons for whatever might be coming.

"We'll go in for a real battle in a few days," she told them. "Whatever that looks like, we still need to be careful. These men, whoever they are, have deliberately attacked dragons in an attempt to eliminate them with Weeping Disease. If they've already learned that we have a cure, we can only assume they'll find another way to fight us that might be even deadlier—and instant."

"We know how to fly," Nicole said with a nod. "And how to fight."

"Yeah." Farb snorted. "Someone thought it was a good idea to show us how to up our game."

Raven studied the two dozen faces of her fellow STAR legionaries and shrugged. "With decent timing, too."

The mood within her division was still as easygoing as ever despite knowing their new orders to head out in two days to engage an enemy they didn't even truly understand yet. Raven was surprisingly proud to be part of a team like this, where each legionary was ready and willing to do their part. No one argued, brooded, or seemed remotely hesitant to join Mage Alby and Dr. Welby against this new enemy.

At Fowler, I had my friends. Four of us at school and William when he could help. Now I have an entire division of elite riders and their dragons willing to follow me. I wonder if that would change if we didn't have orders from Kauler to handle this. It's a good thing he took Chui and me seriously.

Her thoughts persisted through dinner and when the entire Airborne Legion settled for the evening while their dragons took to the sky to mingle and do what free dragons did at the end of a long workday. She still hadn't quite managed to feel as excited and determined as the rest of her cohort.

We still don't know exactly what this foreign army is capable of. If they built catapults for the black fungus to infect dragons, they must have built something else to use against mages. And, of course, they have magic and Smithheart ore to make it stronger. I understand why Kauler's only sending STAR in to deal with this at first but it might not be enough.

That night, as she lay in her bed on Level Six and listened to Nicole flipping through the pages of another book on her side of the room, she wondered exactly how they would manage to stop even a small army with more than a few extra tricks up its sleeves.

Not every Legion dragon can breathe fire. And Leander's the only one I know who can summon blue fire. That's the only thing that'll take care of the fungus. But now the ore's an even bigger problem. We need a way to destroy that.

"Are you okay over there, mage?" Her roommate smirked at her over the top of her book.

Raven sat, pushed her hair out of her face, and nodded. "Yeah. I just had an idea."

"Uh-oh." They both laughed before the blonde legionary returned her attention to her book. "Don't worry, Alby. If you gotta jump out of a window again, I won't stop you. But don't tell me that's what you're doing 'cause it's hard to lie about something like that."

"Ha. No. I'm not going anywhere." She spread her hands in front of her and muttered, "*Loquimi magus* Henry Derks." The casting window of the Full Appearance spell opened between her palms with a shimmer, and the first thing she saw was a swarm of toy Pegacorns hurtling toward her with their horns lowered before they swooped through the spell on Henry's end and disappeared.

"Ah! Come on!" He swiped at the toys and batted a leaping wooden goat out of the air instead. "How many times do I have to—oh! Jeez, Alby." He gave her a sheepish grin and ruffled his hair vigorously. "It's been a while since you snuck up on me with something like this. How's it going?"

"Well, right now, everything's fine." She scanned the semi-dark interior of Magical Madness behind her best friend, where all the enchanted toys and magical joke items showed no inclination to settle for the night like the owner of the shop wanted them to. "But I wanted to ask you about your inventions."

"Uh-huh." He snatched another Pegacorn out of the air and tickled its belly before it fell limp. "Like what?"

"Remember when we talked about whipping something up for the military?"

"Seriously? I thought that was a joke, Alby."

"Yeah, but you looked like you were considering it."

Henry's mouth opened for a retort but he stopped himself and sighed before he muttered, "I did consider it and even started to play around with a few new things that might fit the bill. Hey, you look like crap. Was it a rough day at work?"

Raven glanced at Nicole, who'd since lowered her book into her lap and now stared at the Full Appearance casting window with her jaw hanging open.

"Something like that. Listen, Derks, do you think you could put something together that might...I don't know... act like a miniature transportable forge or something?"

"You mean fire?"

"Fireworks."

"Yeah." He frowned at something she couldn't see, then shrugged. "Yeah, I can do fire. What's it for?"

"Protecting the kingdom."

The young wizard laughed. When he realized she was serious, his smile vanished before he cleared his throat. "Of course it is. I almost forgot who I'm talking to. You know, your comment about giant fart bombs got me thinking and working on something fun. Deadly, yeah. I'm sure I can throw fire into the mix too."

She grinned. "Deadly fire that could melt metal?"

"Ha! That's merely a side effect. Hell, Alby. Fine. You convinced me. I guess I'm breaking into military weapons too. If you don't have any other specs, I'll start work on these. How many do you need?"

Raven wrinkled her nose in thought and shrugged. "As many as you can have ready in two days. We'll be in town then to pick them up."

"Yeesh! You're serious, aren't you?" He didn't even let her confirm that because he was already putting his mind to work on this new invention project that wasn't technically sanctioned by the Legion.

And he doesn't need to know that part. Not now, anyway.

"Lemme tell you, Alby, you're lucky my production spells have improved so much in the last couple of months or I'd tell you this is impossible. But I won't."

"If anyone can do it, Henry, it's you."

He snorted. "You're gonna give me a big head. I'd better get to work. See you in a few days."

When she finished the Full Appearance spell, she lowered her hands into her lap and turned to look at Nicole. The blonde woman hadn't budged. "Do you think you can keep this one to yourself?"

Her roommate stared at her for a moment, snatched her book up again, and pretended to read. "I have no idea what you're talking about, mage. I didn't see a thing."

"Well, that's a relief."

After that, she finally managed to calm herself enough that sleep didn't seem so impossible. Now she only had more waiting to do until they began the serious business of healing sick dragons, eradicating the fungus, and ensuring that foreign invaders from who knew where didn't turn their powerful magic and their machines against Lomberdoon.

CHAPTER TWENTY-FIVE

Two days later, Raven and Leander watched the main avenue of Harpertown fill with local townspeople and citizens from the surrounding towns and villages for the meeting the Legion had called. The entire STAR division stood in formation behind her.

Every legionary had dressed in full battle gear for the second part of their mission once the meeting was over. Their dragons had done the same and donned thick leather saddles and harnesses with the STAR patch emblazoned on each and with their riders' preferred weapons attached at the sides instead of saddlebags. The young mage, thankfully, had been cleared to also arm herself with Sarah Alby's war mage sword and now wore it proudly at her hip.

The people of Harpertown, however, seemed to think a contingent of Airborne Legionaries and their armed dragons taking up half the main avenue was more for intimidation than tactical purposes.

Children stared with wide eyes at the dragons who held their long necks regally toward the sky. Mothers pulled them back. Older men and women gathered in small clusters and whispered to each other while they stared at the STAR cohort with wonder and curiosity. A good handful of people scowled in suspicion and didn't bother to hide their disdain at having military troops and so many free dragons stationed there for a simple town meeting.

"Look at them," one man snarled. "Strutting around our town like they own the place."

His companions nodded and offered their dubious remarks in support.

Raven felt Leander's broad, warm shoulder beneath her hand and it steadied them both.

Ignore them, he told her. *They change their tune when they remember how much they need us.*

That's what we thought would happen when King Vaughn declared Lomberdoon dragons were now free. She swallowed. *Some of these people don't look like they've learned anything.*

It doesn't change what we will continue to do for them.

No. You're right about that.

Finally, when it seemed all the townspeople from surrounding towns and villages had settled for the meeting, the Arbitrator Mage from the king's fortress in Havendom stepped up with Chui at his side to begin the announcements.

"Thank you for coming," the mage said and his voice carried through the main avenue. "We're here to discuss the issue with sick dragons across Lomberdoon's southern region—"

"They're not sick," one of the dragon-doubting men bellowed. "They've lost their minds."

"Destroying our ranches and homes."

"Spooking the animals."

"They can't be allowed to roam around like that. If this is what free dragons look like, we don't want it!"

More people in the crowd shared these sentiments than Raven had expected and Mage Ectorio, who'd come to answer questions on behalf of Havendom, raised his eyebrows and let them voice their frustrations.

The vet scowled and scanned the crowd. Behind him, Gruene turned sideways to study the angry townspeople before she lowered her head to whisper something into her mage's ear.

This isn't even starting the way we wanted.

The young mage wanted to interrupt and tell people what they needed to hear in the same way she'd had to do years before when no one wanted to listen. But the rest of her division stood tall and motionless around her, none of their dragons affected by the vitriol that spewed from angry, frightened mouths.

I can stand here with them and hold my ground, no problem. They'll get the picture eventually.

Mage Ectorio raised both hands and shouted, "I know most of you have your concerns about this issue. But to be clear, this is an issue of a dragon disease spreading quickly through close contact and exposure to a certain—"

"Disease?" a woman shrieked. "Is it contagious?"

"Yes. Highly. But only to—"

"Then get rid of them!" More outraged cries rose through the crowd. "We can't let them infect us."

The man looked like he was ready to turn and walk out of Harpertown forever without another word. Raven met Chui's gaze across the avenue and he grimaced before

Gruene uttered an almighty bellow that silenced the panicked crowd instantly.

"Thank you," he muttered and brushed his hand against her black flank before he stepped forward. "Mage Ectorio, if you have no objections, I'm happy to take it from here."

"Even if I did," the other mage muttered, "I wouldn't be able to get a word in edgewise." He gestured for Chui to continue, and the vet took the overturned crate serving as a makeshift stage in the center of the avenue.

He folded his arms and began. "My name is Dr. Chui Welby. As a veterinarian, I specialize in caring for dragons. That has always been my calling. First and foremost, however, I am a mage. And this"—he gestured with a sweep of his arm toward Gruene—"is my familiar Gruene." She lowered her head in what would have looked to the untrained eye like a bow of respect.

She's as pissed as he is. At least they hide it well.

"I understand that many of you have reservations about the place dragons have in our kingdom now, even after almost two years," he continued. "You're concerned for its effects on daily life in Lomberdoon. You may even be wary of the unknown and the changes of the future. But let me assure you, this disease Mage Ectorio mentioned only affects dragons. This isn't the first time we've seen such an illness in Lomberdoon with such devastating effects.

"Weeping Disease causes far more harm to the dragons who contract it than to us— yes, even with property damages, noise, and a little fear. But please try to open your minds beyond the separation between humans and dragons. What they need right now is our help. Our dedication to healing them and keeping them safe and our promise to do whatever it takes to eradicate this disease and eliminate this problem for all of us. At this point, we are the only ones who can help."

The avenue fell silent.

"How are we supposed to do that?" someone asked.

Welby nodded. "I've developed a cure for Weeping Disease. It's the first of its kind but it has been tested and proven. We know it works. At this point, the illness is spreading far too quickly for me or any of my team to administer this cure effectively and within the necessary time frame, which is why we all have to come together to help dragons the way they've helped us for centuries."

"They aren't helping us now," another man shouted and brandished his fist. "They're destroying our land!"

"My neighbor lost half his sheep to one of those beasts."

"We want them out of here."

Raven grimaced and was on the verge of running across the avenue to stand beside Chui and support his claims.

They have to pay attention. I thought we'd moved past this insane fear of anything that isn't on a farm. Why can't they listen?

In that moment, the vet looked at her with nothing but defeat behind his eyes and his shoulders sagged.

She drew a deep breath to call out but she was cut off by Leander's blood-curdling screech.

The red dragon spread his wings wide, beat them twice to rear on his hind legs, and bellowed, "Humans of Lomberdoon! Listen to me!"

The startled citizens clutched each other in surprise and whirled to face Raven's giant familiar who had thrust himself to the center of attention. A few small children whimpered and scurried away through the crowd but so far, no one dared to turn their back on a dragon who'd spoken to all of them out loud.

"Before I had a rider, before I found my mage, and before I ever took to the sky with my wings," Leander shouted, "I was not free. The dragon trainers who took me in did the best they could with what little knowledge they had. I was separated from my mother and my clan. I was almost impossible until Raven Alby found me and decided my freedom and my choice were the only way to reclaim my dignity."

He lowered his head toward Raven to fix her with an inquiring glance. *Should I tell them?*

Surprisingly, the crowd seemed to hang on the red dragon's every word.

She nodded. *You might as well.*

He stretched his neck toward the sky to tower above the dozens of citizens who'd come for answers but thus far had only shouted accusations. "Listen to the dragon doctor. These dragons acting strangely and making you doubt the promises between us and humans have no intention to hurt anyone. They are infected with a mind-numbing plague that debases them completely—no choice, no freedom, and no dignity.

"And then they die. Many of them have. But that is not the greatest threat we all face right now. A force of human men not from this continent have breached the shores of Threndor and vanished beneath the Brightsbane Mountains where they have found the black fungus growing in the old Swarm tunnels. They know its properties and its deadliness to dragons, and they have built machines to attack us from the ground. They are deliberately infecting us."

A low murmur of surprise passed through the crowd, but no one interrupted the massive red dragon who addressed them as if dragons and humans had held meetings like this for centuries already.

"Whether these humans mean to weaken Lomberdoon with the loss of so many dragons or merely to distract us from what's truly happening, it is no accident. It is an act of war. Without dragons, Lomberdoon cannot defend itself the way it has for so long. And without humans—without all of you—we dragons will not survive this plague. We need your help.

"The free dragons who have chosen to remain at your sides face a terrible death. Wild dragons who have upheld their side of the agreements made among both our kinds now rely on humans to find them and to deliver the healing cure Dr. Welby discovered. This is not the first time we all have a common enemy." He spread his wings and instantly made himself look even larger as he stepped forward once before he pawed the ground. "It should not be the first time we turn against each other to let that enemy destroy us."

When he finished, he snorted and folded his wings against his back again. The townspeople stared at Raven's dragon familiar with varying expressions—surprise, suspicion, and realization. Some of them looked like they were ready to turn on any and all dragons with pitchforks and the use of everyday magic they'd learned to wield over the last few years. The rest nodded thoughtfully and looked at their neighbors for silent reassurance regarding the truth they'd heard from a dragon's mouth.

Chui cleared his throat. "Thank you, Leander."

Raven grinned and patted his shoulder. *That was more eloquent than I could have put it.*

A dragon is always eloquent, Raven.

The other Legion dragons chuffed and pawed the ground as well. Their riders smiled at Leander, impressed by his ability to address a gathering of so many humans who still doubted almost everything these days, even years after the entire world had changed with magic and free dragons.

"Now you've heard what we face," the vet continued. "We need all the help we can get to find every infected dragon within the kingdom borders and deliver them this cure. I ask anyone who is willing to join us in this to meet with Mage Ectorio and myself over here, and we'll hand out doses of the potion to be administered to those dragons. Whatever you can offer, whatever skills or resources you possess, we need them all."

Almost two-thirds of the gathered townsfolk followed the vet as he stepped off the overturned crate and regrouped with Mage Ectorio and the dragons who'd carried the vials from Havendom. The rest of the citizens who'd heard their proof but still didn't believe shook their heads, cast the Legion dragons wary glances, and filtered away along the town's main avenue to return to their daily business, muttering under their breath.

"That didn't get us nearly as much support as we'd hoped for," Raven muttered.

Leander lowered his head over her shoulder to reply in her ear. "It got us enough."

"I hope so." She met Chui's gaze again from across the avenue, where the vet stood beside Gruene and helped hand out the massive number of cure vials a separate Legion unit had brought to arm civilians against the Weeping Disease. He smiled at her and nodded in both appreciation and what looked like silently wishing her good luck on the second half of their mission now that the meeting was over.

And now it's time for us to move.

She turned to address the STAR division still standing in smart formation behind her. "This is the part where we—"

"Mage Alby! I'm looking for Mage Alby! Where is she?"

Raven spun again as the furious thudding of a horse's hooves raced down the cobbled avenue toward the gathering. A few townspeople pointed at the STAR division, and her eyes widened at the sight of Bella Chase barreling toward her on horseback.

"I guess there's one more thing to take care of," she told her division and headed toward her old mage school friend.

CHAPTER TWENTY-SIX

"Bella. What—"

"I'm glad I caught you before you left." The dark-haired mage reined her horse in and nodded. "I have a lead on Connor."

"What?"

"It's weird, Raven. But I trust my sources."

"Where is he?"

Her friend looked at Wesley as her firedrake familiar wheeled overhead, his scales glinting in the sunlight. "My network at the capital sent word that he made contact with War Mage Athena three days ago. She left her post at Havendom after that with a small party of her soldiers, apparently headed this way toward the mountains. The only explanation she gave anyone before she left was that she was leaving to 'help an old friend.'"

"That certainly sounds like it could be him."

"Plus reports that someone's been actively collapsing the tunnels along the base of the mountain leading into

Lomberdoon's borders," Bella added. "Including the Swarm mines south of here. Like they're trying to—"

"Keep someone from pushing through into the kingdom. Yeah, that certainly sounds like him. Is there any way to know for sure?"

The other young mage smirked and shrugged from the saddle of her horse. "Besides heading into those tunnels to see for ourselves?"

"I've already been in those tunnels and we don't have time to search them right now. We're heading out across the mountains to—"

"Seriously weird forces who aren't supposed to be here?"

Raven laughed, not at all surprised. "You've heard about them too, huh?"

Bella's smile widened. "I hear about many things, Mage Alby."

"I bet. Thanks, Bella. I'll have to look into that but right now, I have to get an entire Legion division across the mountains."

"Hold on." The dark-haired mage dismounted fluidly, slipped what looked like a small scrap of parchment paper into one of her saddlebags, and slapped the horse on the rump to send him galloping away from Harpertown toward the main road.

"What are you doing?"

"Come on, Raven. You didn't seriously think I'm not gonna jump at the chance to head into something this big with you. Again." Bella dusted her hands off and nodded. "I'm coming with you."

"You know we're flying, right?"

"Yep." The other mage glanced at all the Legion dragons waiting for their STAR mage's order to move out and swallowed. "But I see Leander's finally wearing a saddle. So I'm willing to suck it up if you are."

Raven chuckled and nodded toward her division before both newly robed mages returned to the Legion contingent ready to cross the mountains and engage an unknown enemy.

"This is Mage Chase," she shouted at her fellow legionaries. "A friend and another independent contractor Havendom is lucky to have working for the king from time to time. She'll ride with me."

Nicole nodded. "It looks like we have two Legion mages now. I like it."

"Most certainly not." Bella snorted. "This is a one-time mission. I will not join the military."

A few of the legionaries chuckled as she approached Leander, who lowered himself onto his belly so she could climb into the saddle. "Mage Chase," he rumbled.

"Hey, Leander. I know I walked into this all on my own..." She stepped into the stirrup and swung a leg over to sit at the back of the saddle with a grunt. "But if you feel like taking it easy on me this time around, I'd appreciate that."

He curved his neck to fix her with a glowing yellow eye. "As long as you keep fighting with us. Try not to scream."

She threw her head back and laughed.

Raven was about to step into the stirrups as well—something she rarely did but had to now that she and Leander would carry an extra passenger—when another shout from the complete opposite end of the town's main avenue made her stop.

"Alby! Hey, Alby! Don't go yet. I did it! I freaking did it!"

Henry Derks waved one arm wildly over his head and the other tugged on the reins of two horses laden with massive, bulging saddlebags as he pushed through the crowds.

She grinned. "He did it."

"I thought he owned a toyshop now," Bella muttered.

"He does but he might be branching out into something else. Derks!" She waved her best friend forward and Henry dodged the townspeople lining up to receive Weeping Disease cures from Dr. Welby. He did a double-take at the vet, who acknowledged him with a nod before he returned his focus to his mission.

When the owner of Magical Madness and his two horses reached the STAR division, the young wizard wiped the sweat from his forehead and sighed. "Man. I cut it close, didn't I?"

"A little, yeah. But it's never too late."

"So you brought your dragon-doctor friend and Mage Chase to help with this, huh?" Henry smirked at Bella. "How come I didn't get the memo, Alby?"

"You got it two days ago."

"Yeah, I guess that works. Look." He unfastened one of the saddlebags and tried comically to hold his two mounts under control as they tossed their heads and stared at the two dozen STAR dragons lined up behind her. Finally, he managed to reach into the open bag and pull his newest invention out. "I did it."

"Is that…" Raven leaned toward his hand and squinted. "A beetle?"

"An exploding beetle." Henry grinned. "Kinda. I got my inspiration from a hell of a scary bug that surprisingly enough exists. It's brilliant. The little guy has a couple of compartments in its belly, right? One of 'em holds this chemical called—"

"I'd love to hear the whole rundown, Derks. Honestly." Raven clapped him on the back and nodded. "Later. Right now, we have to get going."

"Right. Yeah, yeah. Sure. You take these with you and —hey!"

Farb and Maximilian had already approached the horses to start removing the supplies of the wizard's new exploding-beetle invention.

"Come on, guys. Be careful with those. They're ridiculously flammable!"

Farb stopped with a heavy saddlebag in his hand and nodded at Henry. "What do they do? The short version."

"Uh…right. Get these guys on the ground, and they'll… spray a few chemicals that light themselves. Not exactly fire per se but the heat reaches over twenty-six hundred degrees at least—"

"That sounds about right." The legionary turned and headed toward the rest of the division to start handing the exploding beetle toys out.

Nicole took one and flipped it. "How do we get them to work?"

"Well…" Henry scratched his head. "I guess you simply put them out there and let 'em take care of the rest. The critter I modeled these after usually has to feel threatened to release this stuff, but I guess being in a major battle is threatening enough."

"Is there a way to direct them?" Raven asked.

"Not really." He smiled sheepishly at her. "But if this other army doesn't have dragons, at least you'll be safe in the sky."

"He should come with us," Demy suggested as she filled her saddlebags.

"Whoa, whoa. What?" The wizard gaped at her.

"You know, in case we need a little more instruction from the weapon inventor." The legionary grinned at him and he cleared his throat.

"I don't—"

"No, it's a good idea. You created them, Derks." Raven nodded. "And you did an incredible job on such short notice. But we need them to work and you're the only mage who knows how it all comes together. I wish we had time for a demonstration first but we need to leave."

"He can ride with me," Demy added.

"Sounds good."

"Aw, come on, Alby." Henry spread his arms in protest. "I wasn't trying to get caught up in the military."

She grinned at him. "How about getting caught up in helping your best friend save the kingdom, huh?"

Bella chuckled. "It sounds exactly like the last four years, doesn't it?"

Henry rolled his eyes, sighed, and moved toward Demy and her dragon. "I can't say no to this. Hey, make sure someone gets my horses to the shop, huh? Murphy will see to 'em."

With Demy's help as her dragon lowered to the ground,

he scrambled a little clumsily into the saddle and groaned when they stood again. "I like horses. They stay at one level. And you always know where the ground is if you do fall off."

Demy's dragon Mal rumbled and swiveled her head to look at him. "I'll make sure you don't fall off, mage."

"Ha. Thanks."

"All right." Raven finally stepped into Leander's saddle, which felt a little crowded with Bella seated behind her. She called to her division, "Wings Out, Legionaries!"

Some of them laughed but they all echoed the phrase as one before Leander spread his wings with a screech and launched skyward. The STAR division followed suit and dragons leapt into the air and settled into their much-practiced flight formation to head southwest toward the Brightsbane Mountains and the open lands beyond.

Bella gasped and wound her arms around her friend's waist with crushing strength. The red-haired mage grimaced and patted her arms. "Loosen up a little, huh?"

"I can't help it!"

As they soared over the first ridges of the mountain range, searching both for any infected dragons near the Brights-banes and for any sign that this foreign army had crossed Lomberdoon borders, Raven didn't know which issue held more of her attention. Her thoughts continually shifted between heading out to engage these foreign men who'd intentionally infected dragons and knowing Connor Alby was somewhere in these mountains with War Mage Athena, blowing tunnels up.

She knew without a doubt that it was Connor.

That's whose magic I felt in the mines—the warning Chui and I got before the first cave-in. I can't believe I didn't recognize it. And we left him in there.

A hard lump formed in her throat but she pushed away the terror of what might have happened to her grandfather and focused instead on their flight path.

"Why not ask him yourself?" Leander muttered.

Bella leaned forward in the saddle. "He's talking to you, right?"

"Yeah. And that's a good idea." Raven raised her hands in front of her, knowing the spell she meant to cast now couldn't possibly hurt her grandfather since she knew where he was and what he was doing.

"Raven!" Bella shrieked. "Hands on the harness!"

"Seriously?" She looked over her shoulder to see the other mage grimace at her panic.

"Right. Sorry. You don't need that. I keep forgetting."

"Hang tight for a second. *Loquimi magus* Connor Alby." The window of the Full Appearance spell glowed between her hands and her grandfather's haggard, dust-streaked face peered at her.

"Raven. What are you—"

"Are you in the mountains?"

He frowned and gazed around a dark location interspersed with dim patches of silver light. "I'm sorry?"

"The Brightsbane Mountains, Connor. The Swarm tunnels and the mines. That's where you are right now, isn't it?"

"Yes, Raven. I suppose I shouldn't be surprised that you already know, but now isn't the time."

"It is, though. We're flying west across them right now. I have my entire division with me. I assume you found the men camping in those tunnels already, but listen. They've used the black fungus in those tunnels to attack dragons and infect them with Weeping Disease."

"Attacking the dragons?" Connor's eyes widened and he scowled as he tugged on his wiry gray beard coated with dust.

"I don't know what they want," she continued, "but—"

"They're mining the ore. Raven, listen to me. These men are from Malenspire—across the sea. I don't know how they got here undetected, but they've been mining the ore too."

"I know. Because the Smithheart ore is covered in fungus."

"It's not Smithheart ore." He shook his head. "It looks like it but it's not. That ore is powering their magic, Raven, and makes them stronger. It replenishes magic and heals wounds like I've never seen. They're taking it to—"

Shouts rose from somewhere behind the casting circle and Connor glanced over his shoulder. "Be careful, Raven. If the Malendesh have all the ore they mined with them, they won't be easy to stop."

Before she could say anything further, War Mage Athena entered the window of light.

"They're coming. Let her go. We have to—"

A burst of brilliant blue light rose behind both mages in the tunnels, followed by a chant shouted by dozens of voices as one. Attack magic streaked through the air and ricocheted off the tunnel walls. Athena turned and shouted something unintelligible before a blaze of white light erupted from both her hands.

"Connor!" Raven shouted. "Connor, how far in the tunnels are—"

Her grandfather ended her casting of the Full Appearance spell and the window of light disappeared.

She stared at the space where his face had been and clenched her teeth. "He's trying to fight an army under the mountains. With what? A handful of other mages?"

"That doesn't sound like the biggest issue right now," Bella muttered. "If the ore is healing them…"

"Then we're gonna have to turn the heat up. Legionaries!"

The dragons in formation behind Leander screeched in reply.

She looked over her shoulder to see Nicole and her dragon Kileen move beside them. "New intel on the enemy. Spread the word in the air."

Once she'd finished telling her fellow legionary what Connor had told her, the woman nodded and fell back into formation before she shouted it to the riders closest to her. The news spread from rider to rider and dragon to dragon, and no one questioned what they were supposed to do now that they rode to engage an enemy who could power their magic and heal themselves with the ore from Threndor tunnels.

We'll have to go in and do what we do best. That's our only option.

CHAPTER TWENTY-SEVEN

Despite how prepared the STAR division was, none of them expected the sudden onslaught of attacks from the ground the second they'd soared over the last of the peaks that separated Lomberdoon from the open lands. At first, Raven thought she was imagining things when she heard a heavy metallic thump, the creak of wood, and the burst of something heavy being released.

A giant black ball seemed to drip sludge as it streaked toward them.

Leander screeched and dove to avoid the projectile. "They're here!" he bellowed.

The other Legion dragons screeched in reply and the formation broke away to dive toward the ground and engage the enemy no one but him had seen.

Bella screamed and tightened her hold as the red dragon tucked his wings and plummeted toward the enemy force. Their numbers were in the hundreds now, and at least a dozen catapults flung balls of black fungus at the STAR dragons.

Fortunately, Raven's division had been training for something like this for months now, despite not knowing exactly what they'd face when the time came. The dragons split their ranks and evaded the projectiles that hurtled toward them as their riders drew their weapons and prepared to swoop in for engagement.

Leander spread his wings to pull up at the last second beside the thickest grouping of men in strange clothes with darkly painted eyes. His fire breath rumbled in his throat and he unleashed a massive column of flames at the Malendesh forces.

Men screamed and ran, their loose clothing instantly ablaze. Guttural shouts erupted from all sides, followed by crackling blue light directed at the STAR mage and her familiar.

"*Verecundia!*" She launched attack magic at the men, joined by Bella who shouted the same spells behind her to blast men aside as Leander's powerful wings buffeted the Malendesh formation.

His next column of flame caught one of the wooden and metal catapults, which blazed instantly and crackled with fire before he pulled up into the sky. All around them, Legion dragons attacked with fire while men fled in all directions.

The red dragon veered away and the other STAR dragons wheeled into the sky to join him and regroup. It didn't take long before the entire division saw how accurate Connor Alby's warning had been.

The wounded enemy troops reached into their robes to mutter spells or those who had not been wounded ran to them to perform the healing the old mage had mentioned.

And yes, they held small glowing chunks of the ore in their hands.

Raven cursed. "We have to find where they're keeping that ore. We can't fight them with it."

"It's in their clothes," Bella said.

"What about the beetles?" Maximilian shouted from his dragon.

"Derks, you said your stuff burns at over two thousand degrees?"

"Almost three," he shouted in response.

"It sounds hot enough for metal. Let 'em loose!"

Legionaries reached into their saddlebags to retrieve Henry's exploding bugs and lobbed them at the ground.

From behind Demy on her dragon, Henry cried a protest and stretched down like he could stop his new invention from plummeting. "What are you doing?"

"Exploding bugs," someone shouted.

"Not if you break them first!" He clapped both hands to his head. "What a waste."

"You mean we have to get them on the ground?" Raven asked and stared at him with wide eyes before half the division had to bank sharply to avoid more fungus flung at them.

"Yeah, Alby! Sorry. I didn't realize that one detail before we got here, okay?"

She thrust her fist in the air. "Legionary Fender. Take a unit down to distract them while the rest of us get these bugs on the ground. We'll take the fight to them there. Left-wing and right-wing split!"

The division dove in three separate formations, exactly as they'd practiced through months of drills. Nicole and four other legionaries targeted the Malendesh army and their dragons sprayed fire and ice and buffeted the catapults and the stacks of woven baskets holding fungus balls.

The rest of STAR broke in two and wheeled away from each other to descend on opposite sides of the enemy. Before their mounts had even landed, the legionaries lifted handfuls of Henry's exploding bugs from their saddlebags and tossed them as gently as possible onto the dirt.

"What do we do with them now?" Raven asked him.

"Dump them and let them do their thing!" he shrieked.

A roaring battle cry in a completely different language rose from the Malendesh forces and a huge group of the enemy army broke away to engage the legionaries on the ground. They shouted and gestured with their hands to launch crackling blue magic across the field as they surged forward and drew their wickedly sharp weapons.

"Fine. The bugs might need to feel threatened but we don't." Raven leapt from Leander's back and drew her sword before she thrust it high. "Take them down!"

Legionaries dismounted as one and their dragons became airborne to join the others in destroying the Malendesh from the sky. It was impossible to tell who started the cry of, "Charge!" but she honestly didn't think it was her.

She sprinted forward with the rest of her division anyway, Bella Chase beside her and flinging battle magic at the oddly dressed men who looked like they were grinning before the two forces clashed.

Magic and swords clashed violently and Henry practically screamed from the back of the line, "Watch out!"

After a series of quick pops and a sound like a large vial

being violently uncorked, the quick rush and spray of liquid filled the air.

The beetles had finally joined the battle. The tiny toys unleashed the chemicals separated in their bellies and sprayed the combination—thankfully at the enemy and not at the legionaries. The effect was as disastrous as Raven had hoped.

Malendesh screamed and dropped to their knees. Their clothes caught fire, although there were no flames to begin with. It was merely ignited by the heat of a chemical reaction launched from the back of a beetle-shaped toy.

"What the—" Farb staggered back as the first line of men who surged toward him were swallowed in instant flames. He grinned. "That's the coolest thing I've ever seen!"

"Stay away from the beetles," Henry shouted, jumped over one of his inventions, and retreated as it scurried toward the enemy lines. "If you hear a popping sound—"

Right on cue, dozens of beetles emitted a series of quick pops before they unleashed their deadly chemical heat. The stench of burning flesh and clothing was almost unbearable, and the wind picked up to send the thick clouds of smoke racing across the open ground toward open land beyond the mountains.

The STAR dragons overhead without their riders wheeled and continued to attack the Malendesh army's collection of ore and black fungus being loaded into the remaining catapults. Raven caught a glimpse as Leander surged over the enemy with blue fire spewing from his open mouth onto the fungus. That would destroy it but they still needed to get rid of the ore.

"We need more beetles over there!" she shouted and pointed with her sword toward the baskets of glowing ore.

A screaming man with blood already streaked across his face raced toward her, lifted his curved sword above his head, and swung it viciously. She barely managed to deflect his blow with her sword, then extended her hand and shouted, *"Verecundia!"*

Her spell caught him in the chest and he catapulted back.

"Henry, how do we get these bugs over there?"

"I don't know. Drop them where you want 'em!"

Her teeth gritted, Raven raced toward the thickest part of the enemy lines where they kept their supplies, slashed boldly with her sword, and delivered perfectly aimed battle magic in an attempt to fight through. Bella was at her side in an instant, and they at least managed to push the enemy back enough to get a clear line of sight at the piles of ore.

Leander, I need more of those beetles. Can you get them on the ground near the ore?

Her dragon surged across the Malendesh forces again and spewed a massive column of blue flames that consumed another catapult and two more baskets of fungus projectiles.

If I had hands, mage, I would throw them right now.

I'm coming.

Before the two mages could get halfway to their target, hundreds of dragon cries rose all at once and resounded along the mountain passes before their silhouettes darkened the sky.

For a moment, she had to stop and stare at the glorious

sight—hundreds of wild dragons surged over the tops of the mountains to dive onto the enemy they all shared.

And these all got the cure. They're safe.

With renewed hope and the support of wild dragons who wanted to see these invaders suffer for their crimes against dragons as much as Lomberdoon, Raven fought her way even farther toward the baskets of ore.

Leander swooped up to meet a small purple dragon in the sky. Before his mage could comprehend what was happening, one of his saddlebags glowed with purple light, opened, and released a swarm of Henry's exploding beetles toward the ore and the remaining cache of fungus. The toys glowed with the same violet light before they landed exactly where the Legion needed them most.

"How the hell did that happen?" Bella asked before she blasted two more screaming Malendesh who surged toward them.

Raven deflected a burst of blue enemy magic and grinned at her friend. "All dragons are free and some of them have magic."

The effect of the newly released swarm of Henry's weapon beetles was instantaneous. Stuttered pops and loud thumps filled the air to release the noxious chemical mixture from their enchanted backsides. The enemy forces screamed and erupted in flames. A good portion of the chemical weaponry landed on the cache of glowing ore mined from beneath the mountains.

When the enemy saw this, they became completely unhinged. Some of them tried to beat the fire away from the ore but they stepped on even more beetles and made things worse for their forces and themselves. A few realized the threat and began to run simply to escape the mixture that set everything ablaze.

The two young mages fought through the enemy and blasted Malendesh aside before they could attack the wild dragons in the air with their magic. When Bella engaged a snarling Malendesh man with two curved swords, Raven raced to her friend's side but was thwarted by the flash of a small blade that passed mere inches in front of her.

She stopped short and turned to a large man who stalked toward her. His face was coated in black war paint and two massive rubies were embedded in his left ear. He sneered at her and strode forward, his hand extended to either throw another knife or cast a spell. His outstretched hand was mangled with burns that continued beneath his sleeves.

"*Verecundia!*" she shouted.

The man dodged her spell and continued his advance as he drew a wickedly curved blade from the belt at his hip and swung it to strike.

Raven barely had time to defend herself with her mother's sword and the clash of their weapons sent a painful ripple up both her arms as the clang of metal resounded across the valley.

Her attacker moved quickly, struck repeatedly, and drove her into the fray again. She managed to deflect each of his blows as she ducked, dodged, and parried, but he didn't give her a chance to retaliate or release her weapon to cast an attack spell.

When she finally began to think she might have gotten in too deep with this scarred Malendesh man who simply wouldn't give any quarter, she heard the rapid pops of multiple exploding beetles behind her and knew she had only a few seconds to move quickly.

I'm coming! Leander screeched in the sky but she didn't dare look up to search for him. He already knew what was happening.

She lifted her sword at the last second to catch another crushing blow from the man's curved weapon. The pops behind her grew even louder. She darted to the side and leapt blindly, hoping with everything she had that her familiar had been fast enough for both of them.

Her foot landed on his lowered head as he swooped over the dirt and his claws raked the grass. Before her boots touched the saddle, the beetles unleashed their spray of chemical fumes and ignited the scarred Malendesh in a fiery blaze that killed him instantly. His weapon fell and she gasped for breath.

Leander wheeled so she could retrieve her sword that had fallen beside the bonfire her adversary had become.

"Thank you," she muttered.

"I'm always here for you. Even when you don't look up to judge the distance."

"Ha. You know what, I think we're going to—"

A massive explosion from the base of the mountains rocked the entire valley in the open lands. The force of it caught the red dragon's wings and hurled him sideways. Raven was flung from his back and toppled six feet to the ground before she rolled in the scorched and blood-flecked grass.

The ringing in her ears drowned everything else out, but when she managed to push up and turn, she saw

Connor Alby, War Mage Athena, and half a dozen black-clad mages following them into the battle.

He made it. Right on time, Rider Alby. As always.

Her familiar landed beside her but kept his wings spread wide.

"Are you all right?"

"What?" she shouted at him.

Are you hurt?

No, but I'm very sure we hurt them.

With the stores of fungus projectiles consumed by Leander's blue fire, the cache of mined ore melted and destroyed beneath the heat of Henry's exploding beetles, and the majority of the Malendesh army without their weapons or the bolstered power from the ore, ending the battle was a quick affair.

Connor and War Mage Athena had created enough of a distraction for the STAR legionaries to overcome the enemy. The wild dragons overhead had performed exceptionally well and destroyed the rest of the catapults and any weapons and supplies the Malendesh had kept with them to prepare for the battle.

In the end, the legionaries had three wounded riders and one wounded dragon. They were escorted across the mountains first before the rest of the division got to work with what was left from the fight.

The old dragon rider and the war mage helped to take the surviving Malendesh as prisoners, although there were only thirteen at this point. Whatever fungus and ore the legionaries found was systematically destroyed and finally, it was time to return to Havendom to make a report of their success.

Raven's grandfather found her in the field where she'd retrieved her sword from beside the pile of ashes that had been her last attacker. "Did you do this?" he asked.

"It's more like I got out of the way before he was sprayed by a toy beetle's rear end." She sheathed her sword and wiped stray hair from her face. "Thanks for the help."

They embraced each other tightly before he stepped back and scrutinized her intently. "I'm sorry I didn't reach out to you sooner, Raven. I didn't know what I'd gotten into and by the time I did, there was no possible way—"

"It's okay. I understand."

"Yes. Yes, well, I'm glad you reached similar conclusions on your own. Look at you, STAR mage."

She grinned. "It's been worth it so far."

He chuckled weakly. "I'll say."

"We still need to get those tunnels taken care of. And all that ore. If they stay open, we're merely asking for a repeat of all this. Then there's the fungus that needs to be burned away."

"Kyrie and I have already discussed the proposal we mean to take to the Consortium for that." He looked over his shoulder at War Mage Athena, who stood over the gathered Malendesh prisoners with her arms folded and scowled as the legionaries bound them with rope and hauled them to their feet. "We'll take care of that. And I imagine you'll see that these prisoners are escorted swiftly to the capital. They'll want to know how a force as large as this managed to circumvent all our defenses and reach our shores without anyone in any kingdom knowing a thing about it."

Leander growled behind his mage and pawed the ground. "We should kill them all, Raven."

Connor's eyes widened, but he said nothing.

"I know you want to," she said, her gaze fixed on the prisoners. "A part of me does too. But this is for a bigger cause. And we have to find out how many Malendesh are still here, if any. There are so many unanswered questions, Leander." She rested a hand on her dragon's shoulder and nodded. "We did this the right way and that's what we'll continue to do."

He growled again and lowered his head, but he didn't argue her point.

This was how they worked as a STAR mage and her dragon. They were one part of a bigger whole, and it wasn't up to them because they hadn't done any of this alone.

Connor nodded at the wickedly sharp, curved sword of the Malendesh who'd almost killed her before he'd burned. The grip was inscribed with intricate symbols she couldn't read and three smaller rubies were set into its top above the blade. "I'd take that back with you, Raven."

"A sword?"

"If I had to guess, it was made from the same ore these men were mining to magnify their strength. But I do know that the man who held it was in charge of this entire force here."

"What?"

"Take it with you to Havendom when you tell them what happened." He placed a hand on his granddaughter's shoulder and nodded. "I'm proud of you. You'll hear from me soon."

With that, he turned and walked away to join Athena.

Raven stared after him for a moment, then stared at the Malendesh sword in the grass.

"I just took down the leader of an entire army trying to invade Threndor and kill off our dragons?"

Leander's laughing hiss was sharp in her ear. "I believe it was the rear end of an exploding beetle that took him down."

She nudged his snout away playfully and stooped to pick the sword up. The grip was still warm and the weapon was as heavy as it had been when it swung toward her in its wielder's scarred hand. "I guess we don't need our past reputation to help us make a new one in the Legion, huh?"

"We will always have a reputation, Raven."

"Ha. Yeah. Only this time, I'm very sure no one's gonna try to keep it quiet or forget what happened."

"Not if they know what's good for them."

There's a very particular kind of wisdom that comes with crossing the sixty years old line. I'm sixty-two by the way. It's the realization that if I'm not going to change now, it's probably not going to happen.

Back in my thirties it was super easy to tell myself that at some point, on some day in the future I would get the hang of dancing at weddings, leaving the chips in the pantry alone, cooking fish so the skin is crispy, gardening. There's more on the list but you get the idea. I have recently conquered the fish thing so cross that one off the list but the dancing and leaving snack foods alone still elude me.

However, there's an even bigger item that's perpetually been on my 'maybe someday' list since I was thirteen and has only taken breaks for a handful of years at a time.

Losing weight, getting in shape – and staying that way.

Now that I am in that last part of life – which hopefully will last another thirty years, give or take – a few things surrounding all this body stuff has gained a lot of clarity.

Like looking back over the varied landscape of weird diets I've been on and how ridiculous it all looks now. I wanted a quick fix that I was always hoping would hold, but really makes no sense. Remember the Scarsdale Diet? There was a day where all you were supposed to eat was cheese. A bonanza of cheese.

It wasn't until my fifties that I threw in the fad diet towel and went to see a nutritionist. Biggest takeaway was how little I knew about the right way to eat. How did I get that far and not know what a proper portion size was? You're reading this thinking you know, but I'll bet there are more that don't, than do. Frankly, I grew up in a pretty poor household and portion size was whatever you could grab and that was it. No more food till the next meal. (I've also had to learn to eat more slowly – another relic from my childhood because seconds went to whoever got to them. Our home version of the hunger games.)

Until it was pointed out to me, I didn't get that some part of me was thinking that portion size is whatever I'm served.

Back in the 70's that was kind of okay but these days in a restaurant what we're served is often enough for three people.

Here we are in the present and I'm 62 and going through a year of chemo infusions and it's really struck me between the eyes. What I eat, and how I move is really going to affect not only the quality of life I have for the remaining years but also how many years I get.

How's that for motivation?

I'm seeing a nutritionist who specializes in ultraathletes and cancer patients, and he has me on a low-glycemic diet (starve the cancer) and daily exercise. In that patient, stern doctor voice he explained that three days a week wasn't going to cut it. Not even five. I was to decide what I really wanted out of this and if I want the best chances – get up and move every day of the week.

Unlike my earlier years of go big or go home, this time I've been looking for sustainable exercise that I actually like with the goal of a lot of options. Swimming at the local Y, Hatha yoga at a nearby yoga place where the last 15 minutes are meditation, a new bike that I'm still learning how to ride (no, it is definitely not like riding a bike), a portable boxing setup – Quiet Punch - in my house along with TRX straps also set up in my house. Kayaking is on there as an occasional outing that I hope happens more often.

All of those are things I don't hate doing and therefore I'm more likely to keep doing them long term. If I can't get to swimming one day, I can go box. If I'm tired of boxing, I can go hang out on the TRX.

Seems so obvious but I don't think I took it seriously enough when I was younger to really think things through. I took the most convenient types of exercise and slugged it out till one day I just didn't want to go anymore.

But, that needs to change and this time, for good. There are no more 'maybe someday I'll get this' years left. Either I learn how to be consistent now or lose some mobility, some strength – little by little – and look up one day to realize I don't get out as much as I used to.

Nope. I'm going to be more like my cousin, Norie who

still works her four acre garden at ninety-two. And maybe I'll even learn how to dance wildly at weddings. More adventures to follow.

First, thank you for not only reading this story, but these author notes in the back as well.

Since Martha admitted her age, I'll admit I'm 53. While she is the elder of the two of us in this relationship, don't for a minute believe she is the elder statesman…

Wait…wait. Actually, *yes* – you should believe that part. She is very wise and learned in her years and willing to be patient with people (such as myself) who have not quite figured out which annoying personalities one shouldn't be upset with.

"You just let it go… Let it goooooo…"

(Let the emotions of wanting to choke someone who desperately deserves it *GOOOOOO….*)

Now I know where the writer for the Frozen movie got the song concept from.

Because Martha considers larger issues in her personal life, I often receive a bit of wisdom when it is my time to provide MY author notes. Unfortunately, the best I have to offer right now is to realize that you can design your own finish line when you run your own race.

Meaning no one can beat you.

There is no 'I have to beat the Joneses' if the Joneses have a different track to run on than you do. Plus, there is no way for them to beat you. They can't find your finish line, ergo they can't win against you, either.

In short – there is no need to be *compared* to anyone.

Although some thrive on the effort to be better than someone else (and I have and did do this), it became tiresome after a while because *it changes my daily tactics to fit a strategy that doesn't fit my life.*

I'll give an example from my life. In 2017 or so, there was a huge push for indie authors to 'get your letters.' This means to become a best seller on either of the big national newspapers who declared which books were selling the most. If you see a book with "NY TIMES BESTSELLING AUTHOR," then that author is a 'lettered' author.

It was never the goal of my race to become a lettered author. But, I was hooked into the emotions of those who wanted that to be a part of their race. In short, I was allowing my race (and finish line) to be changed.

Once that happened, my brain naturally started to consider some of the projects I would have to become a part of to become lettered. The efforts began to stress me out.

Additional stress I didn't need.

Finally, I realized what was happening, moved my finish line BACK to where it was supposed to be. I dropped the mental gymnastics and frankly was a lot happier.

This effort to run my race yet want someone else's

results do tempt me from time to time. I consider where my finish line is set now (because you can change the location by accident or on purpose). Then I can walk life with fewer stresses and worries.

So, LMBPN is working toward our own goals to become a story-production company in multiple mediums, genres, languages, countries, and distribution methods. Whatever the future offers, we want to provide just a bit of enjoyment across this world.

Exactly where our finish line will be? Well, I'll have to get back to you on that.

Have a great week or weekend, and talk to you in the next book!

Ad Aeternitatem,

Michael Anderle

JOIN THE ORICERAN UNIVERSE FAN GROUP ON FACEBOOK!

BOOKS BY MICHAEL ANDERLE

Sign up for the LMBPN email list to be notified of new releases
and special deals!

https://lmbpn.com/email/

For a complete list of books by Michael Anderle, please visit:

www.lmbpn.com/ma-books/

Made in the USA
Monee, IL
27 April 2022

95512909R10196